C.P. BIRD

THE PORTAELLEN WAR CHRONICLES

VOLUME I – THE INVASION

novum pro

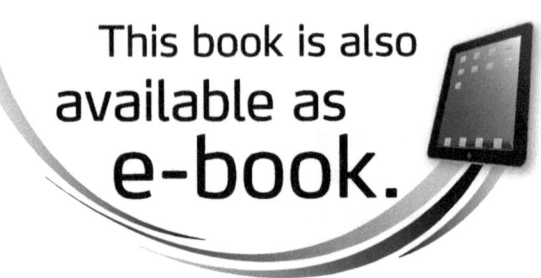

www.novum-publishing.co.uk

© 2021 novum publishing

ISBN 978-3-99107-273-7
Editing: Hugo Chandler, BA
Cover photo:
Robert Adrian Hillman | Dreamstime.com
Cover design, layout & typesetting:
novum publishing

www.novum-publishing.co.uk

For, my Helen Clare.
Thank you, for your support,
of my leap of faith.

Contents

Portaellen Portal Facts

for Everyone

1. Only Dual Bloods', with Portaellen ancestry, can pass through, a Portaellen portal.
2. A Portaellen portal, will only transport flesh, bone and body fluids. Everything that constitutes, a living form.
3. If, it is your first time, exiting a Portaellen portal, you will land in the other world naked. (See point two).
4. If, it is not your first exit, you will land, wearing the clothing and the items, that you had with you, upon entering.
5. You will not remember, your journey through the portal.
6. There is one reported portal, on Earth. Two in Portaellen, which are connected directly, to the one Earth portal. No internal link, between the two Portaellen portals, exists.
7. The distance between Earth and Portaellen, is incalculable. It cannot, be measured. If, you were to ask some Dual Bloods that very question, you would get a tongue in cheek response.

'How far, is the distance between Earth and Portaellen, you ask?' A momentary silence, would usually be followed by a smirk, or even sarcastic laughter, before an answer would finally be given. 'About five hundred years!'

Some, of the above facts, are centuries old. Passed down, through the generations. Hopefully, they will help any Sole Bloods, who will never experience a Portaellen portal journey. Or other Dual Bloods, yet to have an experience. It will also save you from getting a sarcastic response, from a Dual Blood.

It is important to remember, that today, over five million Portaellen Dual Bloods, live amongst us. Only a small percentage, know of their lineage. An even smaller percentage now travel between the two worlds.

Are you one of them?

The Last Knight of Fantaellen

An ode to a warrior
An ordinary man

He is an ordinary man,
A father, a son, a brother,
A man of this life,
A man of the next life,
He is of this world, and another,
He is alive, he has died,
He is yet to be born,
He is all men, yet one man.

On this day of his destiny,
He stands alone.
Around him, a battlefield,
In his hand, his bloodied sword,
having sent many, to their death,
His armour, having defended
against an enemy, so brutal,
and great in numbers,
And yet, he still stands alone.

He is an ordinary man,
A father, a son, a brother,
A man of this life,
A man of the next life,
He is of this world, and another,
He is alive, he has died,
He is yet to be born,
He is all men, yet one man.

On this day of his destiny,
He still stands alone.
Around him, a battlefield,
Seen or unseen, he knows
the enemy surround him,
Therefore, his defiance is roared
long and loud,
He now no longer, feels alone.

This ordinary man is ready,
This father, this son, this brother,
The man of this life,
The man of the next life,
The man of this world and another,
He is alive, not dead,
He has been born,
He is all men, yet one man.
He is ready.

And, into the storm he charged,
with sword in hand,
That one-man war,
The last knight of Fantaellen.

Prologue

The Beginning

Across, the many lands of Portaellen, there is a legend, that has been passed down, from generation to generation. Every word, every line, has stayed the same since its first telling. It would become known, as the 'The Beginning'.

The world of Portaellen, was created by Ramazen, a Guardian, (a God). He was given an atom as a gift, with which, he decided to create a world, for his two argumentative sons, Zada and Yetus.

Firstly, he made the portals between Earth and his newly created World. Then, came the land, fertile and green. Followed, by a river, clear and clean. The elements quickly followed, wind, rain, snow, with two suns and two moons, spawned in honour of his sons. It would take him five hundred years, to develop and form his World. On final completion, he gave his creation, a name. The axis, of Portaellen, now rotated, for the very first time.

Now, that he was happy, with his creation, he presented it, to his son's, with the hope, that they would work together, to establish and create, a brotherly bond, between them.

From the start, the brother's ideas were different, on how to run their new world. Quickly, arguments turned to conflict, as brother fought brother. Other Gods and warriors from Earth, were recruited for the fight, as all-out war, was declared. It would become known, as The First War.

Their Father, finally intervened, when he had seen enough. Ramazen, angrily split the world in two, by creating a sea. He named it, The Stoirim Sea. Each brother was banished to the land, either side of the stormy, body of water.

Even, this did not work. Zada and Yetus, gathered massive armies, and many ships, in the hope, of invading the other's land. War raged on, on either side of the Stoirim Sea. Countless, warriors and Gods died. And finally, after years of unyielding conflict, a stalemate existed.

In, what was to be the final battle, both brothers were killed. Their blood was said to have soaked the land, of what would become known, as the country of Wulfdaeden.

On hearing the news, of the death of his son's, the grief stricken Ramazen, annihilated, what remained of both armies, with bolts of fire and white-hot lightening. No living creature was left alive.

The scorched earth, remained empty, for many future centuries. Before, Ramazen disappeared, (never again, to be seen, at the God's table), he had said, that he hoped, that future generations, of Dual Bloods, would one day inhabit, the world that he had created. And, that there would be peace.

★★★

It was late, in the Earth year of 1919, when the first rumblings, of another possible conflict, in Portaellen, were being spoken of. Many Dual Bloods, were tired of war, having fought in the First World War, on Earth.

Many, Fantaellen's and Wulfdaeden's, (the two biggest countries, in Portaellen, and mortal enemies), had fought on the Western front, as comrades. Rivalries, of the past forgotten, as the war raged on, in the mud, for four long, and bloody years. Men, who had fought in that mud, and the trenches, as allies for their Earth country, now looked likely, to become enemies.

Most Dual Bloods did remain sceptical though, of a Third War in Portaellen. The Second War, some hundred years previous, had lasted, just two hours. It had dragged, all nations of the Portal World, large and small, onto opposing sides, once Wulfdaeden and Fantaellen, had declared, war on each other.

When, the two-rival generals, had met on the battlefield, for, what was to be, the first and only time, they both dealt each other, deadly, fatal blows, and died of their injuries. Because, neither army, really knew why they were fighting, the armies dispersed, and the Second War of Portaellen, was over.

So, entering a new decade, the talk of a Third War in Portaellen, was still being brushed aside, as Earth became used, to its new-found peace, in the winter of 1920. Even, the rumours, of the sovereign of the Portal World, banishing his twin brother, from Fantaellen soil, the previous year, in an incident, that remained a mystery, did not ring, any alarm bells.

Since, being small children, the twin brothers, had always stuck up for one another, and been inseparable.

With the death of his beloved wife, as she gave birth, to their twin children, a son and a daughter, the sovereign, received his greatest comfort from his twin brother, who was there with him, through the hardest times. However, it would be a grief, that he would never, fully recover from.

When, the reports, filtered through, of the exiled twin, having fled to Wulfdaeden, and quickly amassing, a huge fleet of ships, in the ports, facing the coastline, of Fantaellen, those alarm bells, did start ringing. Loud and clear.

In the first few weeks, of the Earth year of 1920, a First World War veteran, and proud Dual Blood, received his call to arms. JJ Quixall, (James, Jonti), or Jonti, as he liked to be known, had sworn, that he had seen enough death and destruction, in the trenches of Belgium and France, to last a lifetime. The official, piece of paper, in his hand, told him otherwise. He was weary and tired but knew he would get over it. His second country needed him. He would answer the call. That would never have been in doubt. Ever.

Now, with the feud between two twin brothers, once again, bringing Portaellen, to the brink of war, the portal world's, century of peace, looks likely to be broken, and men like Jonti, will once again, have to answer the call to arms.

Every story has a beginning. This is ours.

PART I
THE COMING STORM

Chapter One

The unpredictable swell of the coastal waves pushed a small rowing boat, over the crashing breakers of the Stoirim Sea, and onto the sandy shore. Six hooded figures, with their faces blackened, quickly jumped clear of their vessel, before running at a pace, up the sands, through the black, inky darkness, of the dead of night, towards the shelter of some rocks, up ahead.

The hooded figures, remained in the shadows of the rocks for a short while, as they watched and observed for any enemy, sentry movements on the headland and the high ground, that overlooked the beach. The dark horizon before them, was illuminated by the two Portaellen full moons, in the star strewn sky. The beams of both moons were extended beyond the higher ground, and were rested, just in front of their hiding position. The hooded figures remained as still as possible, as their eyes continued to scan the high ground.

The order to break cover, was finally given, with a hand signal. The six figures now made their way across the sand towards a grassy bank. Every man, watching, observing and being careful, to stay as low as possible, as they ran.

Within a short distance, they became spooked, when two sentries suddenly appeared, at either end of a path, on the headland, and proceeded to walk towards one another. All six, instantly hit the sand, and remained still and silent, for a moment or so, as they observed the sentries, walking towards one another.

The two sentries, eventually came to a halt, when they met, on the high ground. For several minutes, they spoke. Their voices carried faint, on the wind. The six hooded figures waited patiently. Their existence on the sand, engulfed by the darkness and the shadows, just beyond the reach of the moon beams. There, they stayed, observing the enemy sentries, not a muscle twitching. Their breathing controlled. Their blackened faces watching and waiting for their moment to move.

As the two Fantaellen sentries parted, and began to walk in opposite directions, the order was given by several hand signals, for the group to split up. Two, were sent in the direction of one of the sentries, and two sent towards the other. The final two, made their way, along the beach, towards a grassy bank.

The larger figure, a man who had a prominent scar, across his forehead, that was red and swollen, was the leader of the group. He watched closely, as his men moved into position, ready to attack. He then turned to the younger man, who was a lot smaller in stature, and carried a satchel, which he looked into checking the contents.

'Do you think, you have enough poison, to get the job done?' enquired the leader.

'Yes. More than enough,' replied the younger man.

'Good. You must not be seen entering. Remember, present yourself, as if you've been there for a while. Learn all the routes quickly, through the passageways and corridors. No one must suspect. When you have completed the mission, send the signal. And don't forget. If you need them, we have someone, on the inside.'

'Yes sir. I remember their name.'

'Excellent. Our ships in the fog, are relying on you. The signal, must be given.'

'Yes sir. I will not let them down.'

'Right. Excellent. Now make ready. The sentries, are about to be dealt with.'

The two now watched, as simultaneously, a hooded assassin, crept out from the shadows to stand silently behind each sentry, before forcibly placing a hand over their enemies' mouths.

Instantly, there was a flash of a small blade, followed by a thrust of the weapon, deep into the lower back. Quickly, but silently, the two sentries were pulled to the ground, where their throats were then slit. The hand of the assassin was only released, when their victim, showed no signs of life.

A signal now came from the high ground. It was time to move.

The leader now watched, as the younger man stumbled at first, before making his way up the grassy bank, towards the summit of the high ground. It wasn't long, before he disappeared from view completely, having run into a large, wooded area, on the northern edge, of some distant headland.

The rest of the group of assassins, now listened intently, as their leader gave them his order's. They had cleared the immediate path of danger, for the lone assassin, and they now had a mission of their own. Nobody would hopefully know of their existence, till morning, when the lone rowing boat would be found, and the bodies of the two Fantaellen sentries were discovered.

Quietly and silently, five hooded figures swiftly vanished into the shadows of the night, away from the light, cascading down onto the headland, from the two Portaellen moons.

An unknown enemy had landed on Fantaellen soil, undetected and intent on fulfilling their deadly mission.

★★★

A dense, heavy, menacing fog had descended during the night, about a mile or two, out to sea. The sentries on the cliffs, beacon points and the walls of the coastal fortifications, that guarded the entire length of the Fantaellen coastline, had watched as the thick white blanket, enveloped everything around them. Many, anxious, nervous eyes, scanned the Stoirim Sea, looking for the enemy ships, that they knew were there, as the waves slammed into the rocks and shoreline, below.

Captain George Corder, the officer in charge of the South Western Fortress, walked out of the main gates, towards the coastal path, that ran along the edge of the cliffs, of the headland. The high point of land had been battered by the winds and waves of the Stoirim Sea, for centuries, and he looked out towards the coast of Wulfdaeden, which on a clear day, can be seen.

The fog had made any visibility impossible. The captain looked for the waiting armada, riding the stormy waves, out at sea. Unable to see very much, he walked a little further, looking for the rock formation, known as Needle Point Rock, a weather-beaten chunk of chalky, white rock, about half a mile out from the main coastline. On a clear day, it could be seen standing proud; a first line of defence in the swells, of the merciless waves of the Stoirim Sea.

As he looked to the east, a brief opening appeared in the white murkiness, and the captain spied the Corridor Of Arches; another rock formation of twelve archways, attached to the mainland, where the elements and thunderous waves, passed through and out one end, to build up and be driven, back onto the coast.

He watched the archways disappear, into the murky white blanket, as he continued his walk, acknowledging the salute of his sentries, with a smile, as he passed. He could sense the tension in his men. He knew his soldier's, would look to him, for leadership.

The captain was middle age, standing six and a half feet tall, thick set, with broad shoulders. His commanding stature, his face, worn from war and conflict, and his reputation, as a killer and a leader of great repute, made him, his sovereign's first choice, to organise the defence of the country's, most vulnerable point.

As a soldier and a ranger, fighting the Wulfdaeden's, and other enemies, he had earned his reputation. Many of his men, had fought beside him, before. The ranks of his battalion were then swelled with proven fighters, from other battalions, and young, raw recruits, who had grown up, listening to tales of their captain's exploits.

The truth was, he too, felt uneasy. Like the worries that you get on the eve of battle. He hated the fact, that he couldn't see the enemy. It always, made him a little nervous. They would come. He knew that. The fog bought them time.

The captain had readied his men, the best that he could. Being garrisoned, at the tip of the south western coast, directly facing the Wulfdaeden coastline, meant that it would be the likeliest place, for the start of the attack. Like the general's, he was sure of this. The other defence points, along the coast, were also on high alert. Now, all he and his men could do, was to sit and wait.

Looking up at the sky, the captain spied a lone bird; a hawk, its wing's spread, gliding on the contours of the gusting winds that blew onto the coast. Fascinated, the captain watched as the hawk, made its distinctive hoarse screech, before being swallowed up, by the thick, white mass of fog.

The captain now chose this moment to pray. It was something he always did, when needing comfort, or to gain fortitude. Closing his eyes, he muttered a prayer, asking for guidance and the courage to lead his men.

Then, with purpose, he strode back to his fortress, to check on the final preparations. The fog would lift in the coming hours. The Wulfdaeden Blackhearts will come then.

***

The lone hawk finally breached the other side of the wall of fog. Below, in the dark unforgiving waves, floated an incredibly large mass of ships, that stretched across the entire channel, that separated Wulfdaeden from Fantaellen. Every ship had their oars raised, as they waited for the signal.

Upon, the grandest looking ship of the fleet the admiral grew impatient. He cursed the fog out loud, as he collapsed his telescope. He knew, that Fantaellen coastal fogs, can last for days, and this one, was thicker than normal. He had been pacing the bow for hours, growing more and more impatient, as time passed. His officers had given up telling him that the landing party, had only just landed. Their departure had been delayed by several hours, due to extremely rough currents and waves. The admiral had grown impatient, and eventually yelled at his officer's, to get the boat in the water, as time was precious, telling them that the fog, would provide the perfect cover, for the landing party. The strong Wulfdaeden oars, would glide through the merciless waves, he reasoned. So, against his officer's better judgement, the boat had been lowered into the water. The mission had to begin. The signal had to be given.

The fog provided the Wulfdaeden armada, with the perfect concealment. The admiral knew that the Fantaellen's would know that they were there. The surprise, would be the size of the fleet, and the completion of the mission, of his master's shadow assassin's, the landing party.

If the God's were with him, then the fog would hold just long enough, for the admiral's ships to remain concealed, before the sight of the lit beacons, came into view, along the Fantaellen coast.

This would be the signal, that he and the hundreds of Wulfdaeden ships waited for. The lit beacons. The completion of the assassin's mission. The signal for the invasion, to begin.

★★★

Stefan, the King of Fantaellen, and the crowned Sovereign of Portaellen, was very ill. What, had started as an ordinary fever, had progressed over the past few hours. The Royal Physician, Henri, a tall, lean man of advancing years, had tried everything to help the ailing king. His servants were running back and forth with bowls of cold water, which he used to try and bring his sovereign's soaring temperature, down.

He had tried proven medicines, but nothing seemed to help, as the king's health rapidly deteriorated. His body, had reached dangerously high temperatures, resulting in violent convulsions, and frothing at the mouth.

Henri now quickly put his sovereign, onto his side, and watched, as another spasm gripped King Stefan's body. Henri was gravely concerned.

'He cannot die Henri.' One of the king's advisors had said, as the royal physician had spoken to a group of important looking men, when they had entered the Royal chambers, unannounced.

'It's only a fever!' One of them called out.

Henri looked up briefly, after recognising the voice, and saw his friend and King Stefan's chief advisor; Robert Scotten, stood with his arms folded, a concerned look on his face.

'I cannot bring his temperature down Robert,' Henri began to explain. 'The infection is escalating.'

Robert Scotten could hear the frustration, in Henri's voice. He watched, as the royal physician, was stooped over their sovereign, gently wiping his brow, as another violent convulsion, pulsed through his debilitated body.

Henri could only watch in horror, as his sweat drenched king and sovereign, suddenly turned onto his back, his body becoming rigid and taut, before collapsing onto the bed.

The convulsions had suddenly stopped. The king appeared to be breathing still. Only just, Henri noted, as he checked his pulse. It was weak and very faint. Almost absent.

The door closing behind him, instantly woke Henri from his trance. Turning to see that Robert, and his advisors had left the royal chambers, bought him some relief. He had not welcomed their presence. He had heard them, whispering and talking in hushed voices, behind him. He had not heard, what they had said, nor had he chosen to, as he had more pressing matters.

Henri looked at his king and sighed. What type of infection was this? He asked himself. His thoughts, now turned to other causes and different treatments, as his mind, processed, his thinking.

Deep in thought, Henri was suddenly interrupted by a young servant, who bought in a fresh jug of water. Henri thanked him. He did not recognise him, but had seen the young man, several times, as he had replaced the bowl, during the passing hours. The servant smiled, nodded his head, and left the chambers, closing the door behind him.

★★★

The young servant, quickly hurried away, from the large gathering, outside the enormous, gold rimmed, white oak doors, of the royal bed chambers. Panic and mayhem ensued, as servants, footmen, and maids ran around, the corridors of Guinlance Castle, with orders ringing in their ears, from worried looking, generals and lords.

In a quiet corner, away from the commotion, five men dressed in the royal purple, tunic and breeches, of someone in office, stood talking amongst themselves, quietly, but with purpose. These men were the king's advisors.

Robert Scotten, a large, giant of a man, was the chief advisor. He and King Stefan had become close, when Queen Annabelle, had died during the birth of the royal children, the twins, Joshua and Madeleine.

'Our king and sovereign is gravely ill. It does not look good, gentlemen.' Robert paused for a moment, as the other advisors, moved in closer.

'Is he really going to die?' one of them asked.

No answer, came from the chief advisor, as he rubbed the top of his bald head. Briefly, he closed his eyes, before opening them to carrying on.

'Listen.' He continued in a low tone, as the other advisors stared at him, their gaze unflinching. As always, Robert held court. He had their attention. Just, as he liked it. They listened, waiting, for his every word.

'We are within hours, of a Blackheart attack. Their invasion fleet, led by our king's Judas brother, is sat in the Stoirim Sea Channel, waiting for the fog to clear. When, the word of the king's death ...' Robert, now saw the look of horror, creep onto their faces, as the last few words, hit home.

'He is going to die!' cried out, one of the advisors.

'Look. We have to prepare for the worst,' another advisor suddenly stated.

'We do,' agreed Robert. 'We need to get our best men, to the portal. The twins need to be taken from the safe house, and bought back to the castle, before their uncle plans to take them. They are our future gentlemen and must be kept safe.'

When, the queen had died, King Stefan had placed his children, into the care of his younger sister. Unconfirmed reports had come through over the years, that she had been turned. These reports were dismissed, after a lengthy period of time, when it was established, that the children, were still within the confines, of the safe house. So, it was determined, that they were still safe.

The fact was, that the king had the problem, of his twin brother, to deal with, and other pressing matters. He had visited the twins when he could. Under a strict armed guard, he had always left, from Guinlance Castle, through the portal at Ingress Hill, out the other side, at the Ring of Stones, and to the safe house. The armed guard was always led, by his most trusted knight, Jonti Quixal.

Unfortunately, King Stefan had not seen his children recently. The talk of war and an invasion force led by his exiled twin brother, had been at the forefront of his mind, for the last few months.

From the moment, the king had watched his brother ride away, from the courtyard of Guinlance Castle, shackled and under an armed guard, he had known there would be war. His younger twin had told him. In fact, he had screamed in the face of his brother, his king and sovereign, that he would be back.

All that Robert Scotten could now think about, as the other advisors, spoke amongst themselves, was the young prince, who had been exiled from the castle, where he had grown up. He had grown into a man, who had been turned, and now had an armada of ships, an invasion force, waiting for the fog in the Stoirim Sea Channel to lift.

Invasion and war was now very close.

★★★

Startled, by a sudden noise, Henri lifted his head sharply, upon waking from a deep sleep. He was sat on the corner of King Stefan's bed. He cursed under his breath. Despite, not having any sleep, for the last two days, very little food or water to drink, the royal physician, had stayed by his king and sovereign's bedside.

Henri quickly realised, that the king was gasping for air. He was evidently, struggling to breath. He had the death rattle, in his throat. His body, now swiftly contorted, as he raised his arms in the air, his twisted fingers, grasping at the air, before his hands turned into a fist.

The blue eyes of the king opened for a brief moment. His head remained on the pillow, as his back, arched violently away from the bed. His face was covered in perspiration, and his mouth was open wide, showing a blackened tongue. Suddenly, he let out a terrifying scream of pain before, his body collapsed onto the bed.

Henri carefully leaned over the stricken body, of the sovereign, and saw that his pupils were fixed and dilated. The king's arms were limp by his side. His mouth open wide.

Henri now felt for a pulse. Nothing.

Gently, the royal physician pulled the eyelids of his king, over his lifeless eyes, and closed his mouth. He then softly kissed his sovereign's forehead, before wearily pulling himself away.

Turning a final time, to his king and sovereign, Henri bowed. Tears flowed down his face. He was suddenly so exhausted, to the point of collapse. He felt so helpless, alone and vulnerable.

Would the king's advisors blame him? Make him into a scapegoat? Questions now flashed through, his exhausted mind.

His king and sovereign had just died. He had been unable, to save him. And, he had never seen a body react, to a fever, like that before.

Wiping away his tears, the royal physician slowly walked towards the door of the royal bed chambers. Before turning the door handle, he took a deep breath, prayed to whichever God listened, and then turned the handle.

The door to the royal bed chamber, slowly opened. Henri appeared in the doorway, with his head bowed. Conversations now stopped abruptly, and the whole corridor outside the king's bed chambers, presently fell silent.

The royal physician took a deep breath. He then lifted his head.

'It's,' he stuttered, 'with regret, that I have to report …' The words began to stick in his throat. Henri coughed, and then swallowed, to coat his dry throat. '… that King Stefan, our king and sovereign, has died.'

Silence. Nobody moved. Everybody stared at him. Henri now felt extremely uncomfortable and suddenly vulnerable.

'God rest his soul!' came a sudden, and unexpected shout.

Groups of servants, maids and lords embraced one another, as a collective grief, instantaneously, gripped the gathering. Many now had tears in their eyes, others, their heads bowed, as the enormity of what they had just been told, sank in.

Robert Scotten beckoned to his fellow advisors to follow him, to his office. Through the crowds of tearful, grief-stricken courtiers, they walked, the chief advisor, striding ahead. Thoughts, and hastily laid plans, racing through his head.

He quickly ordered a communication to be sent, to the coastal defences. They must be told, about the death of their king. The enemy would know, soon enough, he reasoned. There were spies everywhere. And, once that fog had lifted, the Blackhearts would come.

'An attack is imminent,' Robert started, when they reached his office. 'Once, the news of the death of the sovereign, reaches the enemy fleet they won't care about the fog. The news would be enough, to drive them through the fires of Hell, and out the other side. They would be unstoppable.' He paused for a moment, as a thought entered his head.

I need to buy the coastal defences, some time. Yes. That's it!

'Put the castle on a lockdown,' he suddenly, blurted out. 'Nobody is to leave, or enter, without my written permission.'

This, would hopefully, buy the coastal defences, a bit of time to ready themselves, for the attack, Robert reasoned. Whenever, it did come.

Robert Scotten, being the most senior advisor, within Guinlance Castle, was now the Guardian of Fantaellen. A title suddenly bestowed upon him, by the death of King Stefan. He was not of pure blood, but he was the most senior man, in the country. The whole of Fantaellen, would now look to him, for his experience, leadership and strength of character. Just, what his country needed, right now.

★★★

The two Portaellen suns were rising, on a new day. In a wooded area, just to the south of Guinlance Castle, five horsemen, waited. They had hidden in the wood, for a few hours now. They were tired and impatient. Their faces were blackened, their heads, covered by the hood, of their black robes, and their blades stained, with the blood of the enemy.

'There!' one of them, suddenly called. 'The signal.'

The larger man of the group, who had a prominent scar across his forehead, dismounted his white steed, and ran towards, a clearing up ahead.

As he looked up, he saw it in the dawn sky. The fire arrow, released from the roof of the southern ramparts, of the royal quarters. The signal.

The arrow, whistled through the air, as the flames danced on its tip, before it thudded, into some soft earth, up ahead.

The large man, then quickly ran towards the arrow, before pulling it out of the ground, examining it, then extinguishing the flames, with his hand. He did not cry out in pain, or wince, as his skin sizzled, and smoke came from his hand.

The King of Fantaellen, the Sovereign of Portaellen, was dead. Killed, by an assassin of Wulfdaeden. The message was now on its way, to the armada of Blackheart ships, in the Stoirim Sea Channel. Carried, by five black hooded, horsemen.

Their king and master's plan would now begin. Fantaellen, was at the mercy of Napoleon Victory. The once, Prince of Fantaellen, the younger twin brother, of the deceased, King Stefan.

Chapter Two

England
1920

The shooting star, that flew across the clear, crisp, night sky, caught the eye of a lone figure. A creature of the shadows. A troll.

Normauss is a troll, with questionable morals. He is a tenth generation, Fantaellen mountain troll. His ancestors once came from Wulfdaeden. They were captured and cleansed, in the Great Cleansing. More, than five hundred years ago. Normauss preferred the seclusion of the shadows, as he could move about, virtually undetected, and would only show himself, in the daylight if he had to. He was a very good tracker. One of the best.

He is built like many of the males of his tribe. Short in stature (about four feet tall) and as strong as an ox. He has an enormous head, with a dark beard, that covers his chin. Above his round, dark eyes, his bushy eyebrows protrude, and arc around the top of his eye sockets. His hair is dark, and long, and is parted in the centre, which allows it to hang, either side of his head, before touching his broad shoulders. His mouth is wide, and supported by pointed, yellow teeth. He has a brawny, hairy chest. Short, stubby, hairy legs and arms. Normal shaped, hairy feet, with two large toes on each.

Normauss's personality, differs from his kith and kin. Fantaellen mountain trolls are a peaceful tribe, who will only use violence, if provoked. Normauss, is the opposite. He carries the mutant, evil gene. He is highly strung, unpredictable and would use his strength, to kill anyone or anything, that got in his way.

Napoleon Victory, his king and master, had not bothered to have Normauss turned. He had said that the troll did not need turning. He was already evil. His heart was already black.

Normauss, cursed out loud. He was still several miles from the portal. He shook his head, at the stupid complexities of the Portaellen portals. He hated them, so much. It hadn't helped his mood, when the frost on the ground had appeared, and began to chill his feet. Onward, he continued though, determined to reach the portal, quickly.

Normauss had made good time, and he briefly had to stop to rub his hairy feet. They were numb with the cold. Desperately, the troll began to roughly massage his toes, to get some blood circulating through them. He was so fed up. This was mainly due to his last trip through the portal when it had been warmer. Therefore, he only wore a cotton shirt and short trousers, on this winter's night.

The troll watched, as another shooting star flew across, the clear night sky, before it disappeared towards the horizon. Gratefully, feeling the circulation slowly returning to his feet, Normauss began to make his way, again. He was in a hurry. His king and master waited for his intelligence. The troll's mind began to race.

The sudden stress of his situation began to instantly engulf him. Normauss began to shake violently before screaming and cursing, as he ran towards a tree and punched it.

'Ouch!' he screamed. The pained troll immediately regretted his impulsive response.

Shaking his throbbing hand vigorously, Normauss fell to the floor, and burst into tears. He was frustrated and angry.

Time was busy running out for him. The cold weather: primarily the frost, had slowed him down. He wished, he'd worn his boots, as he had on the previous journey. Now he cursed his own stupidity, before desperate thoughts engulfed him, once more.

'Altoa! I am so sorry,' he suddenly cried out, before collapsing, in a heap.

It did take him, a few moments to compose himself. When he was ready, Normauss started to walk quickly, that suddenly turned into a fast run.

The portal was several miles away and, his master waited.

'Come on Normauss! You can do this,' he called out. 'I can do this!' he told a curious fox, who watched him cautiously, as he ran past.

So, Normauss the troll, his feet now thawed out, made his way, towards the Ring of Stones. There, he would enter the portal, before exiting at Hells Point, in Wulfdaeden.

The troll wasn't sure, how his master would use his intelligence once he had received it. It would be all part of the bigger plan.

A bigger plan, that would see the total annihilation of Fantaellen. Of this, Normauss was sure.

★★★

The dirty windows of Meadowlands Cottage were covered in a severe, white frost. The air was still and freezing. A silent, icy mist had descended upon the hard ground. Nothing stirred, as the weak, wintry sun began to rise, on a new dawn.

Through the threadbare curtains of the windows, the meagre rays of the sun steadily trickled through, to faintly illuminate, each and every dark corner, of the cottage.

The early light, of the new day, woke the large woman, from her sleep. Stretching and grunting, she cursed, the delicate light, as it gradually crossed the room.

Aunt Grimshaw was not happy. She never was. She hated the daylight. It repulsed her, so much.

Cursing the orange hue, on the rotten ceiling, above her head, she lay there staring. She did not want to get up. Her whole body ached.

From the side of her bed, she reached down and took hold of a broom, with an extremely long handle. Slowly, lifting it up, she shoved it, towards the ceiling. As it impacted, on to the rotting beams above, she was instantly covered in a light dusting of mould, decayed wood and spider webs.

'Get up!' she screamed, as the thud of the broom head, hitting the ceiling, echoed, throughout the room. She then threw the broom down hard, next to the side of her bed.

Grunting and groaning, Aunt Grimshaw, now struggled to lift her large frame, from her bed. She tried several times, before she succeeded, in finally heaving herself up.

She stood stretching, and as her body creaked and cracked, her mouth opened wide, with the first yawn, of the day. This was followed by several larger yawns, numerous groans, and countless curses.

Eventually, after deciding that she could not hear, any movement from upstairs, she lit a candle, and began to negotiate her way across, the mess on the floor, of her downstairs bedroom.

The moment, that the bedroom door creaked open, and Aunt Grimshaw appeared in the doorway, a black cat, instantly shot up into the air, as it growled and hissed at her, before it arched its back, and showed its teeth. With a look of pure terror, on its face, the cat was frozen to the spot. The feline could do no more, than quiver with fear, as he stared at the wart covered face, the colour of death.

'It's me, you stupid cat!' she hissed. 'Look!'

The cat did not know what to do. So, it chose flight. Off it ran, as fast, as its little legs, would carry it. Screaming at the top of its voice, as it shot past, the large woman, in the doorway, and up the stairs.

'You'll come back when you want feeding!'

★★★

Josh stirred from his sleep, as a result of the commotion and the raised voice, from downstairs. Half asleep, the young boy, looked around the room. He could see his breath, as he breathed. He shivered. It was so cold.

From the corner of his eye, he unexpectedly watched, as the bedroom door, creaked open slightly. He, then heard a scurrying, across the wooden floor.

As, he looked at the foot of his bed, Josh saw Samson, his aunt's black cat, as it suddenly jumped up and landed in an undignified heap, onto his thin, threadbare duvet.

'Ouch!' cried Josh.

Samson had dug his claws, into the young boy's, bony legs. The thin duvet offered very little protection, as the black cat, stared at him, with a startled expression, etched on its face.

'Get down Samson. You're hurting me.'

With the brush of his arm, Josh managed to persuade Samson, to leave his bed. The cat jumped and then fled, under a chest of drawers, in the corner.

Josh pulled back his duvet, shivered, and climbed out of his bed. As the pale, gaunt looking boy, shuffled towards a pile of clothes, on the floor, he coughed.

Quickly, so as not to feel the cold, he took off the rags, that his aunt called nightwear. His thin, bony body shivered, as he hurried to dress. He then washed his dirty face, with freezing water, from a bowl on the dresser, before running his wet fingers, through his unkept hair, to tame it.

With the first signs of a new day, coming through the ice-covered windows, Josh knew that his aunt, would be screaming out, his and his sister's name, any moment now. She had obviously, startled Samson again. Just like she had done, for the countless mornings, ever since she had changed.

Josh needed to wake his sister.

'Maddie. Wake up,' he called softly.

'I'm already awake,' whispered a croaky voice.

'Right, you two!' Bellowed a voice from downstairs, 'Time to get up! Did you not hear, your alarm call?'

A door suddenly slammed downstairs. Presently, there was a pounding on the floor, right below Josh's feet. This was followed, with the abrupt opening of the same door downstairs.

'That's your alarm! Again! You have two minutes!' The last three words were now screamed, before Josh and Maddie felt the door slam, once again, through their floorboards. 'Now move it!'

Brother and sister quickly embraced. A small discreet tear ran down the little girl's face. She tried to hide it, but her brother knew.

'Don't cry Maddie,' he whispered softly.

'I'm not,' she cried out defiantly. 'I've got something, in my eye.'

There was no holding back the tears, for the little girl. She felt so desperate, so lonely, despite her twin brother, being there. With the tears, streaming down her pale, dirty face, Maddie, tried desperately to compose herself. She hated to show weakness, even at her young age.

'I miss father, so much,' she suddenly said.

'So, do I,' replied Josh.

'Especially today. It is our birthdays' today? Right Josh?'

'It is Maddie.' Josh smiled at his sister, as he stroked her long, unkept, blonde hair. 'Happy tenth birthday, Maddie.'

'Happy tenth birthday, Josh.'

Josh knew that it was their birthdays' today. Despite the removal of a calendar and clocks, from the cottage, he had put notches onto a piece of paper, as the sun had risen, and then gone down, on each and every day.

They had been only babies, when they had been put under the guardianship, of their aunt. Their father used to visit regularly. When he came, he had told them wonderous tales, of his adventures, and he always had a gift for them. He also told them, of their mother, when they asked. Neither child, had known their mother. She had died suddenly when they were born. Their father, always chose to change the subject, when asked when and how. Their father's visits became less frequent, as time passed. Not since the day, after their ninth birthday, had he last visited them. And it wasn't long after, that last visit, that their aunt changed.

For many years, she had been a loving and attentive lady. She had cared for the twins, as if they had been her own children. Her appearance, and that of the twins, was always immaculate. She lived by the virtues, of godliness and cleanliness.

Since their father's last visit, her niece and nephew, had seen a dramatic change in their aunt's personality, and general appearance. For someone, who had been a loving, caring person, it had been a quick and severe change. And, it was the twins, who bore the brunt, of that change.

'Come on Maddie. You must get dressed. Before, the dragon screams at us again.'

36

Quickly, his sister dressed, as Josh tried coaxing Samson out, from below the chest of drawers. The frightened cat was having none of it.

The twins heard the kitchen door swing open, and the heavy footsteps, of their aunt, across the hallway. Josh and Maddie, stared at each other, and waited for the bellowing voice, to scream at them.

'Get yourselves down here!' roared their aunt. 'Sharpish! Otherwise, there will be no supper tonight, for either of you!'

The kitchen door, instantly slammed.

'What! No watery soup and mouldy bread, for supper,' cried Josh sarcastically.

This bought a smile, to his sister's face.

'Come on,' Josh started. 'Before, she takes away the lumpy gruel, for breakfast, as well.'

Both children chuckled to themselves, as they closed the door, to their bedroom behind them. Whilst they made their way, quickly across the dank and dark landing, towards the stairs, they noticed, that the air had become thicker. Neither child, now smiled.

In the kitchen, their aunt waited. At her feet, were two metal buckets, filled with hot water, and a scrubbing brush, for each child. On the fire, a thin, but lumpy, liquid boiled. The sickly smell filled the kitchen.

Only, after countless chores, could breakfast be eaten. A breakfast, that neither child, relished.

Chapter Three

The Wulfdaeden Portal Point
Portaellen

Normauss had sprung out of the portal at Hells Point, (an inhospitable place, located in the wild north, of Wulfdaeden), wearing only the dirty cloak, he had been wearing, upon entry. He looked dishevelled and angry. This, as you will come to realise, is the troll's normal look. If, at any point, he is being nice, he is only adapting to his situation, until he can return, to his more natural state.

Normauss glanced back briefly to watch, as the window of the portal, slowly closed until it was completely gone, from view, in the dark sky.

It had just begun to drizzle. Normauss shivered, as he pulled the hood of the cloak, over his head.

Making his way cautiously down the dark, rugged corridors of the ravine, the troll, remained vigilant. He felt a constant need to look around, at every nook and cranny that he could see, through the fine rain and darkness, as he continued, along the path. Normauss tried not to think about, what could be lurking, in the cold inky blackness, that his eyes could not penetrate. It felt, as if the rock formations and the night, would swallow him up, at any moment.

Normauss suddenly halted, in his tracks. He could see four red eyes, transfixed on him. The troll took the impulsive decision, to remain, where he stood. He was shaking. The combination, of the fine rain soaking him to the skin, and fear, caused his body to tremble. A cold shiver shot down his spine. He knew, who those red eyes belonged to.

The four red eyes were set into the two skulls of a creature, as black as night, who patrols Hells Point. It, is a two headed, black hound, built of pure muscle and power. The creature is thought to be, the only type of its breed. A deformed mutation.

He was found wandering through Hells Point as a puppy, lost, lonely and near death. It was thought that the creature, was abandoned by its mother. So, it was taken in by the local regiment, of Blackheart knights. They trained him, to hunt, track and kill. They watched, as the creature developed and evolved, through his early years.

Eventually, upon reaching adulthood, the hound was put to good use, guarding the ravine. Here, he developed new skills to survive the conditions, that he lived and hunted in. The name given to him; was Beorn. He would become known as, The Hound of Hells Point.

'Good evening Beorn,' Normauss called out. His voice wavered ever so slightly when he first spoke. 'It's me,' he continued, 'Normauss.'

Slowly, the troll walked towards the four red eyes, his hand gingerly held out, in a gesture of friendship. He had hoped, to feel the touch of the creature's wet fur. And, not to lose his hand.

Normauss whimpered slightly, as two sets of yellow fangs, and four red eyes, suddenly crept closer, towards him, through the dark. Beorn, then let out, one deep and extremely aggressive bark, that shook the troll, to the core. The hound looked ready for the kill, as he came into view. The copious amounts, of foaming saliva, dripping from his fangs, did little to quell, the troll's fear. The two sets of red eyes now narrowed and Beorn began to growl.

He looks possessed, Normauss thought to himself. The troll could now sense that the hound wanted blood.

'Don't, come any closer Normauss,' a deep voice said, from the shadows. 'You know, he'll rip you to pieces.'

'I thought, just maybe, he would recognise me, for once,' Normauss whined.

'You know, he loves troll meat,' came the instant reply.

Normauss, did not answer. He chose instead, to stay perfectly still, as he eyed every move, that Beorn now made.

'Stay there troll. Do not move.'

Normauss, listened to the advice, and remained rooted to the spot.

'Beorn. Heel. Good boy.' The command, from the shadows, instantly bought the creature, to a standstill.

Normauss breathed a huge sigh of relief. He now watched, as Beorn turned slowly, to face the other way, and walked towards the voice. He listened, as the hound, continued to growl, whilst dragging his heavy feet, across the rock-strewn floor, towards the voice.

'Good boy,' the voice, was now a lot calmer and soothing. 'For you.'

Normauss, suddenly heard something heavy, thud to the ground. Moments later, came the sound of gnashing teeth, and the tearing of flesh. Followed by the grinding of bone. Hearing the sound, of the corpse being consumed, caused the troll to shudder once more, and slowly retreat, back on himself, into the relative safety, of the darkness.

Normauss watched, as four men promptly appeared from out of the shadows up ahead. They were dressed, in the red robes of Wulfdaeden. They wore black armour on their upper bodies that showed the symbol of their country's flag. The Tri-Lance.

One of the men, a knight, of obvious strength and agility, with a scar of significant length, going down his left cheek, stepped forward, as a loud rumble of thunder, echoed through the ravine.

'We have orders, from our master and king, to bring you urgently, to the Fortress Of Fear. He impatiently awaits your report. He threw, Normauss a blanket. 'For you troll. Put it on.' He growled, 'We wouldn't want you getting a chill.' The knight's tone was sarcastic, as he finished, 'Would we men?'

'No,' mocked his men, as they replied together.

'All right. Thanks. Saves me a walk,' replied Normauss, as a stupid grin, suddenly emerged, across his face. He, then proceeded, to pick up the blanket, and throw it over his soddened robes. 'Nice blanket. Thanks.' As he spoke, Normauss winked at the knight, who had thrown him, the blanket.

The knight didn't seem impressed with the troll's childish remark. As, he grabbed Normauss's wrist, he scowled at him, before sharply pulling him, past Beorn.

Beorn, was not interested in Normauss, anymore. The hound's heads were still ripping apart the carcass, that had been given to them.

Normauss watched briefly as the two headed creature, ripped flesh from the bone. He shuddered, once again, as one head, suddenly turned, to stare at him.

'Come on troll. We have no time to lose,' stated the knight.

Normauss, suddenly gasped, as the dark sky, unexpectedly exploded, with a white flash of lightning. It lit the whole ravine briefly, to reveal the secrets within, the darkness, and its shadows.

For a fleeting moment, the troll saw the narrow corridor, of the ravine, through the jagged, black rocks that seemed to go on forever, into the blackness, and beyond.

The drizzle had now turned, to heavy rain. Thunder, suddenly exploded overhead, like a thousand cannons, echoing down the ravine. Normauss, covered his ears. He hated the thunder of Hells Point, more than its lightning.

Without any warning, the troll was abruptly hoisted, onto the back, of one of the knights black steeds.

A lightning bolt, then shot from the dark, rumbling sky, and hit a gnarled old tree trunk, that hung from a ledge above them. The trunk instantaneously burst into flames and came crashing down onto the ravine floor.

One of the black steeds, became spooked, and reared up, on its hind legs. Its rider was almost thrown, as he struggled to stay on his mount.

'Time to go,' came, the instantaneous order, as another rumble of thunder, exploded above their heads.

As, they sped away, down the dark, and narrow, rocky ravine, of Hells Point, Normauss held on, for his dear life.

Looking up, at the inky, night sky, the troll shook, as the angry, sky exploded once more, with all its fury.

Normauss, thanked the Gods, that he was leaving this place. The place, where those same Gods, had positioned, Wulfdaeden's one and only portal.

★★★

The foreboding sight, of the Fortress Of Fear, came into view for the riders, as they reached the brow of a steep hill. Negotiating, the unpredictable terrain, as they made their way down the treacherous slope of the hill, proved tricky, for the riders and their steed's. The ground was soft and uneven, and littered with stones, that tested the hooves of the knight's mounts.

Normauss, was being thrown around, like a rag doll. He became nervous, every time the back legs, of his ride slipped.

The troll had only been to the fortress, once before. And, this was the first time, that he had seen it from the north. Viewing it from the vista, of the steep hill, had enhanced the dominant look of the enormous structure, and its high, soaring towers, that disappeared up, into the night sky.

According to legend, the towers in the four corners, rose high above the clouds, strong and proud. Each, with a Tri-lance flag, proudly raised.

The fortress has high, thick stone walls that were a mile wide on all sides. Inside, the impenetrable walls, is a city. The whole structure is built into the side, of a granite cliff, that disappears up, into the dark sky.

The area is known, as the Badlands. The capital, of Wulfdaeden.

As, the riders reached the flat, muddy ground, that surrounded the fortress, Normauss could see a strange mist, that looked as if it was going to surround them. He quickly noticed that it had developed, some density.

The thick, choking fog, rapidly enveloped, everything around it, as it swirled and danced amongst them, with menace.

Nervously, the troll strained his eyes to see. He, suddenly twitched, to his left, when he heard, several faint, and barely audible moans and groans. They began to grow in volume. It wasn't long, before there were moans, groans and voices speaking, all around them.

Normauss, had heard about the fog before. This was the first time; he had experienced it. Other trolls had told him about it, around the campfires, back home.

Tales were told of innocent trolls and Fantaellen's being captured, tortured, then killed, in the fortress. The fog is said to be, the faceless, souls of those beings, and is called, The Fog of Lost Souls.

The further, they rode into the fog, the thicker it became, and the more amplified, the moans grew. Periodic screams startled the troll which, were followed by crying, and voices of despair and pain.

What, Normauss experienced as he rode towards a meeting with his master, made him feel such pain and despair, unlike anything he had ever felt before. The troll, uncharacteristically, began to cry. Something, he never did. Even, as a young troll.

'First time, through the fog?' growled, a Blackheart knight, who could see the troll's anxiety.

'Yes,' Normauss mumbled.

The thick fog slowly dissipated, and the riders could see a little further into the distance. This was the moment that the imposing, and grandiose magnificence, of the Fortress Of Fear, suddenly came into view.

Normauss the troll's eyes opened wide, in wonderment, and he instantly gasped, at the incredible sight before him. Words, defied him, at this moment. All he could do, was stare.

It wasn't long, before the riders, came into the view of the Blackheart guards, along the battlements. A call suddenly rang out, from inside the huge, thick walls, to lower the drawbridge.

The enormous drawbridge of the fortress was slowly lowered, as the riders approached. The enormously long, iron chains, that pulled the extensive structure, creaked and groaned, as they took the weight, and the tension.

When, the drawbridge, was close to the ground, it was suddenly dropped, and an instantaneous, loud impact, violently shook, the earth. Hundreds of black Ravens, immediately scattered from the battlements, startled by the thundering noise.

Normauss, himself, was rattled and shaken. His mount had reared up upon the impact, which had caused the ground beneath them to violently shake.

The startled troll had held on to his rider, for dear life, whilst, the Blackheart knight, controlled the panicked animal. Eventually, with the stroke of its mane, the calm hand, had worked.

As, the riders made their way towards the drawbridge, Normauss, strained his neck to see. Looking up, at the black stone walls, that seemed to go beyond, the dark sky above, the troll, could just about see, the guards on the walls, and hear the orders, being called out. His attention was taken, by the flickering torches, and movement, from the windows and arrow slits, spread across, the enormous structure.

The drawbridge, seemed to go on forever, as the hooves of the riders, thundered towards, the main gate. The extremely high, stone built arch way, lit by torches, fixed on to the stonework, now opened up, as the portcullis, was raised, by its chains.

The troll's heart began to pound in his chest. His short, stocky, hairy legs, turned to jelly, as they neared. Suddenly they rode through, the stone arch way of the main gate coming to a halt in the dark, dimly lit courtyard.

Normauss now felt the sudden overpowering feelings, that he had experienced, the first time he came to the fortress. He had hoped, that on his next visit, the feeling of dread and fear, would not have taken over his senses, and reduced him to a nervous wreck. He had been wrong.

Without warning, the troll, was suddenly and unceremoniously pulled from his mount, and before he could protest, he was thrown to the ground. Normauss gasped, as he hit the hard, stone cobbles, with such force, that his whole body jolted on impact.

A couple of the Blackheart knights laughed, as they watched the troll struggle to compose himself as a sharp pain, pulsed through his body. Defiantly, Normauss got to his feet, whilst gasping for air, gulping it in, as he struggled to breath.

'This way troll,' came the order. 'Now!'

A forceful shove from behind, propelled Normauss forward. For a brief moment, he stumbled, before regaining his footing. The shaken troll suddenly grabbed hold of his left hand, which had begun to shake.

'I'm going, to rip your heart out,' he mumbled to himself, and to nobody in particular. His hidden fear had now turned to anger. His hand, had all of a sudden, stopped shaking.

Scornfully, the troll stared at a Blackheart knight, as he was marched past him, towards a large wooden door. The guard didn't even notice the small troll, who cursed and mumbled as he passed.

Normauss, became breathless, upon reaching, the top of a long, spiral staircase. His short legs had struggled the climb up, as the stone steps, seemed to go on forever. At certain points, the troll became quite claustrophobic. Especially, when the stairs narrowed. It felt as if the walls were closing in on him. He did have to stop on several occasions to regain his composure, whilst, behind him, several Blackhearts, pushed him, ever upwards.

Normauss, had been marched down several long corridors when his nervous feelings started all over again. His left hand, began to shake, once more. Anger, was once again, replaced by fear.

What is that?

The troll could hear something, albeit, very distant. The hairs, on the back of his neck, had begun to stand up. It was faint at first, but slowly became, more pronounced. They were, indeed, voices, he told himself.

Either side of him, shadows slowly appeared, that instantly formed, into human shapes. Visibly, they seemed to be dancing, within the torchlight on the walls.

Then, without warning, the shadows raced along the walls and ceiling, towards the other end of the corridor.

'Come,' they hissed. 'Come, this way, to the master's War Room.'

A shadow, above Normauss's head pointed the way. The troll watched as a faint and undistinctive face suddenly appeared in the dark form. The featureless profile quickly disappeared before the shadow, raced along the ceiling towards the other end of the corridor.

They were swiftly surrounded on all sides, by more shadow figures, who spoke in whispers too, that became more audible, the further they walked. Normauss, could not work out, what they said. It seemed like, an ancient, Wulfdaeden language. It was all around them now. The further they walked, towards a lone doorway, at the bottom of the corridor, the louder, the voices became.

Suddenly, the chorus of voices started to chant repeated, unclear words. The troll watched, as human shapes, formed into shadows, and danced on the walls. The chanting became louder and louder, to the point where, Normauss had to cover his ears.

Then, without any warning, the shadows, swiftly disappeared. It became eerily silent and still.

Down the corridor, an icy, cold wind blew, and the torches on the walls, flickered.

Normauss shuddered, as he was shoved, down the corridor, towards the only door, at the far end.

One of the Blackheart knights beat his big, heavy fist, once, on the large wooden door. He then, stood back and waited, to be called in.

Silence.

'Knock again,' came a faint voice, from the shadows, behind them. 'You must always knock, three times.'

Three heavy knocks at the door, one after the other, vibrated down the corridor.

'Enter!' a voice boomed.

Normauss was encouraged, with the tip of a blade in his back, to open the door, by one of the Blackheart knights. Reluctantly, the troll turned the handle, and then took, several cautious steps, into a dimly lit room.

Though, he could see very little, Normauss ventured further in, constantly looking around, as he did so.

He was always vigilant in every situation that he found himself in. But he was feeling very vulnerable for the first time in a while.

Normauss, began to feel as if he were suffocating. A panic, took over, as his pulse raced. It felt as if his heart would explode.

'I have, to get out of here,' he mumbled.

The troll was just about to do just that when he heard deep breathing from somewhere in the room.

'Hello!' he called out. 'Who is there?'

Normauss thought that he had heard movement to his left, so he swiftly turned on his heels.

'Normauss,' came, a low whisper, from over his shoulder. This caused the startled troll, to cry out, before his legs and feet became lead, and he was rooted to the spot.

From behind him the troll felt a cold hand suddenly grab his neck. This was quickly followed by a heavy crack on the back of his skull.

Almost instantly the lights went out in Normauss's world as his body slumped onto the floor.

Chapter Four

An urgent and important message had just been delivered to Captain George Corder at the South Western Fortress. Straightaway he recognised the handwriting. Turning it over, he broke, the red, Fantaellen royal seal, before unfolding, the paper and reading its content.

Upon finishing he placed the paper on his desk and dismissed the messenger with his thanks, and a heavy heart.

'It won't be long now, before the Blackheart's attack,' he said aloud as he stared out of his window, at the thick, bank of swirling fog, that had thus far, shown very little sign of diminishing.

The captain's thoughts suddenly turned to the previous night. The noise of a great sea battle, going on, behind the curtain of fog, now filled his ears, once more. He and his men, had listened, and feared the worst for their country's ships and sailors, who would have been, hopelessly outnumbered, if the reports of how many Wulfdaeden ships were ready to engage in battle, were true.

In less than an hour, the cries and the screams of the dying abated, and the straits of the Stoirim Sea, had fallen silent, once more.

Unlike the night before, this one had been quiet, thus far. Captain Corder had spent his time alone, in the officer's quarters, going through his official correspondence, and the plans for the defence, of their coastline. He had prayed that the fog, would stay, just long enough, for him to do the final checks of his fortress, and ready his men, for the upcoming battle, and the war, that would inevitably follow.

They would be ready. They had to be ready.

There was another knock at his door. It woke him from his thoughts.

'Enter,' he calmly, called out.

Captain Corder had asked for his officer's to present themselves in the officer's quarters.

'Gentlemen, please.'

He gestured for a couple of his officers to join him as they entered the room.

They were dressed in their purple battle robes, an officers' tunic, a gleaming metal breast plate and greaves, to protect their legs. At their side a sword of the finest Fantaellen steel.

'Excellent,' remarked the captain. 'Ready for a fight, then boys?'

'Yes sir!' the officers said, in unison. It had been, an immediate, and eager response, which had pleased, their captain.

Within moments, all the officers were present. Small talk was briefly exchanged, as the captain, encouraged his officers to feel at ease.

For a very brief moment he stared at the young men in the room. They looked so smart so young and eager. Yet not one of them had been tested in battle. Their armour had not a single scratch or dent on it. Unlike his armour that hung on an old wooden stand by the door. His sword, that his father had given him, when he became a junior officer, also hung proudly next to it. He hoped that one day, at least one of these young men would stand where he was, talking to his subordinates. Having survived the hordes of Blackhearts now waiting to attack their homeland.

'I have a message, in my hand for you all.' Captain Corder held the message aloft, in his hand. 'In fact, it is a message for all our fellow countrymen, up and down the width and breadth of our coastline, and our fortress's inland.' He briefly paused for a moment, before continuing.

'King Stefan, is dead.' A stunned silence now existed in the room. 'He passed away suddenly, in the early hours of this morning. We all know that the Wulfdaeden spies will be working in the shadows. Their joyful message, currently heading to our coasts. Once, their fleets out in the Stoirim Sea, receive the news, the Blackheart devils will attack. Fog or no fog.'

Captain Corder walked from behind his desk and approached his officer's. He then, began to look every one of them, in the eye. He wanted to stare deep, into their souls.

'Good,' he said. For, he had liked, what he had seen. 'No fear. That is what I need to see. We must be cool, and calm gentlemen. The men will look to us, for leadership and we must deliver.'

As, he walked over to a wooden table, in a corner of the room, he grabbed a candle, and began to unroll a map.

'We are now at war. Make no mistake. The enemy will attack soon. The Blackheart ships, that sit just beyond the wall of the fog, just shy of the range of our Trebuchet's, await their signal. We have a limited amount of time before they come. We have gone over our plan of defence, many, many times. We must make the most, of what time we have.' Captain Corder began to straighten the map out, on the table. 'Come.' He beckoned, to his young officer's.

Swiftly, they joined their captain round the table, before he continued, his briefing, choosing not to miss, a single detail, as he spoke. Such was his meticulous and exhaustive diligence always, to every little action, and possible outcome.

'That was where, the discarded rowing boat was found, along with our dead sentries. As you can see. It was only, a mile away. Is that their attack point?'

He pointed at one of two coves. Not one officer spoke.

'Well. It could be here too?' He pointed, at the other cove. 'Or both? That would be my guess gentlemen.'

Captain Corder began, to go through the defensive plan, that had been put into place, for when the attack commenced. Once again, he picked out every detail, to them. Each of his officers, knew the plan inside and out. But still they listened to his every word. They had done military exercise days, where every man was made aware of their role in the defence of the fortress. In theory, they were ready. Ready to defend the south west coast of their homeland.

Fantaellen would soon be under attack. War was indeed imminent.

★★★

Dazed and with a severe throbbing pain across his skull Normauss suddenly awoke from the darkness that had taken him. As, his senses slowly returned, it felt as if his head would explode. He suddenly realised, that he lay prone on the cold stone floor. He could taste blood and dirt. His skull pounded uncontrollably, and as he lifted his head, he realised, that he could not see properly. Normauss winced, when a red-hot pain, unexpectedly, seared through every fibre, of his body. It took his breath away.

Still, dazed and groggy, Normauss wobbled, then staggered, as he tried, to pull himself up. As a direct consequence, the troll, instantly decided to remain seated, rather than trying to stand up. For now, the effort required, was too great.

Rubbing his head, that felt like a smashed rock, he began to, cautiously look around. Within, the dimly lit room, the troll could make out, blurred shadows, and shapes.

As his sight now gradually returned, Normauss became aware of a cloaked figure, in a corner of the room, hidden by the shadows. The figure seemed to be standing, with their back turned to him. A large hood, over their head.

The cloaked figure turned to face Normauss from the shadows and stepped forward. The troll now realised, how tall, the person or the creature was. He could not make out any facial features apart from two icy blue eyes that stared directly at him.

Normauss's gaze, quickly became fixed on a poor wretch of a creature that the cloaked figure had hold of. Over its mouth, was a hand. At its neck, a small blade. The troll, instantly gasped when he realised, who it was.

'Altoa!' he screamed, as he started to charge towards the cloaked figure, who, on seeing the troll moving at a speed, pulled the blade closer, to the creature's neck. The creature, immediately winced, as the blade, drew a little blood. This stopped Normauss, dead in his tracks.

The troll now slowly backed away, in a show of retreat, and submission. His hands held out in acceptance.

A stalemate now prevailed. Nobody spoke. Nobody moved.

★★★

Napoleon Victory, the King of Wulfdaeden, and his most trusted General, Cedric Grafton, were marching, down the cold, dark corridors, of the fortress of fear. The general listened intently, as his master, relayed his order's, spoken with an impetus, and a motivation, born from some information, that he had received, 'on the wing', as he called it, just moments ago.

'Do you think, the poison will have killed him, by now Sire?' asked General Grafton.

'Well,' began Victory, 'the hawk, that was chosen, to bring back the intelligence, is the fastest of his breed. You are still looking, at several hours though, for the crossing. The bird's release signals the poison's administration. He should be dead by now. The signal to the fleet will be actioned soon. I am sure.'

General Grafton, smiled coldly, at his master's response.

The two men were dressed in their Blackheart armour. At their sides, their sheathed broad swords. Both men, cut a figure of power, as their heavy footstep's, echoed down the corridor.

Their stride, presently lengthened, as they neared, their destination. They were both desperate, to hear the intelligence gathered, by one of their spy's.

Napoleon Victory trusted General Grafton, with his life. Together, they had planned and executed the coup, which had seen the whole Blackheart army, turn against its king, resulting in his gruesome death. It was a bloody business, with heavy losses. Both men, had bled for their cause, and they had the scars, to prove it.

General Grafton's left ear was missing. Taken clean off his head, by a Fantaellen sword. Napoleon Victory had a long scar on his left cheek, from the corner of his left eye, right down to his lower jaw. Skilful surgeons had managed to save his eye, which he wore a patch over, to cover it.

Both men, had other scars, that defined their look, of a fierce and war like warrior. Their hair was shaved to the bone, as a sign of masculinity. Their presence was truly powerful, and nobody, ever challenged their orders.

Victory and his general, suddenly stopped, as they came to, a large wooden door. The two, Blackheart guards at the doorway, immediately snapped to attention. Their acknowledgement, of the presence of their master and the general, was greeted by a nod from General Grafton.

One of the Blackheart knights directly opened the door for them, and the two men, promptly entered the room.

Napoleon Victory smiled coldly, when he saw Normauss, at the other side of the room. He then nodded, at the cloaked figure.

'You may go now,' he growled.

The cloaked figure, side stepped towards the door, whilst still holding the blade, at the throat of his captive. His icy blue eyes stayed fixed on the watching troll, as he slowly made his way, towards the entrance.

Normauss stared, not daring to move, as the cloaked figure left the room, his blade still not moving, from the throat of his terrified captive. The troll's eyes, followed them, as they left the room, and continued to until the door slammed behind them.

'That, young Normauss,' Napoleon Victory started, 'is a little reminder. We will spill her blood, if we have to, my troll friend. I'm told female trolls, bleed very well.' A cold, calm and calculated smile, now came over his face, as he waited, for the troll, to react.

Victory suddenly sniggered when he saw Normauss grimace, and then touch, the back of his head.

'Ah yes. The whack on the head. Well, that was not my doing. My cloaked friend insisted. Sorry about that.'

Victory closed in on the troll. Having chosen, to stand in front of the creature, to intimidate him, with his size and stature, the King of Wulfdaeden, now knelt, in front of Normauss, and stared into his soul.

The troll showed no sign of weakness, his stare unflinching, even though, it felt like his master's eyes, were going to bore a hole, right through him.

'I see you Normauss,' Victory hissed, winking at the troll, and grabbing him by the chin, he pulled him close.

Normauss immediately flinched, at the awful smell, of his master's rancid breath.

'Let me down. And she dies.' Spittle hit Normauss's face, as Victory said his last few words.

'Then, I will find the rest of your family and I will massacre them.'

The troll instantly cried out in shock and in pain, when he was suddenly poked, in his left eye, with such force, that his head shot back. Normauss, now lowered his head, and began to rub his eye, as a painful tear, quickly followed.

'You, I will keep alive, troll. Just.' Victory's breathing had increased, and he had become, more excited. 'Not before taking your eyes. One, at a time.'

Normauss struggled to break free, as Victory now forced open the troll's mouth.

'Then, I will take your tongue.' A wicked, evil smile crept over his master's face, as he released the troll's tongue. Normauss choked and spluttered, as he pulled away, in desperation.

'Finally, I will have you thrown into the deepest, darkest dungeon, to rot. Remember Normauss the troll. You are Mine! I own you!' The last few words were spoken with such vitriol, that it shook Normauss, to the core.

In an instant, Napoleon Victory's tone changed, and the wickedness on his face, had suddenly been replaced, with a look of concern.

'You're shivering.' He remarked softly to Normauss, who said nothing.

He just stared. His eyes unflinching and determined, despite the unbearable pain, in his left eye, that was extremely red and weeping uncontrollably.

'Listen,' Victory had a gentle hold of the troll's arm. 'I do appreciate, what you do for me. For our cause. You have been my eyes and my ears, on the twins. So please. Tell me everything. Since Agent Grimshaw, was persuaded to look after them, on my behalf, have there been, any problems?'

'No Sire,' Normauss started, 'there has been, no enemy activity around the area. It has been very quiet.'

'Good. That means, that the dying king, or should I say, my hopefully, now deceased brother, seemed to have no idea, of our sister's betrayal.' Victory sniggered to himself, once more.

'That's good Sire,' remarked General Grafton.

'It is General. It is.' There was a pause, as Napoleon Victory, gathered his thoughts, whilst pacing up and down the room.

Normauss was nervous. He had told, his master the truth. The twins were safe. The troll still felt guilty though. As, if he had lied. He hadn't. But, the unpredictability of Victory's moods, made Normauss feel, suddenly vulnerable, and guilty.

'Anything else to report?' Victory suddenly asked.

'No Sire.'

Normauss, now watched nervously, as his master, continued to pace the room. The troll could normally read a situation but this time he was not sure if his master believed him.

The troll's nervousness, came from a story, that he had made up, to cover his whereabouts, on a mission, a few months ago. He had lied to Victory, and he knew that his master knew. Normauss was sure, that Altoa, had been paraded, in front of him, just moments earlier, as a warning. For it had been his little sister, who he had visited, when he should have been watching the twins. He was willing to bet, that the person in the hood with those blue eyes had followed him and reported back to their master.

The man in the hooded cloak was known as the Assassin. Normauss hated him with a passion. He was sure that the Assassin, felt the same way, about him too. They were rivals. Bitter rivals.

They were both, Victory's best spies. Each working in the shadows to achieve their mission. Normauss had once sworn, to kill him one day. He hoped that day, would come soon. Nobody holds a knife, to his little sister's throat, and lives. However, that was a mission for another day. Normauss could be patient when he had to be.

Napoleon Victory stared at the short, stocky creature in front of him. He was carefully thinking about what function the troll could serve him next. The King of Wulfdaeden knew of the reputation of the trolls of the Fantaellen mountains. Their cunning, and their abilities to hide in the shadows made them the best trackers in the World of Portaellen. When in battle they also made a fierce adversary.

Even though the troll looked so vulnerable at this moment Victory could still see a fire in the creature's deep, dark eyes. That fire was the reason that the troll still served a purpose. Victory just had to make sure that he kept him on his side.

A Blackheart guard entered the room with some new clothes for Normauss. As the troll began to dress, Napoleon Victory passed him a sheathed dagger. On the handle, was a raised emblem, of the Tri lance banner, which the troll rubbed his fingers over, as he unsheathed the weapon.

'Keep that dagger, hidden on your person', began Victory. 'I am sending you to where you can be of the most use to me. I am sending you back home. You will be my eyes and my ears in Fantaellen. You will report to General Grafton, who will join you in Fantaellen, within the next few days, because any hour now, our warships will receive the signal, to attack the Fantaellen coastline. The invasion will then begin.'

Normauss quickly dressed. He had been given a white cotton shirt, a pair of black breeches and a black hooded cloak. He had also attached, his sheathed dagger to his belt. He was ready.

'You may go now Normauss.' Victory had now closed in on the troll, once more. 'I expect you to comply. Remember I hold somebody most precious to you.'

'I won't forget,' snapped the troll, his dark eyes, instantly widening.

'Good. Control that anger, you have. Use it properly.' Victory suddenly gestured towards the door. 'Now go,' he snarled.

Normauss hurriedly made his way towards the door. As he turned the handle, he briefly glanced back at his master. The look of pure hatred that he gave Victory managed to stop the King of Wulfdaeden's black heart, for a split second. The ferocious and chilling anger in the troll's eyes, the catalyst.

Victory, instinctively sneered at Normauss, which was followed, by a look of pure distain for the creature, before nodding his head, in acknowledgement of the look, he had been given. He then turned his back, on the troll.

As Normauss closed the door behind him the troll swore, that he would be back one day to bring his sister home.

With Normauss now gone, General Grafton was quick to voice his concerns to his master, about the troll.

'I know, you don't trust the creature, Cedric. But he is ideal for the job. Besides we have him held to ransom now. My hope is that once Fantaellen is on its knees, we can bring the rest of the trolls to heel. Normauss will be our way of doing just that.'

'I still don't trust him, Sire.'

'He will comply,' came the sharp reply. 'He has too.'

Napoleon Victory began to speak to his general about something more pressing. The twins were now an important piece in his jigsaw. And, he had a plan.

'I need you to speak to Wulfrik,' Victory stated.

'Yes Sire.'

'The Fantaellen's will be looking, to take the twins back to Guinlance to keep them safe. Wulfrik and his Wolfdogs are on standby. They await my orders.'

'Yes Sire.'

'Send them with half a dozen of your best men to agent Grimshaw's home. They must bring the twins back here. Alive.'

'Yes Sire. I will see to it.'

Napoleon Victory was desperate to be The Sovereign of Portaellen. He also needed heirs. Compliant, true blooded ones. He figured that he could make both twins true Wulfdaeden's by nurturing their minds, their souls, and most importantly, turning their hearts. Just as he had been. The twins were his hope of continuance. The children of a pure, true blood of the direct descendants of the original Portaellen Sovereign.

Victory's thoughts suddenly took him back to the throne room at Guinlance Castle. The words of his older twin brother ringing in his ears as he was banished from Fantaellen, forever. For a crime that his brother had said was an unforgivable sin. A sin that only the two brothers and the queen knew of.

Before he dismissed his confidant and general the two men went over all their plans and strategies once again. General Grafton watched as his master and friend became animated as they carefully went over his invasion plans.

Upon, dismissing the general the two men embraced, and shook hands.

'The invasion needs to be fast and lethal,' Victory stated. 'Our enemy will then be brought to their knees.'

General Grafton saw the passion in his master's eyes as he spoke. His pupil's widened as he finished, 'Fantaellen will burn! The blood of its people will fuel the flames.'

General Grafton saluted his master, with a thump of his fist on the breast plate of his armour. Then, turning on his heel's the general marched out of the room.

Cedric Grafton, General of his master's Blackheart knights had his orders. As he made his way down the cold dimly lit corridors of the Fortress Of Fear he did so with purpose. The blood raced around his body and his evil; black heart pounded in his chest. Never had he felt so alive.

Time was short. Orders to be given. An enemy to bring to its knees.

★★★

Henri, the Royal Physician had been summoned to a riverbank a few miles outside of Guinlance Castle. The last daylight hours had faded quickly, and the evening chill had kept him awake.

He had only managed a few hours' sleep since the death of the sovereign. A combination of guilt worries and questions consumed his tired mind.

Henri had been told that a body had been found by a patrol of knight's returning from the coast, and that he with his medical background would be needed to ascertain what had happened to the victim as foul play was not only suspected but certain.

As he dismounted his steed Henri gently patted the horse's head before walking the creature towards a tree where he tied the reins around the trunk. He then grabbed his medical bag and accompanied a knight who now directed him towards a small, wooded area.

It was eerily quiet. Just a single hoot from an owl disturbing the gentle sound of the River Leife lapping at the riverbank.

'One of my men spotted him,' revealed the knight. 'We haven't touched the body. Thought it best that we leave it for you. A couple of us recognise him from the castle. We think he was a servant.'

Henri was suddenly curious. 'How did your man, spot the body from the track?'

'Bit of luck sir. A call of nature.'

'I see,' replied Henri.

They walked the distance to the site of the body in silence which allowed Henri to survey the surroundings. They appeared to be walking deeper into the trees towards the river when he spotted a clearing and a glimpse of the riverbank.

'Just over here, sir.'

As they neared the body, Henri noticed that it was lying prone with a large pool of blood that had congealed, around the head.

He knelt next to the body and began to roll it over.

'Here. Let me help you, sir.' Offered the knight.

Together, the two men rolled the body over.

Henri instantly recognised the dead man. Somehow, he suppressed the urge to gasp or say anything.

After gathering himself together Henri studied the body with more intent. All the time staring at the lifeless face as he did so.

'He has an obvious wound to his neck,' Henri confirmed. 'A knife wound. A deep cut, from left to right.'

As Henri examined the body further, he found a large amount of blood all over the man's right hand. In all likelihood the victim's he concluded. Probably the final act of a dying man trying to hold his neck together. As he wiped away the blood his heart suddenly stopped when he saw the blackened fingertips.

Oh! No!

Henri tried to remain calm and carry on his investigation as the events leading up to the death of King Stefan flashed through his head.

A few feet away he noticed a dagger on the ground most likely the dead man's as only a very panicked killer would leave their weapon behind Henri deduced.

'Are you all right, sir?' enquired the knight who could see that the royal physician was visibly shaken and a little distracted.

'Yes, I'm fine. The sight of dead bodies still gets to me. Strange isn't it? My profession and I still can't get used to seeing one. I will be all right, shortly. It will pass.'

'No problem, sir. I can give you a few moments.'

The knight had been called over to speak to one of his men. So that now left Henri alone with the body.

Henri continued to examine the corpse. Strangely he noticed that the deceased's left hand was inside his tunic. As Henri pulled out the hand to examine it he could see a chain entwined within in stiffened fingers. The royal physician began slowly prising it from the tightened grasp.

The bloodied chain was a dull silver with a small, engraved pendant that appeared to have a prominent raised symbol on the back of it. Craftily, Henri placed it in his pocket. He did not recognise the symbol, but he knew that it did not belong to the victim.

The victim had been an assassin. A killer with blackened fingertips. The mark of a poisoner. And the probable killer of a king and a sovereign.

Walking away from the body Henri had one question in his head. How did this probable murderer of his sovereign get out of

Guinlance Castle when it was supposed to be in lockdown? The victim appeared to have no official paperwork upon his person to allow him to leave the castle. So how did he get out?

It was not long before the royal physician had more questions than answers whirling around his tired mind as he rode his steed back towards Guinlance Castle.

He did, however, now know that King Stefan's death was definitely not a natural one. He believed that he also knew how and what poison was probably used. Furthermore, in his pocket he had a bloodied chain prised from the fingers of the dead man that had a symbol of some significance of which Henri was not sure of yet. That chain held a possible clue to the identity of the killer.

A killer who was either safely hidden behind the walls of Guinlance Castle or was away in the wind and back in the shadows. Were they friend or foe?

Henri had no clue.

Chapter Five

In the dead of night, a small band of Fantaellen knights, urged their steed's, through a large, and densely wooded area. The crisp and clear light from the waxing crescents, of the two moons, in the star covered sky, lit their way.

The knights had left Guinlance Castle, in a hurry, a few hours earlier, with the orders of the highest secrecy, given to their captain, by Robert Scotten. They wore, the silver armour, and the purple robes, of the royal battalion of the king's knights. These men were the best knights of the royal bodyguard. Their mission was of the utmost importance and secrecy.

Their captain was Jonti Quixall who had been attending to family business back in England when he had received his papers to return to Fantaellen; immediately. He was a man who had been so highly thought of by King Stefan. He had been missed by his sovereign for a few years. The knight's services were needed in a terrible war in his other world. Thereafter on his return everywhere that the king had gone Jonti had been there. He was a decorated knight. A leader of men. A warrior.

His Sergeant, and second in command, Geremi Hammam, was a decorated knight. The younger knight was also Jonti's oldest and dearest friend.

The two men had saved each other's lives, countless times. More recently, in the trenches of France and Belgium. Then, after the Armistice, both returned to their world of birth, to continue their normal duties, of guarding the king and sovereign. As children, they had become friends, after a chance meeting, and as young men, they had trained, side by side, growing stronger and smarter, each day. On their right wrist, both bore a cut, which bound them together, as blood brothers. An oath, to be broken, only by death.

With the last, of the trees behind them, the knights raced towards their destination. Over fields, past villages, across streams, and up and down, hills they rode, stopping for nothing.

Nearing the coast, the smell of the sea air, filled their lungs, and the dense, thick fog, that hung out at sea, gradually crept up on them. As they continued, for several miles, they followed a rocky path, that kept them quite close, to the coastal headland. Not once, did the fog break.

Upon taking, a sudden north west turn inland, their urgent pace continued, through fields and past sleeping villages, until they reached a riverbank. They crossed the River Leife, to the opposite side, before Captain Quixall, ordered his knights, to dismount and take a rest. He remained on his steed, as he looked around, at the quiet countryside, that surrounded them.

The captain was presently joined by his second in command.

'Anything wrong?' Geremi asked.

'No. I am always cautious, around the portals. Especially Ingress Hill. The portal is less than a mile away, straight up that hill. When I see that tree stump on the brow, it makes me a little nervous. You never know, who is watching from up there, or waiting for you.'

'True,' replied Geremi. 'We have had a few surprises, over the years.'

Jonti, then briefly noticed, a fresh cut on Geremi's hand, as he pointed towards the tree stump.

'How, did you get that cut?' he enquired.

Geremi, seemingly caught unawares, by his friend's unexpected question, now came me up, with a vague answer.

'Oh! You know?' Geremi did not look at his friend, as he continued, 'Sword drills. An over enthusiastic pupil.'

'You should be more careful, my friend.'

'Yes. I should.'

Geremi, suddenly looked nervous. Jonti could see his friend fumbling with his collar. He now knew why, he had been vague, and caught off guard, with his question. Jonti now moved, to reassure him.

'You will be fine. Portal journeys are not that bad,' he said softly.

Geremi, nodded at Jonti. He looked like; he was about to be sick.

'You've got your pendant, for good luck?'

Geremi nodded, once more.

'You will be fine, then.'

Jonti watched, as Geremi fumbled around, inside his tunic. He had a confused, then a sudden, horrified look on his face.

'Are you sure, you are all right?' enquired Jonti.

Geremi, did not reply, as he frantically searched, through his pockets, clearly looking for something.

'I am fine!' he suddenly snapped.

With that, the young knight angrily turned away, from his captain, and strode towards his steed, cursing as he went.

'All right my friend,' Jonti called out.

He had seen, Geremi react like this on numerous occasions, just before a portal journey. So, he dismissed his outburst, as the usual nerves.

Glad, I don't suffer from portal sickness.

Captain Quixall now signalled to the rest of his men, to mount up.

The riders were soon on the brow of Ingress Hill. A magnificent, silent, starry night sky surrounded the inconspicuous landmark. With, the two waxing crescent moons, sat high in the dark velvet, providing the perfect, back drop. It was eerily beautiful and quiet.

Jonti Quixall, suddenly felt so small, and insignificant, compared to the enormity of the panorama, and the magic of Ingress Hill, that surrounded them. He was, in complete awe.

It wasn't long, before the captain and his men, were dismounted and marching towards, the window of the portal, that slowly opened up, for them.

Captain Quixall suddenly felt exhilarated, as he always did when the portal window, began to open.

'Come on!' he called, to his men. 'Time to carry out, our orders.'

The future of Fantaellen, rested squarely on his broad shoulders. Silently, Captain Quixall prayed, that they would get there on time.

★★★

Henri had not slept well, that night. His mind had been racing. He knew that he had to do the right thing, and tell Robert, what he had discovered, last night. Over and over, he had gone through, numerous conversations, in his head. Different scenarios, playing through his mind. Some, sounding plausible. Others implicating him, in the murder of their sovereign.

'If only, I could have spotted the signs of the poison,' he suddenly blurted out, as he lay, wide awake, staring at the ceiling.

He knew, that was impossible, as the particular poison that he thought was used, was normally undetectable. Those facts did not stop, a heavy guilt, wreaking havoc, on his weary mind, as the dark, small hours, had passed.

So, it was no surprise, when Henri entered Robert Scotten's office, the next morning, looking weary and extremely troubled.

The Guardian of Fantaellen, was busy, making final arrangements, for King Stefan's funeral, the following day.

He had also just dismissed, two of his general's, who had given him, their daily reports. As, he quickly, read over the contents, he did not look up once, to acknowledge, that Henri had entered the room.

Henri waited quietly and nervously. He watched, as his friend, suddenly stood up, and walked over to another, larger table, that had several maps, strewn across it. There, he placed the reports.

At this point, he walked over to Henri, and greeted him, with a formal handshake. The two, old friends, had not spoken to each other, since the day that King Stefan had died.

'You look tired.' remarked Robert.

Henri said nothing. He just smiled awkwardly. To Henri, the greeting had been uncomfortable and cold, but understandable. His friend had a lot of responsibility. Robert, had to put any friendship's aside, as running the kingdom, and the inevitable war, with Wulfdaeden, was his number one priority. His new position, even if, only temporary, would also mean, that he could favour no one. He had to be distant. Henri also felt that his friend, could have blamed him, for the death of their sovereign. It was that feeling, as he started to talk to Robert, that made him, uncharacteristically stutter.

Robert Scotten had ignored Henri's initial faltering words, and he stood listening to him, as the physician composed himself, and continued. His eyes were completely fixed on Henri, as he began to tell him, about the body on the riverbank, and what he had discovered.

Once, Henri had finished speaking, Robert suddenly turned, and walked to the other side of the room, shaking his head, in obvious disbelief. He quickly became agitated. His face, swiftly contorted with anger, as he looked at his friend.

Are you telling me, that the death of our sovereign, as catastrophic as it is, was murder!' He slammed his fist down, on the large table, in front of him. 'Zada!' he exclaimed, 'And, to make matters worse, you saw a black coating, on the king's tongue, and thought nothing of it?' Robert let out a sigh of disdain, as he nodded his head, in disbelief.

'I have no excuse, for not taking any notice, of the king's black tongue,' Henri explained. 'It was my error. I would not have been able, to save his life. The poison, already had him.'

Robert just stared at Henri. An obvious, incandescent rage began to show, on his tired features.

Henri continued unperturbed, choosing to ignore, his friend's anger. 'I believe that the poison, is from a Death Poppy,' he began. 'It is found, mainly in the remote regions, of the Wulfdaeden mountains.'

The royal physician, began to explain, that some had been seen growing, in Fantaellen. Their seeds probably bought over on the winds, or on the soles of unsuspecting, enemy spies.

Robert, listened stoically, desperately trying to keep his anger in check, as his friend carried on. 'It is only lethal, when the black seeds from the centre of the poppy, are boiled. They disintegrate, into a clear liquid. They have no smell or taste. A fairly short period of ingestion of the liquid, or it being absorbed through the skin, will prove lethal. Also, someone who has touched the seeds, for a certain period of time, will have blackened skin.'

Robert now approached Henri. 'And you?' he sneered.

The physician instantly held out his hands. He did not look at his friend, as he did so.

Henri continued, still unshaken, as his friend stared at him, with doubting eyes, that were so cold and unforgiving. 'The man found dead yesterday, at the riverbank, was a servant, who I recognised, as one of several, who kept bringing me a jug of water, for King Stefan. I gave the king, little sips of the water, in between him, going in and out of consciousness, to help with the fever. When, I examined the servant's body on the riverbank, I found that his fingertips, on one hand, were blackened. I also found this, in his hand.'

Henri handed Robert the chain and pendant.

'It's a travelling pendant. Not sure, if you recognise the symbol? It's not something, I have seen before.'

Robert studied the chain and pendant briefly, before putting it directly, into his pocket.

'No, I don't recognise the symbol, either. I will look, into it.'

Robert's demeanour suddenly changed, as he said, 'I am sorry, Henri,' as he held out his hand to his friend, who took hold of it cautiously, 'I did blame you, for King Stefan's death. I felt that you could have saved him. But, with this evidence, that you have presented to me, I can see, that would not have been possible, without prior knowledge. I am glad, that you have told me.'

Henri felt a relief, come over him.

'I could not, have kept it a secret, Robert. The security of our kingdom is at stake,' he stated.

'Very true. We need to keep this, between the two of us, Henri. We don't know, if the assassin, was killed by one of our own? Or someone, who is yet to surface? Or, indeed, another enemy spy, covering their tracks?'

'Of course, Sire,' Henri agreed.

'Please Henri. I am your friend. In our own company, I am just, plain old Robert, to you.' A warm smile, had now, enveloped his face. The two men embraced.

Over the course of the morning, the two friends spoke at great lengths, about various things, including the arrangements, for their sovereign's funeral, the next day.

Both men, now began to enjoy each other's company once again, the air seemingly cleared, as plans were being put into place.

They were the plans of a guardian, that would hopefully repel, an enemy armada, with an obvious intent, of invasion.

However, the funeral of a king, and a sovereign, also needed to take place, as the Gods had an empty chair, waiting for him, at their table.

★★★

On the eve of King Stefan's funeral, Robert Scotten, spent the night standing guard, over his sovereign's body. He had felt that it was the right thing to do. His duty.

Watching the sun set, through the window, of his personal quarter's, the Guardian of Fantaellen, donned his finest robes and armour. As he left, he grabbed his ceremonial sword.

Entering the quiet sanctity, of the candlelit chapel, Robert dismissed the two knights, who stood, dutifully and silent, at each end of the coffin. As, they turned on their heels, they saluted their sovereign, and smartly marched out of the chapel.

King Stefan's body had lain in state, for the last couple of days. An armed guard, constantly around his coffin.

This was the first time, that Robert had seen his sovereign

since he had died. He looked so peaceful. Almost as if he slept. Robert, spent the next few moments, staring at the coffin. His thoughts, drifting away.

The burden, of governing his country, that was on the brink of invasion and war, suddenly weighed heavy on his shoulders. He wished that his king and sovereign, would suddenly climb out of his coffin, and tell him, that it had all been a ruse, to lull the enemy, into a false sense of security before, attacking the advancing Blackhearts, smashing their invasion, and sending them defeated, back into the Stoirim Sea.

Robert slowly came out of his dreamy state. He and Stefan, as he had been told, to call his king and sovereign, had been close. True friends, who had confided, in each other, about everything. Even when, dark forces had tried to enter Robert's life, his king had helped him fight, them off. The Guardian of Fantaellen, would have died for his king. He wished that it were his body, lying in the coffin. Robert's heart suddenly felt so heavy, and a tear had begun to fall, as guilt overcame him.

It should be me.

King Stefan was dressed in his full, Fantaellen battle armour. His silver breastplate had been polished, with its gleaming emblem, of two rearing steeds, reflecting the calm candlelight, of the chapel. His purple robes were pressed and clean. In his hands, he held the hilt of his battle sword, that lay horizontal, against his body.

As, the night slowly progressed, Robert began to think about the impending Wulfdaeden attack. He wished, he could talk to his king, one last time. He just needed somebody, to reassure him.

The passing small hours, played havoc, with his tired mind. Robert battled his doubts and his misgivings, as he heard numerous hourly chimes, of a distant clock. But, there he stood, unmoved and disciplined. Determined, to do his duty, within the silence of the chapel.

When, the changing of the guard, came an hour or so after sunrise, Robert Scotten, marched from the chapel, with a purpose. He was exhausted, but he had no time for sleep. He had dispatches to read, and his sovereign's funeral to oversee.

Once reading the first of his dispatches, Robert Scotten, knew that the Wulfdaeden attack, was just hours away. For, the fog had dissipated, in certain areas, along the coast, and the Blackheart war drums, had begun their beat.

There was a knock, at Robert's door.

'Enter!' he called out.

The door opened, and a young knight, marched in. He snapped to attention and saluted him.

Robert, stared at the young knight, who stayed silent.

'You may speak!' Robert snapped.

'Sire! Everything is ready.'

'Good. I will be out, in a moment.'

'Sire!'

The young knight, saluted once more, before marching out, into the corridor, closing the door, behind him.

The Wulfdaeden Blackhearts were coming. Yet, the next several hours, were about honouring a king and a sovereign, who had been murdered.

Then, Robert Scotten and his army of knights, would smash the Blackheart invasion force into pieces, before sending their ships, to the bottom of the Stoirim Sea, with Fantaellen trebuchets.

A lesson, given in blood and countless bodies. A clear message given, to a traitorous brother, once of Fantaellen.

★★★

It had been raining since the early hours. The raindrops had been bouncing off the cobbled streets of Guinlance, all morning. The dull sky, unyielding in its attempt, to soak the earth, below.

By the end of the morning, the rain had stopped. The sky remained dark and angry, and a cold wind, whipped the clouds, across the sky.

The streets outside the castle, were packed with people, straining to gain a vantage point. Lines of heavily armed knights held the masses in order. All the windows, of the buildings along the main street, leading up to the castle, were open. Heads sticking out, looking for any signs of movement, from the castle gates. Every face sombre, and tear stained.

The people of Fantaellen, loved their king. The leaked news of his sudden and unexpected death had spread quickly throughout the city, and beyond its walls. The chance, to pay their respects, was the reason why, his subjects had gathered in the rain, since first light. Dressed in their finest, funeral clothing.

Robert Scotten had his head bowed, as he stood, next to his sovereign's closed coffin, just inside the entrance, of the castle chapel. He had stayed dressed, in his finest armour and robes. The Guardian of Fantaellen, would be at the head of the cart, that carried the king's body. He would walk, at a slow step pace, befitting a funeral, of a king or a queen.

One of the suns, suddenly peeked through the clouds. Robert lifted his head, and watched, as its rays, touched the soaked, cobbles of the courtyard. He smiled to himself.

Maybe, it was a sign of hope, he thought, on this sombre day.

Just then, a knight hurriedly presented himself to Robert, with a tired salute, and rushed words.

'Slow down.' Robert ordered, as he interrupted the messenger.

'Sorry Sire.' The knight took a deep breath, before continuing. 'The fog is lifting, along our entire coastline. Reports, are coming in, of thousands of Wulfdaeden warships, up and down our coasts, from the north to the south.' The knight hastily thumbed through some papers, in his hand. 'And, it seems, that the biggest concentration, is on the south western coast,' he stated.

'Any attacks yet?' asked Robert.

'No Sire. Well, at least up until an hour ago when the reports, started to reach us. It's as if they are just sat there, waiting.'

There, was a momentary silence, as Robert took in everything, that had been reported.

'Thank you,' he suddenly said, as he patted the knight, on the back. 'You may go now.'

'Sire!' The knight saluted Robert turned on his heels and left.

The Guardian of Fantaellen, knew that the Wulfdaeden attack, was now imminent, or worse, already ordered. But first, they had a king to honour.

Robert, his mind clear, instantly snapped to attention, and saluted his king. He then marched, out into the courtyard. There, he was greeted, by a guard of honour, that comprised a score of knights, who stood rigid, to attention.

The courtyard was quiet and sombre, as King Stefan's coffin, was now carried to the waiting carriage. As, it was carefully placed on the sumptuous, gilded transport, the twenty knights saluted.

Robert, slowly walked to the front, pausing briefly, to gently stroke, the beautiful, majestic white steed, that stood, almost statue like, at the front of the carriage.

The king's guard of honour, dressed in the most brilliant, shining armour, marched forward in unison, before they split into two groups. Ten men, either side, of the king's coffin.

'Attention!' Ordered Robert Scotten.

The guard of honour, instantly snapped to attention, and unsheathed their swords, and raised them in the air.

'King Stefan! We salute you!' Came a perfect, simultaneous cry. The swords, then sheathed.

'King's guard! Forward!' Robert ordered.

As the funeral carriage, slowly rumbled forward, the disciplined, and unwavering lines of workers from the castle, and their families, remained silent and still, like statues. Their heads, bowed.

King Stefan left the courtyard of his beloved Guinlance, for his final journey, in a coffin, made from the finest Fantaellen oak. The emblem, of the two Unicorns of Fantaellen, proudly etched, into the shield, on his silver coffin plate.

On the eerily quiet streets of Guinlance, Robert could see how much the people loved their king. Men, women and children, had their heads bowed in silence, as a mark of respect. Many sobbed, as they tried to control, their personal grief.

Robert's heart suddenly felt heavy, with his own grief. Unable to control them, the tears flowed down his face, as he sobbed, uncontrollably.

At a slow, and dignified pace, it took an age, for the funeral procession, to make its way, down the streets of Guinlance. The thousands of people, lining the streets of the Fantaellen capital, remained silent, as the king's carriage passed by. The noises, that echoed off the walls of the buildings, were that of the royal carriage, and the marching knights of the king's guard.

The disciplined procession eventually left the capital's streets and began to make its way, through a wooded area, on the outskirts of Guinlance.

Following, the natural route, along the banks of the River of Life, leaving Guinlance, its hill and its castle behind, they made their way, towards the ancient site, of the original castle, and the seat of the original throne of the Sovereign of Portaellen. It is said, in ancient scriptures, that this was the place, that the Gods crowned, the very first sovereign. The ruins, of the castle still stand, and the original stone, that the first throne, was placed upon, is still there. It was here, that the funeral of King Stefan, would take place. Then, in keeping with tradition, his body would be cremated, on top of a funeral pyre.

When, they neared a large rock formation, which was cut out of the side of a hill, and was topped with masses of huge oak trees, the funeral procession stopped.

Robert gave the order, to enter the narrow rock-strewn passageway, that lay up ahead. This would lead them to, the site of the ancient ruins of the original castle. In the distance, a stone archway, to greet all, that entered.

The king's coffin was then unloaded from the carriage, by six knights. Robert Scotten, and the remaining knights, then followed behind the coffin, through the archway, towards the derelict shell, of the original castle. Three, solid looking, high stone walls, now held the structure together, with the eastern facing wall, all but gone.

The pall bearers slowly marched the king's coffin, towards another, magnificent looking entrance, a stone archway, with two rearing unicorns, hanging proudly above it.

Upon entering, the funeral procession, was instantly surrounded by the high stone walls, that reached, up into the sky. There was no roof. The broken, wooden beams overhead, showed where the floors above, would have been.

In front of them, a priest stood, on a large stone, which was embedded in the ground, his head bowed. Robert recognised it, as the foundation stone, of the original throne.

Behind the priest, was a pyre.

The king's coffin was placed before the priest. Whereupon the knights slowly backed away.

For a moment, everyone remained silent, their heads bowed. Robert listened, to the wind whistling through the ruins. He could also hear some distant birdsong. It was so quiet and peaceful. So, calming.

After a lengthy silence, the priest slowly lifted his head, before looking up into the grey skies, and raising his arms into the air, as he began to cry out.

Robert recognised some of the priest's words, as the ancient language of Fantaellen. A mix of Latin and Fantaish, (the original language of Fantaellen). The priest, spoke in an articulate, clear voice, which echoed around the ruins. His deliverance of the words filled the air, with clarity and purpose.

He, then delivered the eulogy in English. He spoke, about everything King Stefan had achieved, and his lasting legacy.

He then ended the eulogy, with a declaration. 'Despite, the gathering dark clouds of evil', he began, 'which, are just a heartbeat away. Every Fantaellen, can take strength, from the king's passing. He will be watching. Guiding. Use his passing, to fuel your courage and strength, for the dark times, ahead.'

He, then asked everyone to kneel, and join him in the Lord's Prayer. The words were spoken in English, and with a purpose. Many loud, clear voices, now directly, resonated throughout the ruins. The words, carried on the wind, and up into the grey skies above.

The priest, then asked everyone, to rise to their feet.

The six pall bearers marched over, to the king's coffin picked it up in unison, and slowly marched over to the pyre, which stood six feet tall.

They placed the coffin, carefully on top. Facing the pyre, the pall bearers, slowly backed away, from the coffin of their king and sovereign, before being brought to attention, by a command, from Robert Scotten.

'Pall bearers! Salute your king!' Came his order.

'We, the king's pall bearers! Salute you!'

Six pairs of heels suddenly snapped together, and the salute was presently given. The pall bearers then marched back into line.

Robert was presented, with a burning torch. The Guardian of Fantaellen, walked over to the pyre, where he immediately raised the flaming torch, in the air. He then turned, to face everyone.

Robert and his knight's, simultaneously, unsheathed their swords and raised them aloft.

The Guardian of Fantaellen, spoke. 'King Stefan of Fantaellen. The supreme Sovereign of Portaellen. We, your loyal subjects, salute you.' There, was a brief pause, as Robert, looked into the eyes of his men. He now saw, what he needed to see. 'Stronivus. Honourous. Couros!' He shouted.

'Strength. Honour. Courage.' Came a concurrent, and instant reply, from his men.

Robert promptly sheathed his sword, and placed the burning torch, under the pyre, before taking several steps back.

Within minutes, the pyre was fully alight, and the king's coffin, was engulfed in flames. Robert watched, as the flames, danced around, and the smoke rose into the air, sending King Stefan, into the afterlife, and to the table, of the God's.

Robert suddenly felt tired. He had to get some rest, he told himself. He had to be able to think, clearly and concisely. The kingdom needed him.

As, he left the old ruins, Robert Scotten once again, felt the heavy burden, of governing his country. For the first time, he felt anxious. His heart suddenly beating quickly, in his chest.

'Come on,' he sighed to himself, as he took, several deep breaths.

In the grey skies above, he could hear the high-pitched cry of an eagle. As Robert looked up, he spotted the king of the sky, soaring way above, in the darkening clouds.

Instantly, the heavens erupted, as a loud clap of thunder, resounded across the darkening sky.

The god's have opened their great door, Robert thought to himself, as he watched the smoke from King Stefan's pyre, reaching towards the sky.

The eagle circled the smoke, and a shaft of brilliant sunlight, pierced the slate grey sky, before engulfing the burning pyre, in a heavenly light.

King Stefan had passed to the other side. He was now at rest. Robert was sure of this.

'Fly high, your Majesty,' he said, as the heavenly light disappeared, and the sky rumbled above.

The Gods had duly taken another Sovereign. King Stefan had entered the house of Ramazen.

Chapter Six

Captain George Corder stared in disbelief, at the sight before him. He stood, with one of his officer's, on the most northern facing rampart, of the South Western Fortress, which looked directly out to sea.

The thick blanket of fog had been lifting all morning. And gradually it had revealed a deadly cameo, of hundreds of enemy warships.

The captain and his men had known that the enemy were there. They had heard them; they could smell them. They had endured, the terrible screams of the Fantaellen sailors, as their ships were rammed, and subsequently were sunk, by the enemies bigger and faster ships.

The fog had hidden the enormity of the Blackheart armada. Captain Corder and his sergeant were just beginning, to see the size of the attacking force, before them, as the last whisps of lingering fog dissipated.

'Oh my God!' the sergeant muttered to himself.

Captain Corder was still staring out to sea, when he gave his sergeant, an order.

'Send out two patrols. One to Rocky Cove. The other, to Windy Cove. No more than twenty men, in each. They must get our beacons lit. I, then want them to observe the enemy movements and report back. They must not engage the enemy, if at all possible. Their numbers are too small. We will need, every man.'

'Yes sir!'

The captain knew that the Blackhearts would look to make their landings, at the two coves, and launch their attack from them. They could not climb, the natural barrier of the enormous cliffs, in front of his fortress. The North wall of the fortress was just a few feet away, from the edge of the cliffs, with a sheer drop, into the crashing waves, of the Stoirim Sea. It had stood strong and proud, against the unrelenting elements, for over a century. This was a tough coast. The two coves were now the captain's weakness.

He knew that the enemy, would want the fortress, as a stronghold, before heading inland. It was pivotal, to his country's defence, or to the enemy's success. Therefore, it had to be defended, at all costs.

The sergeant was dismissed, to carry out his captain's orders.

Captain Corder remained, observing from the battlements, listening and planning a strategy of defence, then attack.

The fog had now fully lifted, and the captain could properly observe, the armada of enemy ships, as they sat and waited, in the unpredictable currents. The Wulfdaeden coastline, was just twenty-four miles away, and it seemed as if the enemy ships, were so numerous in numbers, that they filled every inch of those miles.

Then, the drums started. Wulfdaeden orders, were now being carried on the wind, and their drums of war, started their incessant beat.

George Corder, a captain and a knight of Fantaellen, had observed enough. He was ready. Ready to do his duty.

An invasion force was coming. War was now declared. The South Western Fortress, had to be held, at all costs.

★★★

The patrol arrived at the highest vantage point, above Rocky Cove, just as an incessant rainstorm, blew in from the sea. The officer in charge, quickly dismounted his steed and directly gave the order, for two of his men, to ride eastwards, along the coastal path, to the beacon point. He ordered the rest of his men, to dismount, and to guide their steed's down the often-treacherous path, and onto the shingle beach.

Holding, the reins of his steed, the officer in charge, walked towards the sound of the breaking waves, as they thundered onto the shore. He cursed momentarily, as he wiped the rain and sea spray, from his face. His heart, suddenly stopped, and his eyes widened, in horror.

'Oh! The Gods!' he exclaimed.

As the shoreline of the beach, opened up to him, a fear, that he had never felt before, unexpectedly gripped him, and immediately shook him, to the core.

The open water as far as his eyes could see, was full of enemy ships. The officer quickly noted, the large amount of rowing boats that were either being lowered, or were already in the water, and heading towards the accessible beaches, along the south western coast.

'Ramazen!' He cursed, before turning to his men, to give the order to leave.

The order had barely left his mouth, when a single arrow flew past his head, and whacked into his steed. The beautiful, white creature screamed, and fell heavily to the ground, as blood sprayed from its wound.

'Shields!' Came the cry.

The officer, still had a hold of his steed's rein's when the next arrow, violently launched him, off his feet. With, a Wulfdaeden arrow, embedded in the right side of his throat, he was dead, before he hit the shingle.

A deadly chaos now reigned, as a panic took hold of his men. Several, had quickly formed a makeshift shield wall, facing the west, from where the arrows had come, as the rest, tried to mount their steeds, in a blind panicked, commotion.

Several more arrows, killed three more men, and the survivors, now made for the relative security, of the shield wall.

The shield wall had been formed into a crude circle. There was fear, within its fragile sanctity.

'Where, did those arrows come from?' one man asked.

'From the headland, to the west,' came the reply.

'No. I could have sworn, it came from the east!' another shouted.

'We need to get off this beach, they have Long Bows,' stated another. 'We have to make our way, towards the sandbanks. We must report our findings.'

In a split second, it felt as if all hell had been unleashed, upon the small, confused, Fantaellen shield wall.

From the headland of the east and the west, the sky had suddenly filled with more Wulfdaeden arrows, that quickly rained down, on the small circle.

The shingle around them, was rapidly littered with stray arrows.

Within their wall, two men had died, and one lay screaming in agony. An arrow embedded in his right thigh.

'Turn!' A sudden scream refocused the shield wall, and they quickly turned, to make a line, facing the sandbanks.

A blood curdling scream, instantly came from the sandbanks, as the Fantaellen knights, slammed their shields, into the sand and shingle.

A screaming horde, in black hooded robes, headed their way.

The archers from the headland, now took full advantage of the distraction, and unleashed another, quivering, deadly volley of their arrows.

The Fantaellen shield wall, was instantaneously broken up, into an undisciplined chaos, as many were maimed or had died in the arrow storm.

With no officer in charge, the Fantaellen knights, had suddenly become an undisciplined rabble.

Several now charged towards the sandbanks, and were cut down, in another shower of arrows.

The rest, their shields now down, looked around for direction, as the hooded horde, smashed into them. Razor sharp steel clashed, as swords were flailed around, with a ferocious and deadly intent.

The air quickly filled, with screams of the dying. And, the shingle beach, turned red, with the blood, of many.

The Fantaellen knights, though so few in numbers, held their ground. They had killed many of the hooded attackers, despite their superior numbers. They fought bravely, and with great skill, but the enemy, were too many in numbers. Each Fantaellen, fought at least half a dozen Wulfdaeden's, at once.

It, was not too long, before they were overwhelmed.

The last two Fantaellen knights, died with their bloodied sword's in hand. One perished, as his head was despatched from his body. The other, received several slashes and stab wounds, as he died swinging his sword, wildly.

The bodies of the Fantaellen knights, were checked for signs of life. Any of the bodies, that even quivered, had a Wulfdaeden sword, thrust into their ribs.

The order, to finish off the enemy, had come from a giant of a man, who had barked out the order, as he pulled off his hood, to reveal his terribly scarred face. As, he pulled his sword, from the chest of a dead Fantaellen, he shouted out his next order.

'Put their bodies, in a pile, over there!' He pointed to a vantage point, situated centrally on the beach. 'Pile them high,' he ordered. 'And, then burn them! They, will be our signal.'

Within minutes, Rocky Cove reeked of burning flesh. The signal had been sent.

A burning bonfire, at Windy Cove was already ablaze.

No reports of enemy movements would reach the South Western Fortress.

And, in the waves of the Stoirim Sea, hundreds of slaves, pulled hundreds of oars. The Wulfdaeden war machine was coming. Driven forward, by the incessant beat, of their drums of war.

★★★

Captain Corder had ordered his archers to the ramparts, and his crossbowmen, had been given the order to fire their bolts, down on to the enemy, from the arrow loops, built into the walls. The Long Bows, that he had requested for his archers, had not arrived. As, a consequence, the standard issue, Fantaellen Oak Bow, would have to be good enough, for today.

On the ramparts of his fortress, the captain had ordered, the vats of boiling oil, to be placed strategically, along the battlements. His final order was to bring forward his newest weapon, to the parade ground.

It took a large number of men, several minutes, to manoeuvre the towering platform, into position. As, the wheels rumbled, across the cobbled parade ground, the noise became, almost deafening.

Captain Corder, had never seen the engineers, use this latest weapon. He had heard about its capabilities, in siege warfare. He hoped that the Trebuchet, would wreak havoc, on the Blackheart fleet, that now charged, towards the coast.

A sudden shout, from the battlements, instantly caught the captain's attention.

'Sir! Smoke!'

'Where?' he immediately enquired.

'Seems to be, from Rocky Cove, sir.'

The captain had been on the parade ground, and was quickly up on the castle wall, looking out, across the battlements. He instantly, spotted the smoke, coming from the east.

'That smoke, is not our beacons,' he said to himself, as he raced towards the nearest stairs.

Christ! We need to get them lit! The signal must be sent!

Captain Corder, called out to his officer's, to meet him on the parade ground.

He was shortly joined by his trusted subordinates, who listened carefully, as their captain gave them his order's. He began, by telling them, that his plans had changed. He now swiftly explained, that the changes, had been forced upon him, by the smoke seen from Rocky Cove, and the second call, of smoke coming from Windy Cove.

'So, it appears, that the enemy, is already upon us.' He began, to conclude, 'The smoke, is clearly a signal, to the Blackheart ships, to attack. Our beacons, have not been lit. We need, to get them lit. We must then defend the clifftops, and this fortress. When, our beacons are seen, it will become known, that we are under attack. I have also, sent a rider, to the nearest garrison inland, for reinforcements.' The captain, paused for a moment, before finishing, with a resounding and emotionally filled ending, 'Gentlemen. This coast, our coast. This fortress is our fortress. We will defend them both, to the death!'

'Yes sir!' Came the instant reply.

'Right. Let's make it happen gentlemen.'

Captain Corder stood and watched, as his officer's, barked out their order's.

The fortress was now a hive, of fast paced activity, as knights and officers, made ready.

It wasn't long, before Captain Corder saluted two battalions, as they marched out of the main gate, and onto the windy clifftops. Both battalions, had archers, and knights on horseback, with lances, and foot soldiers.

The two battalions, then parted, and made their way, towards their objectives, Rocky Cove and Windy Cove.

Captain George Corder prayed to the Gods above.

'We will need them.' He told himself, as he ordered the main gate, to be closed.

He had not taken the decision to weaken the numbers within the fortress, lightly, by sending the two battalions, to their possible death. Those beacons did need lighting, and the coastal paths and high ground above the coves, now formed a part of his defensive strategy. He prayed, that his two battalions, could hold out long enough, until the reinforcements arrived. He hoped that some of his men, would make it back.

Ramazen. Please help us!

The reply was instant, as the darkening sky suddenly rumbled, high above the captain's head.

★★★

The young officer dismounted his steed and sighed. He had halted his battalion, when his scout had reached him, and reported, what he had seen. Together, with his sergeant, the three men had rode, along the cliff tops, towards the beacon.

The beacon was completely destroyed. It had been hacked down and lay on the ground.

Two knights lay dead. One, with numerous Wulfdaeden arrows, in his chest. The other, lay face down, with an axe, in his back.

'Sacré bleu!' Cursed the officer, as he checked the bodies. 'There is nothing, we can do here.'

Quickly, they mounted their steeds, and made their way, back to their battalion.

A rider was subsequently sent back to the fortress, to report their findings.

The battalion made their way, towards Rocky Cove.

***

The South Western fortress launched its first missile, at the attacking Wulfdaeden fleet. On impact, it took out the sails of a ship, that had just launched several rowing boats, full of Blackheart knights, before landing on the deck, of another. Within moments, the ship took on water, and began to sink.

The cheers and bravado, from the watching eyes at Rocky Cove was short lived. The sky suddenly turned darker, as hundreds of Blackheart arrows, that had been shot from the sea, by the amassing, angry hordes of black armoured knights, impacted on the Fantaellen lines. The sand dunes ran red with blood, and the screams of the dying and the injured filled the air.

The Fantaellen response, was immediate. Their archers, instantly broke from the cover of their shields, and filled the sky, with their deadly reply.

Their officer watched, as many enemy knights, fell to the sand, as the ferocity of his archer's arrows, smashed through the armour, of the invaders.

He stood, at the top of the coastal path, looking down on to the cove. Below him, his archers fired their arrows, true and deadly.

'Loose!' Rang out his command, every half a minute or so.

The Wulfdaeden's, seemed so many. For every arrow, that hit its target, another crazed Blackheart, charged forward. Their bodies littered the shoreline, and they just kept coming, in their hundreds, as more and more boats, smashed through the breakers, and hit the shore.

The officer glanced fleetingly at his foot soldiers, who were formed, into perfect lines, three deep in front of the sand dunes, their shields, facing the enemy.

To his left, the knights on horseback waited, for their command flag, to be raised.

Their signal came, almost instantly. From the clifftop, a purple flag had been raised. A message for the archers.

The Fantaellen archers, immediately ceased firing. The flag of the knights on horseback, was then elevated.

The knights on their magnificent, white steeds, quickly formed into a single line, across the shingle, facing the shoreline and the enemy, with their lances raised in the air.

In a majestic, strong line, they remained for a brief moment, unmoving, waiting for the command to charge.

'Lances!'

Fifty, deadly, razor sharp lance points, now faced the Wulfdaeden Blackhearts.

Before, he let his men go, their officer, pointed to the now smouldering pile, of their countrymen, that the enemy mocked, as they charged up the beach, towards them.

'That, is what the enemy, did to our fellow countrymen. See! Let the sight of their smouldering remains, fill your minds with revulsion. Let their death's, be avenged, by our lances.'

The officer rode across the line of his knights. Some of the steeds whinnied, in anticipation.

'May the gods, guide our lances, and our swords. For today, we have a date with destiny.' The cavalry officer sharply turned his steed, to face the enemy. He unsheathed his sword and pointed it forward.

'For Fantaellen!' He roared.

Down the beach, the Fantaellen knights charged. At breakneck speed, they advanced as one.

The line stayed straight and true. Their pace, unrelenting. They looked, truly magnificent, and deadly, their brilliant, silver body armour gleamed, the feathered plumes, danced on their helmets and their purple robes flowed, behind them.

Their charge was sent to put fear, into the blood lust advance, of the Blackhearts. The Fantaellen officer, who stood on the coastal path, above the shingle battleground, had shown the enemy, a different hand. He now prayed, that the highly trained, knights on horseback would inflict as much death and confusion, as possible. Before, he sent his foot soldiers, to smash the enemy, back into the sea.

The Wulfdaeden's, tried desperately, to form several squares. Officers, barked orders at the stragglers, who stood in fear, of the enemy charge. Makeshift, squares were hurriedly formed, with a wall of Blackheart shields, suddenly facing outwards. In the middle of each square, an officer, ready to give his orders.

'Hold!' Came the general command. 'Steady!'

The squares now braced, for the oncoming cavalry, and the inevitable, brutality and speed, of the impact.

The Fantaellen charge, just kept coming. Their eyes focused, on the enemy squares. A cloud of sand and shingle kicked up behind them, as they raced down the beach.

The sky in front of the riders, suddenly turned darker. The Wulfdaeden's, had unleashed a storm of arrows, from their Long Bows, that had flown vertically, up into the sky, as a perfect formation, before starting to descend, towards the Fantaellen cavalry, at a deadly, lightning speed.

'Lances!' shouted the cavalry officer, his voice loud and unbroken.

Fifty riders now screamed their aggressive, defiant war cry, as they dipped their lances, ready for the kill. Forward, they charged, as one. Head on, into the Wulfdaeden squares, and arrow storm.

The impact, of the arrows came quickly, and with deadly accuracy. Blood curdling screams suddenly filled the air. The sickening impact, took its toll, on the advancing Fantaellen cavalry charge, as arrow after arrow, ripped through armour, then the flesh, of man and steed.

The cavalry officer quickly looked down the line, as rider after rider, were unseated, and countless steeds went down. He himself, had an arrow embedded, in his leg. The pain seared up his thigh, and he briefly grimaced, as he chopped the majority of the shaft away, with his sword, before screaming an ancient, Fantish obscenity, at the enemy.

The officer, and a dozen or so of his knights, were all that now remained, of their line. Forward, the remaining riders charged, their deadly lances, still dipped.

The arrow storm had suddenly ended, as quickly as it had impacted. The cavalry charge was now a suicide charge. No Fantaellen knight, had ever turned to run, in the face of the enemy. And today, would be no different.

The enemy now taunted the remaining riders, as they continued, to come at them.

'Hold!' Came the cries, from the centre of the squares.

The impact, as the Fantaellen steeds tried to smash through the Wulfdaeden squares, was initially successful, as the heavy weighted momentum of man and steed, carried through, and the deadly thrust of a lance, impaled its victim.

Instantaneously, several riders went down, as individual, Blackheart squares, held their position's. Screams were heard, and the blood flowed, as the downed Fantaellen riders and their steeds, were quickly slaughtered, by sword and axe.

Beneath its hooves, the officer's steed had trampled on several enemy knights, leaving a trail of bodies, as it smashed through a Wulfdaeden square and raced towards the centre.

The officer had just lanced, a Blackheart through his chest, pinning him to the ground. Quickly, he drew his sword, and now began chopping, slashing and cutting, his fine weapon through everything at his front, and at his side. As he took the head, from the shoulders, of a Blackheart, he looked up to see, other Fantaellen knights, desperately swinging their swords, and killing as many of the enemy, as they could. This caused his blood lust to rise, even further.

'For Fantaellen!' He now screamed.

His back, then suddenly arched, and he shrieked in pain, when the heavy blow of an enemy sword, smashed into his lower spine. This caused him, to drop his sword.

Gasping for air, the officer tried to compose himself, as the blood ran down his back, and more of the enemy, closed in on him.

The killer instinct, returned to him rapidly, as he drew another sword, from his side. Instinctively, he hacked, chopped and slashed, his way through, the Blackhearts who charged at him. He killed countless invaders, as the adrenalin in his body, drove him on.

In the other squares, Fantaellen knights were now being pulled from their steeds, as hordes of baying Wulfdaeden's, went for the kill. Their bloodied swords, cut, chopped and slashed, at the charging Fantaellen's, whose attack, remained direct and unequivocal.

There was a sudden cheer, as a Blackheart, held up the bloodied head of a Fantaellen knight, for all to see. Before, throwing it to the ground, and kicking it away, to the chorus, of mocking laughter.

Then, came a blood-curdling scream, as one of the last remaining Fantaellen riders, was set upon, by a large group, who seemed to take great pleasure from every slash and cut, as his blood sprayed through the air. After untold blows, his body lay in pieces, on the shingle.

The cavalry officer was still alive, but mortally wounded. He had taken another powerful laceration, this time to his stomach, from an enemy sword, after losing his body armour, in an earlier clash. He stood leaning on his sword, his hand covered the blood soaked, gaping wound, under his tunic, as if holding his guts in. Momentarily, he stumbled, as the pain racked his body. Next to him, his steed lay motionless. At his feet, many dead Blackhearts. He was now completely surrounded, by a baying circle of Wulfdaeden's.

As, he steadied himself, and stood as straight as he could, with his sword held in both hands, the Fantaellen officer screamed his defiance, at the circle, as the blood gushed from his stomach wound.

From behind him, came the sudden, final blow, from a Blackheart sword, that split the skull of the cavalry officer, in two. Blood splattered into the air, and the baying circle, screamed in delight. His body was then ripped to pieces, by axe and by sword.

***

Fantaellen arrows, once again filled the sky of Rocky Cove. The Wulfdaeden squares, had broken up, and the officers, were now roaring their men forward, up the beach.

The Fantaellen officer, had quickly joined his foot soldiers, and organised them into a shorter but stronger line, three men deep, his second line of men, armed with lances. From behind them, his archers fired their arrows.

'Steady boys,' he said, in a calming tone, as another volley of arrows, were fired from the back of the line. How he wished, his archers had Long Bows.

One young knight next to him, looked frozen with fear. He was shaking, and his eyes were wide, and full of terror. The officer placed a reassuring hand, on his young shoulders, and smiled at him.

The officer himself, was a hardened campaigner of war, having fought in the trenches in the Great War in France, defending his second country against invasion. He had also fought, the Blackhearts, on foreign soil. He too, was only just, three decades old, but war from a young age, had aged him.

The Fantaellen officer, was scared too. He would not show it. He could not show it. The Blackheart invaders were just too many. He had sent a messenger back to the fortress, to ask for reinforcements. He knew they would not come. He, and his few hundred men, were all that stood, facing the thousands of Wulfdaeden Blackhearts, who now charged up the beach.

First, the invaders had to face him and his men. He would make sure, that he and his knights, would greet their ancestors in the next life, with their sword in hand and Blackheart blood, dripping from their blades. This, he swore to himself.

Another volley of Fantaellen arrows, left the back of the line. Many Wulfdaeden's already lay dead on the shingle and were soon joined by countless more. The ferocity and the accuracy of the Fantaellen arrows was exemplary. So much so, that the number of bodies, of the dead or the dying, began to hinder the Blackheart charge.

Still, they kept on coming. Climbing, over the bodies of their fellow countrymen. Screaming, taunting, crazed and blood drunk. Desperate, for the kill.

A cold sweat dripped down the Fantaellen officer's face, and he shuddered, as he watched the enemy charge up the beach. There, were thousands of them. His archers had killed hundreds. For, everyone they had downed, another two appeared. They were close now, he could smell, their stench.

'Shields!' He suddenly ordered. Hundreds of Fantaellen shields, dug into the sand and shingle.

'We hold them here!' The officer shouted. 'Lances! Ready!'

The Blackheart charge was so close now. Close enough, for several Wulfdaeden's to die, from the thrust of a number of eager, Fantaellen lances.

The Wulfdaeden's roared. The Fantaellen lines, roared back in defiance.

In an instant, came the loud crash, as sword smashed into shield, and bodies smashed into bodies. Bone crunching momentum now hit stubborn defiance.

'Hold! Hold!' Screamed the Fantaellen officer. Hundreds of guttural groans and grunts now filled the air, as the Fantaellen line first pushed, then held, as one.

'Lances!' He now ordered.

All down the Fantaellen line, like a well-oiled machine, the man at the front of the wall, moved his shield to the left for a brief moment, and the man behind him, instantly lunged forward, with his lance, hard and fast. Screams filled the air, as many Wulfdaeden's were speared through the neck, or the lower part of their body, where they had no armour. The front Fantaellen knight, then bought his shield back in front of him. Then, with their officer's order, the well-oiled machine, snapped into action again. This aggressive offensive went on for several minutes. The Blackheart bodies quickly piled up, in front of the Fantaellen line.

The second line now dropped their bloodied lances to the floor and drew their swords. The shield wall had now returned to defence.

The Fantaellen wall, was just about holding its line, as their officer screamed his orders. He could see that his men were getting tired, and the line began to feel the strain, as the sheer numbers of Blackhearts increased, and their momentum, began to slowly push the Fantaellen's backwards.

The situation was getting critical. The shield wall began to buckle, as the Wulfdaeden's chopped, slashed, thrust and cut, their way forward.

The Fantaellen officer, shouted out his orders, as best he could. The cacophony of screams, defiant roars and the clashing of swords and shields, made it difficult for him. He knew, it wouldn't be long, before his wall would be smashed, and the melee of killing and death would begin.

When it happened, it was as if something had crashed straight through the middle of the Fantaellen shield wall. The surge for killing, in the Blackheart hordes had pushed many of the enemy forward, on to bloodied Fantaellen swords, whose resistance, had been broken, all at once.

The Blackhearts, charged forward, wildly swinging their weapons, whilst slashing and chopping, at the shocked and surprised enemy. Such was their lust for blood. Nothing was going to stop them from going forward.

With, their shield wall broken, the Fantaellen's were now engaged, in out and out combat, with sword, lance, shield, or dagger.

The Fantaellen officer, had now joined his men, in the centre of it all. At his side, the young knight, who had lost all sense of terror, having now killed, several of the enemy. He suddenly charged, his sword swinging wildly, in his young and bloodied hands.

The officer parried a blow from an enemy sword, before lunging and thrusting his sword, into the back of another Wulfdaeden.

As, he released his blade from the ribs, he swung round, and took the head off the shoulders, of another.

Many Fantaellen's, were now dead. Their bodies, strewn across the sand and shingle. They had fought skilfully and bravely, but the sheer numbers of Blackhearts, had overwhelmed them.

Surrounded by hordes of Wulfdaeden's, the Fantaellen officer was slaughtered, as he lunged at a Blackheart. Three enemy knights took his life with their swords. He was dead, before he hit the sand.

Not a single Fantaellen, was left alive, on the sand and shingle, of Rocky Cove.

The hordes of Wulfdaeden's, now swarmed towards the sand dunes. The Fantaellen archers, who had been ordered to retreat to higher ground, killed many, as they fired their killing arrows, down into the black mass, of the enemy.

The Blackhearts just kept on coming. Their swarm, filled the killing ground, as more and more, joined the charge, up the dunes, towards the deadly Fantaellen archers.

Many archers were quickly running out of arrows and had drawn their swords. They desperately fought the blood drunk enemy, in the dunes. For a short time, they held their line, with their discipline, skill and determination, to repel the invader.

Before long, the archers were overwhelmed and then finally massacred. Their bodies, strewn across the dunes.

Rocky Cove had now fallen, into enemy hands.

Thousands of Wulfdaeden Blackhearts now made their way up to the coastal path, ready to attack their next objective. Their blood lust at its highest.

In their way, of the total domination of the south west coast, was Captain George Corder and his fortress of knights.

★★★

Captain Corder thought about his son and his sick wife, as he looked out at Rocky Cove. Another burning missile had just been shot from a trebuchet, and was hurtling out to sea, as he watched, the amassing, blood crazed hordes of Blackhearts, chargingforward, along the coastal path.

His mind wandered. The noise of battle suddenly faded. He was in a lush, green field, on a beautiful, sunny day. He was chasing his son, who laughed uncontrollably, looking back, as his father chased him. On a blanket, his wife sat and watched, a beaming smile, on her face. George Corder, at that moment, was a father, a husband. He was happy. Content.

A shout suddenly went out from the western rampart. When he got there, the captain could see, that Windy Cove, had fallen too. Thousands of enemy knights had gathered in strength heading towards the fortress.

Captain Corder, allowed himself, one last thought about his family. He prayed, that news of the attack, had reached his village, and his wife and son, had made their way to Guinlance, with the help, of his father, and the elders.

He now made the sign of the cross, like any good Catholic, Dual Blood would, when asking for his God's help.

'Right!' He fiercely whispered to himself, before he turned to one of his men, and grabbed him by the shoulder.

'Let's kill some Blackhearts!' He shouted.

'Yes sir!' Came the immediate response.

'Good man.'

They had a fortress to defend, and the men under his command, now looked at him, to lead them.

Everything was in place. The archers. The oil. Men, on the ramparts, men on the parade ground, ready to reinforce any position. They also had one thing in their favour. Both coastal paths, were narrow. On one side, as you neared the fortress, was high ground, which was very rocky. On the other, a sheer drop, into the crashing waves of the Stoirim Sea. The northern wall, that faced out to sea, backed onto the cliff edge, so no attack could come from there. The main gate, at the southern wall, was the weak point. Facing inland, they would be vulnerable from attack, by any other Blackheart regiments that had managed, to fight their way up country. From the high ground, that surrounded that wall, archers, could also fire down into the fortress.

When the enemy had charged up the coastal paths, (despite them being narrow,) it would then create a mass of bodies, around the sides of the fortress. Giving the Fantaellen archers, lots to aim at. The vats of boiling oil could then wreak havoc, and the enemy dead, would pile up.

The captain had positioned archers and oil on three of the walls. On the sea facing, northern wall, his engineers, continued to batter the Wulfdaeden ships, with burning missiles, watched by half a battalion, of reserves.

From the battlements, the men of the fortress watched, as thousands of Wulfdaeden Blackhearts, were suddenly ordered into small, disciplined lines, on the eastern and western coastal paths. The initial, rather undisciplined charge, of blood thirsty Blackhearts, had been halted, by their officers, who had returned order, to their ranks.

On the rocky, high ground, facing the southern wall, countless enemy archers had been spotted, as they attempted to climb as high as they could, to gain a vantage point. The ledges were treacherous, from the recent rains, and loose rocks higher up, proved dangerous. A cheer went out, every so often, from the battlements, as a Wulfdaeden archer, slipped and fell to his death.

An order, then went out, to pin down the enemy archers. A volley of Fantaellen arrows, quickly followed.

The Wulfdaeden archers, were now pinned down, on their ledges. Several were killed, before they rallied, and sent over their deadly reply which, was met with jeers, from the battlements, as the majority missed. One Fantaellen archer, was taken to the infirmary with an arrow lodged in his leg.

'Archers!'

Countless Fantaellen bows, were now fully drawn. Tension, on bow strings held, as they waited the order.

'Loose!'

The next Fantaellen arrow storm was sent instantaneously.

The sudden and startling, loud eruption, of Wulfdaeden swords, presently being smashed onto their shields, in a fierce, intimidating cacophony of crazed defiance, followed by the roar of frenzied, demented taunts, was enough to send an instant chill, down the spine of every man in the fortress.

It continued, for several minutes. Each loud bang, of Wulfdaeden sword on shield, and every taunt, grew louder and full of fury and vitriol, with every enthusiastic delivery.

Captain Corder remained calm. His attention focussed on something else. Besides, he had witnessed, many Blackheart displays of defiance in battle, in the past. He was closely watching, the eastern coastal path. He had seen, two naked men, wearing Blackheart helmets, being pushed through the ranks of enemy knights, and out on their own, in full view. Around their necks hung a sign, with a word upon it, scrawled in blood. The captain was sure, it spelt the word, coward. Two Blackheart knights, then marched forward, with an axe in their hands. On the order of an officer, they brutally attacked the naked men. Chilling screams were immediately heard, as each axe blow, chopped into flesh.

One was cut in two across his rib cage, the other, almost split in half, with a blow to the top of his skull.

Triumphantly, the axe men then held their blood dripping weapons, above their heads, and roared at the hordes of fellow Wulfdaeden's, before turning to point them at the fortress.

Then, with a chilling scream, the two axe men charged forward, quickly followed by the mass, of thousands of Blackhearts.

'Show them, we mean to make our stand here!' roared, Captain Corder.

The thunderous noise, of thousands of enemy knights, charging at the fortress, provoked a roar of defiance, from the South Western Fortress.

Hundreds of aggressive screams of opposition, to the enemy being on their soil, shot out from the battlements, with the ferocity of an arrow storm.

'That's it lads.' Captain Corder muttered to himself. 'Show them, what the Fantaellen defiance, sounds like!'

To the last man. To the last breath. He and his men would fight to hold the fortress. This is what had to happen, he told himself, as a call suddenly went out, from the battlements. This time, from the south wall.

'Captain! Blackhearts!'

As, he raced across the wall, the captain gave instructions to his archers, to let loose their arrows on his command.

Stopping briefly to watch as thousands of enemy knights, charged down the rocky path, towards their main gate, the captain suddenly felt an icy cold shudder, shoot through him. The enemy had made inroads, inland. His worst fears, for his homeland, had happened. It was a disaster.

'Sir? Your orders?'

The bowman's voice quickly bought him back, from his thoughts. Captain Corder glanced at the archer, before straightening his back, and giving his order.

'Archers!' The captain's voice thundered around the fortress, and across the battlements.

Hundreds of Fantaellen bowmen, on three walls, now nocked their arrows, onto their bow strings.

A fresh roar, of Blackheart hostility, towards the enemy defensive position, was quickly shouted, at the show of force.

Captain Corder held his nerve, as his archers remained unmoving, anticipating his order. Their bows tensed. Waiting, to unleash a storm of deadly arrows.

'Now!' The voice in his head, screamed.

Instantly, the captain roared his order. 'Loose!' as he swiftly bought his arm down.

The sky now turned deadly, as hundreds of Fantaellen arrows, shot out from the battlements of the fortress, in a lethal, disciplined display of bowmanship.

Captain Corder watched, as countless enemy knights, who attacked the south wall, were wiped out in seconds.

The bodies were quickly trampled on, by the black mass, that climbed over them, as the Wulfdaeden charge continued, relentlessly.

'Archers!'

Once more, hundreds of arrows were expertly nocked, onto their bow strings.

'Loose!'

Another ferocious, deadly arrow storm shot out from the battlements.

Captain Corder gave the order, three more times, before he commanded his archers to release their arrows, when ready. This now created a constant barrage of arrows. He was not prepared, to let the enemy get close to his walls, just yet. His oil and fire would wait. Besides, his bowmen were still wreaking havoc, on the enemy charge.

The onslaught of the Blackheart army, on all three attack points, was relentless. There were hundreds of dead or dying Wulfdaeden's, strewn across the reach of the Fantaellen archer's, killing zone. This did not stop, the chaotic and crazed charge, of the black swarm, being driven forward, by a mad, blood lust.

Many dying Blackhearts were trampled to death, by their own, as the baying mass, continued to run into the Fantaellen arrows.

Suddenly, above the intense noise of battle, Captain Corder's attention was abruptly turned to the west. A thunderous, emphatic beat of enemy war drums, that sounded like the coming of a storm, instantly bought the enemy to an abrupt halt. Then, came the beat of drums from the south, and the east. This, was quickly followed by the thunderous crash of shields, being thrust into the earth, on all three sides of the fortress.

From the south wall, the captain watched the hurried mass of shield walls form, just a few feet apart, as far as the eye could see. At their front, the bodies of their dead and dying countrymen.

The order, for his archers to cease firing, came swiftly, as their arrows, now fell short, or bounced off Wulfdaeden shields.

'Save, your arrows men! We'll need them, soon enough.'

The oil, in big metal drums, was now made ready. With two men, for each drum. Their responsibility was to lift and pour, the oil onto the enemy. Each archer, had been given a separate bag of arrows, with a piece of material, wrapped around the shaft, near the arrowhead. Next to them, was a small lit fire. This was the captain's ace. Oil and flame.

★★★

To, the beat of their drums, the Wulfdaeden shield walls, slowly moved forward, as one disciplined mass.

Captain Corder watched with intrigue, as a score of Blackhearts, formed a separate wall of shields. The men from the second row, to the men at the back, now held their shields, above their head. Forward, the lines marched, in perfect time.

The tension around the fortress, was almost unbearable. The captain could feel it. His heart pounded, in his chest. A few of his men, looked a little twitchy.

A lone arrow, was suddenly fired from the south wall, landing just short of a shield wall.

'Hold your arrows!' The captain reminded his archers.

Minutes passed, as the fortress watched the enemy shield walls, creep ever closer. The captain was tempted to use the crossbowmen, as the enemy drew close enough for them to be effective. In a flash, he decided not to give into temptation, as the Blackheart shield wall, would definitely repel their bolts. Instead, an order was despatched to them, to fire, when the shield walls, were broken apart.

'Make ready the oil!' Came the captain's order. He could now hear the grunts and groans of the enemy shield wall's, as they neared.

It wasn't long, before his anticipated order rang out, across the battlements.

'Now! Release the oil!' He screamed.

The black oil was poured by the gallon, from all three walls, onto the advancing shield walls. In an instant, the archers had lit their arrowheads, and they stood waiting for the order.

The Blackheart shield walls carried on moving forward relentlessly, despite the impact of the oil, upon them.

Screams were heard, as crossbow bolts, downed a few Blackhearts, who had become disorientated, after being covered in oil, and had stumbled away from the safety of their shield wall.

The men on the west wall watched, as one particular Wulfdaeden who was covered from head to toe in oil, charged blindly forward, stumbling several times. He was eventually lifted off his feet, by

98

a crossbow bolt, that struck him right between his eyes. He fell to the ground, blood spurting, like a fountain, from his head.

They could wait no longer, Captain Corder told himself.

'Archers! Loose!'

Hundreds of Fantaellen fire arrows, were now fired into the oil. Almost instantly, the red-hot flames consumed anything in its path.

The piercing screams, of Blackhearts quickly ablaze, suddenly echoed around the fortress. Like a wall of fire, the flames enveloped the closest shield walls, that were suddenly crumbling apart, as burning men stumbled around, screaming in agony, the flames engulfing and devouring their bodies.

Many were quickly silenced, by Fantaellen crossbow bolts. Others were left to die in their flames.

Cheers suddenly rang out from the walls, of the South Western Fortress. All, three shield walls had been repelled. The furthest, enemy shield walls had retreated leaving the remnants of the first wall, to be slaughtered by crossbow bolts, and fire arrows.

A heavy rancid smell, of burning flesh, filled the air. Captain Corder afforded himself a slight smile, as he looked around at his cheering men. His plan had worked, thus far. He knew that this was just the beginning. It would get a lot worse. He believed, in his plan, though. He just hoped that the walls of his fortress, would keep the enemy out. They would come again. This time, a lot harder and in greater numbers.

Wulfdaeden drums once again, now beat out their orders. Fantaellen cheers, were suddenly halted, by the beat of the enemy war drums, and the screams, of the battle crazed Blackhearts.

On all three sides of the fortress, the captain's men stood silent, watching the mass of black armoured Wulfdaeden's, taunting and baying for Fantaellen blood.

Then, they charged with their ladders, and their battering rams. Screaming and roaring defiance, at the fortress. From the south, the east, and the west, they came.

Captain Corder had remained on the south wall. He had grown concerned, by a larger, concentrated mass of enemy knights, in the distance. What, had subsequently grabbed his attention, was the large battering ram, held by several, strong, enormous Blackhearts, roaring and screaming, as they charged towards the main gate. At, their backs, hundreds of Wulfdaeden's, their swords and axes, flailing around their heads.

Quickly, he gave the order, for the reserves from the north wall, to support the south wall. He now had to trust the walls of the fortress. He and his men, on the south wall, had to protect the main gate. Their most vulnerable point.

Captain Corder, then gave the order, for his crossbowmen to fire, when the enemy was in range. His last order was for his archers, to make ready their bows.

The black mass quickly charged towards the fortress. The heavy pounding of their feet, and their loud, defiant, blood curdling screams, resonated around the outer limits, of the fortress.

Captain Corder slowly closed his eyes and prayed. He thought of his wife and his son. For those few, dreamy moments, he was at home, with them both. His world, his everything, the three of them together.

A Blackheart arrow, landing at his feet, instantly awoke him from his thoughts. Quickly, he drew his sword, held it above his head, looked down the line of his archers, and gave the order, once again.

'Loose!'

The arrow storm killed many Wulfdaeden's. Despite the impact, of the deadly arrows, for everyone killed, an unbroken wall of enemy knights, still charged forward. Their numbers were continual, and seemingly unstoppable.

On the south wall, the battering ram, just kept coming. One of the Blackhearts, at the front of the battering ram, had several arrows in his body, but he kept on going. Captain Corder marvelled at the sheer size and strength of him. He looked like a giant, a creature, not even a man.

Fantaellen arrows, continued to fly from the fortress. The captain's archers were very effective. The crossbowmen added their fire power.

A charge to scale the walls with ladders, on all three sides, was repelled, by more oil and fire arrows. Yet still the enemy kept coming.

The sheer mass of their numbers carried the Wulfdaeden's forward, towards the fortress. The archers on the battlements, could not fire their arrows, fast enough.

Blackheart archers, on the high ground, had now begun to pick off archers, and knights, on the battlements.

In time, the Wulfdaeden's finally managed, to secure several ladders, at the east and west walls, of the fortress. Many, fell to their death, scaling the runs, slaughtered by swords or arrows, before they could clamber into the fortress.

Nonetheless, with the sheer number of attackers, climbing the ladders, some eventually breeched the battlements, and a surge of fierce fighting now began, as the Fantaellen defenders, fought to repel the invaders.

Captain Corder, and his men on the south wall, fought a desperate battle to hold their rampart. Ladders had been placed at the base, and the battering ram, moved ever closer.

The last of the oil, was ordered to the south wall. The captain, then commanded his archers, to release a concentration of arrows, aimed at the high ground. Quick volleys, before taking cover, were his order's. That was key. He had seen that his men were finding it hard to lift the drums, as they were being pinned down, by Wulfdaeden arrows, from the high ground. The oil had to be used. The enemy archers needed to be silenced.

The sky above Captain Corder, and his men, suddenly filled with arrows. Wulfdaeden Fire arrows.

'Get the oil away!' He shouted, as he ran towards the nearest drum.

A Fantaellen archer, was hit in the chest, by a fire arrow, just a few feet from the captain. His screams soon ceased, as the flames, consumed his skin and flesh, prior to taking his life.

The screams of others dying, engulfed in unyielding flames, caused chaos, and confusion, and provided the Wulfdaeden archers, on the high ground, with easy targets. Several fire arrows had landed in the metal drums, and in the spilt oil, along the rampart. The south wall was quickly ablaze, with small, uncontained fires.

The captain watched helplessly, as all around him, his men died by flames and arrows. He had to do something.

Desperately, he called out, to rally his men.

'Knights of Fantaellen! We hold this wall!'

The breech of the south rampart was quick and virtually unchecked. Like a black, crazed swarm, the Wulfdaeden's poured onto the walkway. Chopping, slashing, cutting and stabbing, their way along the battlements.

Captain Corder pulled two young knights to their feet. They looked so scared and had been hiding from the enemy arrows.

'Time to get those nice shiny swords, bloodied boys.' At that moment, he smiled at them, as they shivered and stared at him. 'We go that way.' He pointed.

The captain led the charge. He hacked, chopped and slashed his way, along the battlements, and through the enemy, with a trained, warrior skill, and his killer born, courage and strength. His determination, not to lose the south wall, evident by the amount of blood on his blade, and the bodies, all around him.

As, he swung his sword, to parry yet another enemy blade, he was suddenly lifted off his feet, by the sheer power and ferocity of the hit from a Blackheart sword, which came like a hammer blow, from behind.

Captain Corder's world instantly turned dark.

When, he opened his eyes, the captain knew he was not dead. He lay prone, on the blood-soaked cobbles of the walkway, staring at the battle, that raged on around him. His senses were smashed. His body battered. At this moment, he wished he were dead. The pain, pulsing through his body, was unbearable.

As he lay, watching his men being overwhelmed and slaughtered, the noise of their screams, echoed through his tired and pained mind. Unable to move, Captain Corder closed his eyes, and allowed the darkness to take him.

The deep, male voice, that suddenly thrust him from the tranquil darkness, screamed at him to get up. To fight.

With, his senses, now somewhat restored, Captain Corder struggled to his feet, and picked up, his bloodied sword. Seeing some of his men, suddenly joining the fight, he ordered them to follow him forward, towards the baying enemy.

Then, grabbing hold of an officer, who had just killed a Blackheart, he ordered him to hold the south wall, at all costs.

'At all costs!' He reiterated to the officer, as he stared deep into his eyes.

'Yes sir!' Came the unflinching reply.

'Good man.'

The captain was already charging, towards the steps, to the parade ground, when he heard an almighty crack, and a thunderous, crashing sound. Instantly, he turned to look at the main gate. Under his breath, he cursed.

As the battering ram smashed through the main gate, hundreds of Blackhearts, now charged forward at once, into the fortress.

The men on guard duty, and a hastily made shield wall, were immediately overwhelmed and slaughtered, by Blackheart sword and axe.

As the Blackheart swarm, surged powerfully into the fortress, they were met by another Fantaellen shield wall. This one, stood strong and unflinching, from one end of the parade ground to the other. In the middle, his voice booming out his encouragement was their captain; George Corder.

The Blackheart swarm now charged towards the shield wall. Their vast numbers filled the parade ground, almost instantly. Their lust for Fantaellen blood, driving them forward.

At that moment, Captain Corder, tried to rally his men, with his words of encouragement. Passionately and with determination, he spoke, as he raised his sword in the air.

'We hold them here', He started. 'The Gods have chosen this moment for us. This time is our time. History, will remember us.'

His voice suddenly became louder, as the enemy neared, their demented screams echoing around the parade ground.

'Shields! Strong and true!'

A strong, masculine grunt, from the men at the front of the wall, was quickly followed by the slam of Fantaellen shields, into the earth. The men behind them, then drew their swords and fixed their shields.

'Lances!'

From behind, the front two rows of the shield wall, Fantaellen lances were thrust forward.

'Hold! Brace!' The enemy were so close, Captain Corder, could now smell them. 'Steady. Steady,' he called. 'For Fantaellen!'

The shield wall braced itself for the inescapable impact, of the enemy charge.

Suddenly, the bone crunching, crash of bodies, armour and blades, smashed head on, into the shield wall.

The initial impact was repelled by the combined strength, within the wall. Even, with the onslaught of more waves of the invaders, the immovable, unwavering line, held strong.

The Fantaellen wall, now went on the attack, as Captain Corder screamed the order.

'Lances! Attack!'

Hundreds of deadly, razor sharp, Fantaellen lances, were instantly thrust forward. The screams, as the flesh of many, was fatally, ripped open, resounded up and down the Fantaellen line. Countless Blackhearts were slaughtered or maimed, as Fantaellen lances, were then quickly retracted.

The second attack was immediate. Captain Corder, having seen the ferocity and impact of his lances, wanted the stunned enemy, to feel more Fantaellen, cold steel.

'Lances! Attack!'

Additionally, he now ordered the men in the first two rows of the shield wall, to break cover, and attack the confused and dazed enemy, in front of them.

They stabbed, slashed and thrust their swords, into the enemy. Many Wulfdaeden's, were slaughtered, before the disciplined withdrawal, back behind the shield wall.

Untold, Wulfdaeden bodies, lay strewn across the parade ground. Their blood ran thick. The sight buoyed up the Fantaellen line.

The captain now saw his opportunity.

'Push shield wall! Push!'

With a guttural grunt, instantly followed by a cry of defiance, hundreds of Fantaellen heels, dug into the ground, and took the strain.

Slowly, the Fantaellen shield wall, now moved forward as one, trampling over the dead and dying Wulfdaeden's, the booming voice of their captain, urging them onwards, into their attack.

The concentrated violence and brutality intensified, as the Fantaellen line, smashed into the Blackheart mass, in a tumult of screaming and shouting, and vicious, bloody, combat.

Still, the Fantaellen line held their discipline, as the enemy tried to break up the impenetrable wall of shields and repel the attack of bloodied sword and lance.

On the battlements above, the Blackhearts were overwhelming the defenders, with the mass of their numbers, and the savage, brutality of their onslaught.

The officer, who Captain Corder had ordered to hold the south wall, still lived. Desperately, he and a dozen of his men, now fought to push back the enemy, and retake the lost ground of the battlements.

A sudden clamber, of more Blackhearts onto the southern battlements, thrust more of the blood drunk enemy, at the officer and his men. A brief glance, over the rampart, made his heart almost stop, at the sight of the multitudinous swarm, now scaling the ladders.

As, he charged at two Blackhearts, the officer cut his sword across the neck of one, before thrusting his blade, deep into the guts of the other.

He was about to attack another when an arrow suddenly pierced the back of his neck. Instantly, he fell to his knees, desperately clawing at the bloodied arrowhead, that protruded from his throat, as he choked on the blood, that filled his windpipe.

A Blackheart knight now pounced, and immediately stuck his blade into the guts of the dying officer. At once, he put his boot on the Fantaellen's chest and pulled out the blade, before charging forward, to attack more of the enemy.

The officer took his final breath, as the last of the Fantaellen resistance on the battlements of the south wall, was unmercifully crushed.

Captain Corder urged his shield wall ever forward, as one unbreakable line. Slowly, the wall pushed, slashed and stabbed its way, across the killing floor, of the parade ground. Countless, Wulfdaeden's were butchered, as lost ground, was taken back.

On the battlements, the Blackheart hordes, had virtually crushed the fierce resistance. Large numbers of blood crazed attackers were quickly charging towards the doorways, that led to the stairways, and into the fortress.

On the south wall, the enemy poured down the steps, to the parade ground.

Captain Corder glanced up at the east wall. He watched, as a small band of his men, fought desperately to hold back, a large mass of Blackhearts.

They were quickly hacked to pieces, by enemy swords and axes, after making their forlorn stand.

It, was not long, before the knights on the west and north walls, had been overwhelmed too.

Captain Corder and his shield wall was all that now stood, in the way of total annihilation, of the knights, of the South Western Fortress. The captain knew that reinforcements were not coming. They never were, he now told himself. Soon, the Blackhearts would be at their front and at their back. The battle would then become a desperate fight to survive, and to try to hold onto the fortress.

He was ready to die, with his sword in hand. He knew, his men were too. This was it, he told himself. Their destiny.

Before, the final beat of his warrior's heart, he would kill, as many Blackhearts as he could. This he vowed, as he ordered his shield wall, into a new formation.

The knights with the lances, were ordered to turn and face the shrieking, roaring mass of enemy knights, that were about to attack, the rear of the shield wall. With, the order given, those men instantly dropped their lances, readied their shields, and drew their swords.

Directly, a new order came, from their captain.

'Shield wall! Attack!'

He had decided to throw his men forward at the enemy. Forced to abandon his shield wall formation, by the dire situation, they were in. Defence, had now turned into attack. He knew that his men were better, than the enemy, in one on one, brutal combat. They would have appreciated the chance to kill, as many Blackhearts as possible. Despite, the overwhelming odds. He and his men now took the fight to the enemy.

Captain Corder swung his sword, and took the head of a Blackheart, clean off his shoulders. Before, that body had hit the ground, he was on the attack again. Parrying two blows, before going to his knees, and slicing away the ankle, of an enemy. Then, he instantly sprang to his feet, and finished him off, with a thrust under the black armour, to the stomach. He, then pulled the blade from the body, and ran towards a group of his men, who were being overwhelmed.

Around the parade ground, there were many desperate battles, going on. Hundreds lay dead or were dying. The smell of sweat, death and blood, hung heavy in the air.

The innumerable numbers, of Blackhearts, were too many for the Fantaellen's. They were gradually, being overwhelmed.

Still, they fought on. Their captain, leading from the front.

★★★

After, many exhausting hours of fighting, a small band of Fantaellen's, were all who remained, in the centre of the parade ground. Completely surrounded, by the enemy.

Captain Corder, and no more than half a dozen of his men, stood, bloodied, battered and exhausted, in a circle, in the middle of the parade ground. Every man, still holding their bloodied sword in their hand.

The fighting had abruptly ceased, and the Blackheart swarm had backed off, when an order had been received, from a Wulfdaeden general, looking down on the battle, from the north wall.

It was an offer, for the brave men of Fantaellen, to surrender. The messenger growled, those exact words, as Captain Corder smiled in disbelief, and shook his head.

'Really? Surrender? Ha!' The captain called out, before directing his final answer, straight towards the north wall. 'Shove your surrender, up your backside! We are Fantaellen's! We never surrender!'

With that, the circle roared its defiance, at their attackers, and goaded them to come at them.

The Blackheart mass, that surrounded them, were desperate to finish off the captain and his men. Yet, they did not attack.

On the east wall, Wulfdaeden archers, swiftly appeared.

As he turned to his men, Captain Corder, pointed at the bowmen.

'I for one, will not die, standing here, doing nothing.' He quickly looked, at each and every one, of his men. In turn, they nodded their agreement, at him. 'Good. Then let us die well, gentlemen.'

The captain instantly led the way. Together, the last remaining men of the South Western Fortress, charged at the invaders.

The archers, up on the east wall, released their arrows, from their deadly Long Bows, into the maelstrom of battle, as soon as the order, was given.

Captain Corder was swiftly knocked off his feet, when an arrow, thwacked into his right leg. He grimaced at the searing pain, before trying to pull it out. The tearing of muscle and flesh caused him to cry out, and eventually halt. The pain was just too much.

Around him, the Blackheart's closed in, and the slaughtered bodies, of the last of his men, lay scattered.

He desperately wanted to stand upright. He had to die, on his feet, sword in hand. He had expected, to have been hacked to death, by now. But no blows had come.

A Blackheart officer pushed his way, through the mass of his countrymen, and approached Captain Corder, as he pulled himself, to his feet. Once again, the captain, was given a chance to surrender. A final chance.

Captain Corder was not really listening, to what the Blackheart, had to say. Instead, his mind suddenly wandered back to his childhood.

He was sat with his father, who recited an old poem to him, called The Last Knight of Fantaellen.

The Blackheart officer instantly stopped talking, when he watched in total disbelief, as the captain pulled the arrow from his leg, and then threw it to the ground.

Captain Corder now began to quote the final few words of the poem. Not a faltered word, spoken.

'And into the storm, he charged, with sword in hand. That one-man war. The Last Knight of Fantaellen.'

Captain George Corder now roared his final, contemptuous and fierce defiance at the enemy. Then, with sword in hand, he took his one-man war, to the Blackheart invaders.

Chapter Seven

The Ring of Stones
Wiltshire. England

In the centre, of the ancient standing stones, stood four hooded men, in dark clothing, their face's blackened, their hoods up, and their rifles, across their shoulders. Nobody spoke. Nobody moved. They just listened and waited. Their highly tuned senses, on alert. Their eyes, scanning the quiet and still landscape.

The energy around, and within the stones, suddenly turned electric. A gusting wind whipped around the stone pillars, for a short time, before calming to a gentle breeze.

'Be ready boys,' their officer ordered, as he began to walk away. 'Keep your eyes on the sky. The portal, will open from the south.'

In the clear, night sky, a small window, a white circle of bright light, swiftly appeared. All four men watched, as the circle became larger, and the energy around them, and within the stones intensified, once more. As, the white circle increased, a high level of kinetic energy, pulsed through their bodies.

'There it is boys. Come on!'

The hooded men now ran towards the light.

Directly, they were ordered to take cover, in a small, wooded area, away from the enlarging, bright circle.

One of the men, produced a sword, from a sheath on his back, and thrust it into the soil, before joining the others, in the cover of the trees.

Now, with their rifles locked into their shoulders, and aimed at the night sky, the hooded men waited.

Soon, the window of the portal, began to envelope the ground in front them. Nervous fingers now twitched on rifle triggers.

'Steady.' Came the officer's calming command. 'Do not fire straight away.' He reminded them, 'We must see the signal, and hear the password.'

The energy around the window, suddenly grew so intense, as it slowly opened, that the hooded figures, had no choice, but to avert their eyes, away from its ever-brightening light.

Then, without any warning, the portal released its travellers.

The half a dozen figures, in dark clothing, their hoods, over their heads, swiftly appeared, and walked out, from the purity of the light, as the portal, began to disappear.

With the clear, night sky returned, and the serenity of the small hours restored, the intense energy, that had encompassed the stones, had vanished. Evaporated, until its use, was sought once more.

Two of the travellers, suddenly ran towards, the wooded area. As they did, they drew their swords, and thrust them into the ground, next to the lone sword. There, they halted.

'Zada!' One of them called out.

'Yetus!' Came the clear response, from the trees.

The rest of their group joined them promptly. Nervous eyes, under dark hoods, now began staring at the trees ahead. Their rifles, ready to be fired, into the unknown shadows of the wood.

One of the portal travellers, now promptly removed his hood, to reveal his blackened face, and beckoned, with a hand signal, for the rest to follow him, towards the wooded area.

From the trees, three hooded figures suddenly appeared. Slowly, they removed their hoods and lowered their rifles.

'Glad you could join us, Jonti!' Came a shout, from the trees.

A large figure of a man now peeled away from the shadows, of the wooded area, and removed his hood, to reveal his blackened face.

Jonti Quixall, smiled to himself. He thought that he had recognised the voice, and now saw the man before him. A friend. A dear friend.

'Hello Richard. Good to see you,' Jonti began to reply. 'Seems an age, since I last saw you, my friend.'

'Yeah, I remember it well,' started Richard, as he approached Jonti. 'I was just about to shoot that Hun, when you promptly told me, that it was all over. The war had ended.'

Jonti smiled at his friend, before continuing, Richard's tale, for him.

'Then you ran off, do you remember? Towards no man's land, like a mad man.' Jonti now had a huge smile on his face, 'You, then dropped your lice infested trousers, and your filthy underwear, whereupon, you proceeded to show a startled bunch of the surrendering enemy, your bare backside.'

'Oh yes,' remembered Richard. 'They deserved it. They started it.'

'Started what?' asked Jonti, even though, he knew what was coming. And, just as he was about to say it, his friend beat him to it.

'The war!'

Both men, now started laughing.

'Come here, you daft fool,' Jonti gestured, as he saw his friend's bi coloured eyes, now light up, with joviality.

The two friends immediately embraced.

Lots of back slapping and laughter followed, with quickly told stories and memories, excitedly spoken of.

Jonti, suddenly realised, that nobody, apart from himself and Richard, knew anything about the events they spoke of. So, he tried to cut his friend short, with the subtle hint, of a cough, as he began to tell, his men about the time, he and Jonti, had stormed an enemy machine gun post.

Richard gradually realised that he was digressing, and quickly apologised. The focus, now returned, to the mission.

'These are our guides for tonight, men,' Jonti began. 'Richard. This is my second in command, my very dear friend, Geremi Hammam. You may remember him, as a very green and impatient young man, at Mons.'

'The Somme,' mumbled Geremi, as he corrected, Jonti.

'Oh yes. That was it,' replied Jonti.

'Are you all right, young man?' Richard, asked.

Geremi, nodded his head, before placing his hand, over his mouth.

'It's portals Richard. Our young Geremi, doesn't like them.'

'He does look rather white, or maybe grey,' replied Richard. He then passed Geremi, a water bottle. 'Here. Have some water.'

'I am all right,' Geremi stated, as his stomach turned once again.

Richard and Jonti, had started to make their way towards the wooded area, as Geremi composed himself. Breathing through his nose, the young knight began to slowly feel better.

Presently, he joined the two men, who were crouched down, and studying a map.

'So, my friend, you can see we are, but a few miles from the twins.' Richard started, 'No major enemy activity, has been reported, around the cottage. Which is good. The twins were seen, just this morning, picking up leaves, in the front garden. So, we are very confident, that they are still there, tonight. However, there is some dispute, over which side the babysitter, is now on.'

'Yes, I have heard,' replied Jonti. 'Reports in the homeland, tell of her being turned. The king's sister, as well.'

'And the Judas's sister too,' remarked Richard. 'So, I am not surprised, that she has been turned. The only surprise, is that the enemy, have not attempted to move the twins.'

'Maybe, their uncle feels, that they are safe there?' Geremi had now joined the conversation. 'Having had the babysitter, turned?' He reasoned.

'Yeah, good point,' replied Jonti.

Richard suddenly rose to his feet, and folded up the map, before putting it, in a pocket.

'Our scouts tell us, that Normauss has been seen there, on several occasions.' Jonti saw the look of disdain, on his friend's face, as Richard said the troll's name.

'We will, get him my friend,' Jonti promised, as he and Geremi, got to their feet. He then placed a hand, on his friend's shoulder.

'I know we will,' Richard replied.

For a moment, there was silence, as the two men stared at each other. Jonti, could see the look of a killer, in his friend's eyes. They were dark, and full of anger and revenge.

Swiftly, Richard turned on his heels, before checking a pocket watch, that he took from his breast pocket. At which point, he gave an order, to one of his men.

'Time to get going, Jonti. I have some transport parked up, about half a mile from here.' His tone had suddenly become intensely serious, as too, his demeanour.

The two men now gave out their orders, before requesting a weapons check.

It wasn't long, before the two teams, made their way, across the fields, and the ancient stones, were quickly in the distance, behind them.

The mission to extract the twins, had now begun.

★★★

The transport, that Richard had obtained, had been borrowed from a farmer, who was a Dual Blood, Fantaellen. He explained that the farmer had owed him a favour, and had been more than willing, to pay back the debt, with the loan of his truck.

The uncomfortable, creaking vehicle shook the bones of its passengers, as it raced through the winding, narrow, country lanes. The driver, one of Richard's men, regularly crunched through the only two gears the vehicle had, mainly, as they came to, then took the corners at a speed. Everyone in the back, held on for dear life, with every turn and jolt.

'He does know that he can use the breaks, to slow down?' remarked Geremi, out loud.

'Hope so. Not that I think, he's used them yet,' replied Jonti.

Suddenly, they banked, into another corner, and Jonti and Geremi, slammed into each other, once more. Both men grunted, on impact, before apologising for the umpteenth time.

The truck wasn't designed, to carry a small group, and their rifles, so it was very cramped. It also offered, very little protection from the elements. A canvas sheet wrap, that was attached to the truck, the only protection.

When they reached the brow of a steep hill, Richard ordered his driver, to slow down, and dim the lights.

'Now, switch off the engine,' he instructed, as they came off the crest, and began to descend. 'Let her roll. We'll go in silently.'

'Sir.'

The vehicle quietly rolled down the hill, till it abruptly came to a halt, at the side of the road, about halfway down.

Richard then turned to Jonti and pointed out of the front window of the truck.

'That's our target. The cottage. See it?'

'Yeah. Got it,' replied Jonti.

The cottage, appeared to be, the only building, for miles. It was in complete darkness and seemed quiet.

The surrounding countryside opened up to them, like a patchwork cameo, as they rolled down the hill. Even, halfway down, the view, seemed to stretch for miles.

'From here, we go on foot,' started Richard. 'As quickly and as silently, as we can.'

Jonti listened, as Richard went through the finer points, of his plan. 'When, we reach the cottage, I suggest that we place one man in the front garden, and one in the backyard. They, will be our eyes and ears, as the rest of us go in. It, will need to be a quick and silent extraction.'

Jonti nodded his head in agreement. He trusted his friend's plan. He knew, how thorough Richard's attention to detail was, when planning a mission. Every action would have been thought through, so carefully.

A voice suddenly piped up from the back of the truck.

'What if the twins, or their aunt, do not want to come with us?' The voice was that of Geremi Hammam, who had been wondering why, they needed the king's sister.

Richard instantly smiled, as he pulled a black and white photo, from his pocket, before producing a small bottle, and a handkerchief, from a compartment, under the dashboard.

'A picture of the king, their father, will hopefully, make the twins trust us. As for the aunt? Well depends on her compliance.'

Richard held up the bottle.

'You see young Geremi, Chloroform. It will make anyone compliant.' He then winked, at him.

'The aunt could be as valuable as the twins,' Jonti began to explain, 'She may be able, to give us vital intelligence. Even, if she has been turned.'

Jonti had moved, to explain the reasoning behind, removing the aunt, as he knew, what his second in command, had been thinking.

'Right. Time to move gentlemen,' cried Richard, as he was handed a Long Bow, and a bag of arrows, by one of his men.

'You still use the bow, I see Richard,' Jonti remarked.

'Definitely. It's still more accurate, than this rifle. Got it made for me, by a master bowyer. And, my arrows, by the best fletcher, and arrowsmith in England. Even in these modern times, there are still, masters of the art around. You've, just got to know, where to go.'

Jonti, saw that Geremi had suddenly put two and two together, and before he could say anything, he pulled the young knight, to one side, after climbing out of the van.

'I never thought about it, till now', Geremi began. 'Even, when I saw his eyes.'

'Keep it quiet,' Jonti hissed. 'He, and his men, are a minority. Do not speak, their name. Especially, in this world. Word gets out, that they are, well you know,' Jonti now looked sternly, into Geremi's eyes, 'they will be hunted down. As far, as the Blackhearts are concerned, they are the sought-after ones.'

'Yes. I do get it!' snapped the young knight. 'Their race, no longer exists.'

'Good.'

Jonti felt bad, about the way, he had spoken to his friend. He had to get his point across, as it was vitally important.

Richard's Portaellen race, had been hunted down, by the Wulfdaeden's, like wild animals, in the portal world. For, they are formidable bowmen, and centuries long, allies of the Fantaellen's. Their homeland had fallen to the Blackhearts, nearly a century ago. The surviving refugees subsequently scattered across both worlds. The name, of their bowmen, and their country, is revered through-out Portaellen, and is not spoken of, by their allies, to protect them.

Jonti, wanted to make sure, his young friend, remembered that fact. He then prayed, that one day, Richard (who will tell people, he is a proud Fantaellen, and secondly, a proud Englishman,) and his fellow compatriots, could return, to their homeland, in peace.

Silently, the men of Fantaellen, made their way, down the dark country lane, towards the cottage. In the far distance, the cry of a fox, and the call of a pheasant, forced them to come to an abrupt halt, as they listened for further noises.

The countryside quickly fell silent once more, and the group, were on the move, again.

As, they finally reached a long privet hedge, that ran the length of the front garden, Richard ordered everyone to crouch down, with a hand signal.

There, they stayed briefly. Listening, and looking, for any signs, of enemy movement.

Richard looked at Jonti, who nodded.

This was it. The time for action, and the execution, of the plan, had now come.

Presently, the two officers urged their men through the front gate, and up the garden path. One man was placed on guard, on the front lawn. Another was then ordered around the back. Jonti, Richard and the rest of their men, quickly made their way, to-wards the front door.

The door was a rather old looking wooden door, that Jonti thought, would have been quite secure, at one time. Not now, however. It had obviously, seen better days.

It wouldn't take much, to take it off its hinges, he thought to himself. But, once inside, the element of surprise, would be short lived.

Richard had already planned the entry. It did not involve, taking the door off its hinges. One of his men, produced a small, thin blade from his pocket, (Jonti recognised it, as a hand combat weapon, called a Gut Knife), which he pushed through the keyhole. It was not long, before the key, hit the doormat. He, then used the blade, to fiddle with the rusty old lock, until there was a click. He, then turned the handle, and the door creaked, as he slowly, opened it.

Two of Richard's men entered the cottage first, with their rifles ready, to be fired. It was pitch black, as they crossed the threshold, of the doorway, and moved into the unknown. Their boots were heavy, on the wooden floor, as they cautiously shuffled forward. To their left and right, there was a closed door. In front, a darkened, partly opened doorway. Additionally, at their front, to the left, the staircase, which was also in complete darkness.

Both men, glanced at each other, before one of them took the lead, and went to enter the room, with the door, that was partly open. Before, he could place his hand, on the handle, the knight took a cautious step back, unsure of what he had just seen.

Was that a shadow?

Unexpectedly, a loud piercing scream, came from the darkened room in front of them. Followed swiftly, by two blades, that flew over their heads, and embedded themselves in the wall behind them.

When Jonti, Richard and the rest of the men, entered the cottage, they promptly took cover, as the blades came their way.

Then, from the darkened room, charged a bulky, shrieking figure, with a large sword, that they flailed around, like a possessed, mad creature.

The two knights, near the doorway, just managed to dodge, the charging mass, before turning to take aim, with their rifles.

'Don't shoot her!' ordered Jonti.

Instinctively, and together, the two knights, now attacked the charging figure from behind, one, by jumping on her back, the other, opting for a rugby tackle.

As the figure, cursed and spat at them, they briefly saw see the evil, in her eyes.

With, a swift, hard driven rifle butt, suddenly smashed into her shoulder, the shrieking, crazed figure, immediately dropped the sword. Still, she fought ferociously, spitting, biting, and punching, as she was being pulled, to the floor. As much, as the two men pushed, shoved and punched her, she would not go down.

Two other knights had now joined the melee, and the four men, were now proving too much for the possessed, large woman.

'Get her down,' Richard ordered.

It still took, a short while, before the woman was supine on the floor, and cursing at the ceiling, her hands tied behind her back, and a gag, eventually placed over her mouth. Even at this point, she was never fully compliant, as she tried rolling around the wooden floor, on her back, her legs, kicking and thrashing around.

'You two. Sit on her,' Richard ordered.

'Sir? Sit on her?' one, knight queried.

'Yes! Sit on her,' came the repeated order. 'And you two, tie them legs together.'

Reluctantly, the two knights sat on the quivering, angry mass, as the other two knights, grabbed her legs, and proceeded to tie them together.

Richard now quickly produced a small dark bottle and a rag, from his pocket.

As, he knelt beside the woman, Richard briefly looked into her eyes. There, he could see nothing but evil, staring back at him.

'I can't believe, you are the king's sister,' he remarked.

He then promptly removed her gag and administered a very large dosage of Chloroform, before she could scream and curse, anymore.

Within, a short space of time, her body was motionless.

Two knights, were presently sent upstairs, to locate the twins.

A whistle was then heard, from the back garden. Richard and Jonti, ran up the stairs, to the landing, and opened a window, that overlooked, the back garden.

'What is it sentry?' Richard called out.

'Headlights, to the north sir. Just coming over the brow of that hill. See?'

'Yes. I see,' replied Richard.

'Time to move?' enquired Jonti.

'Yes. I think so,' answered Richard.

Just then, the two knights appeared from a room, further down the landing. In their arms, they each carried a limp child.

For a moment, Jonti's heart sank, and a nauseous feeling overcame him, as he feared the worst.

'They're alive sir,' one of the knights stated, upon seeing, the look on Jonti's face.

'They have been drugged,' the other knight began. 'Probably for transportation. Look, they're breathing.'

Jonti, quickly looked over the two children. They appeared so small, so thin, and filthy looking. Their small chests, hardly moving.

Not the appearance, of the children of a king, he thought to himself.

'We need to get going,' Richard suddenly piped up. 'We may have company, to the north.'

'Yes sir, came the immediate reply, from the two knights.

They were out the front door rapidly. Two men carried the compliant aunt between them. Jonti, carried the little boy, and Richard, carried the little girl. The rest had their rifles ready, as the group, quickly made their way, back up the hill, towards their transport.

Jonti, did turn briefly, at one point, to watch the set of headlights, heading towards them.

'Come on my friend,' Richard started, 'they must be Blackhearts. Who else, would be driving down, these country lanes, in the dead of night?'

'True,' agreed Jonti.

The race to the Ring of Stones, was now on.

★★★

The silence of the countryside was abruptly disturbed, by the sudden screeching of tyres, hugging the narrow corners, around country lanes.

Halfway up the gradient of a hill, a vehicle was being pursued by another. Both were being driven, at their top speed, as a deadly pursuit, began to unfold.

A shot fired from the pursuer, rang out. The aim, wayward and hopeful.

Jonti and Geremi, were in the back of their truck, crouched down, and watching with concern. The other vehicle appeared to be gaining on them.

'Can't this thing go any faster? cried Jonti.

'We are at full speed,' replied Richard. He had briefly turned around, to reply to Jonti, before continuing to give the driver, some instruction.

'Christ,' Jonti muttered to himself.

Jonti quickly grabbed his rifle and took aim. Geremi followed suit.

Jonti, quickly took his first shot, which whistled past the enemy truck, as it listed, to one side, whilst going around a bend. He cursed his bad luck, under his breath. For, the driver had been, in his line of sight.

Geremi fired next. His bullet pierced the windscreen, and hit the passenger, in the front seat, clean, in the middle of his forehead. The shot had snapped the head back, before the passenger had slumped forward, onto the dashboard.

'Good shot,' remarked Jonti, as he took aim, and fired, his next shot.

An instant return of bullets came from the pursuing truck. None hit their intended target.

Along, winding country lanes, the pursuit continued, towards the portal.

One of Richard's men, was fatally hit, by a stray bullet, that had whistled past Jonti and Geremi, and got him in the throat, just as he had fired an arrow, from his Long Bow. The sound of choking, on his blood, lasted only moments, as Jonti, comforted the young knight, before he died.

Next, Jonti and Geremi set about the task, of laying down a constant line of fire, in an attempt, to pin down their enemy.

It worked. Their disciplined, suppressive volley of fire was almost, going unanswered.

They knew that they were close, to the location of the stones. Any vital time, they could gain, by keeping the enemy pinned down, and slowing their pursuit, would give them the chance, to unload their passengers, and make a run for the portal.

Richard had already told Jonti, that he and his knight's, would form a defensive position, to protect his friend and his men, as they made a run for the portal.

Jonti knew, that they would need this precious time.

With a sudden, and sharp, hard turn, their vehicle, now came to an instant halt, with a screech of brakes, and an immediate jolt.

'Everybody out!' ordered Richard.

As, he jumped from the passenger seat, Richard briefly looked, to see the headlights of the other truck, dancing between the road and the sky, as it made its way, around a twisting lane, and up, the final hill. The enemy were now close.

He smiled briefly at Jonti, as they quickly unloaded the passengers, from the truck. His friend had done well. The suppressive firing, of he and Geremi, had bought them some precious time.

Jonti, winked at his friend, and smiled.

'We will hold them here,' Richard stated. He then stared, deep into Jonti's eyes as he continued. 'The future of Fantaellen, is now in your hands, my friend. Good luck.'

At that moment, the two old friends, saluted each other.

'Sir!' One, of Richard's men, suddenly shouted out.

He pointed, at the advancing Blackheart vehicle. Jonti saw, that the advantageous distance, they had gained, was presently being swallowed up, quite rapidly.

'Time to go Geremi,' ordered Jonti. 'We, must leave our friends, here.'

'Yes sir,' replied Geremi sharpish, before turning, to give his orders, to one of their men. He then picked up, the little girl, and cradled her, in his arms.

Jonti, then picked up the little boy. Two of their men, carried the compliant aunt.

In a very, short space of time, Richard and his men, had formed, their defensive line. He turned briefly, to watch, as Jonti, and his group, made their way, past the stones, towards the location, of the arrival point, of the portal.

Then, with defiance, in his voice, Richard, gave his last order, before they would be engaging, with the enemy.

'This is where, we hold them boys!' He now demanded, of his men. 'Here! At this sacred place.'

All eyes were now focussed, on the Blackheart vehicle. Fingers twitched, on triggers, and bow strings.

'Hold!' Richard called out. Sensing the nervousness, of his men.

The enemy truck, suddenly slammed to a halt, up ahead. Its head lights, enveloping the ground in front of them, shining, straight into their eyes.

Two shots suddenly rang out, and the headlights, were now gone.

'To the last man!' Richard now roared, as he reloaded his rifle, before putting it back over his shoulder, and pulling his Long Bow, over his head. In a heartbeat, he had nocked his arrow, onto his bowstring, and had pulled the tight string back, level with his ear, and taken aim.

Two Wulfdaeden's, had managed to crawl under their vehicle, and had started firing wildly, at them. Richard had killed one enemy knight, with his first arrow, as he tried to jump out of the driver's side, of the vehicle. The dying Blackheart, had spent his final breath's, clawing at the arrow, embedded in his ribs.

Richard now fired two more arrows. One, fell just short of his intended target. The other, took a Blackheart, clean off his feet, as the arrow thundered into his face with such force, that he was instantly pinned to a tree.

A hail of bullets kept Richard and his men busy, as they sought cover. One Fantaellen, who was out in the open ground, tried to retreat, and find himself, any kind of cover. He was killed, when a single bullet, smashed into his frontal lobe. He died instantly.

For several, frantic, deadly, minutes, a fierce fire fight ensued. Knights, on both sides, died. Neither, choosing to break cover.

Then, came the Wulfdaeden offensive. Richard had been expecting it. He, and his men, had been doing their job, thus far. Buying, Jonti and his men, time.

The signal for the Blackheart attack, came in the form of a whistle, followed quickly, by a howl, from a wooded area, to the east, of Richard's defensive position.

Richard, turned to see, several narrow, red eyes suddenly appear from the shadows.

Slowly, a group of four legged creatures, sauntered from the tree line. They had, wolf shaped heads, and pointed ears, a long snout, and a snarling mouth, with saliva dripping fangs. Their bodies were small and muscular, and carried by four strong legs, and huge paws. Their fur, varied in colour, texture and thickness. Two, had black, white and grey markings. One, was completely white. Two, were grey. At the head of the group, was the alpha male. Jet black in colour, his fangs bared, his red eyes, focussed on the enemy's, defensive position.

'Wulfrik,' Richard cursed, when he recognised, the leader of the Wolfdogs.

The Wulfdaeden assault, now began, in earnest.

From the east, charged Wulfrik and his Wolfdogs. Ahead, of Richard and his men, came the Blackheart charge.

Richard ordered two of his men, to open fire, on Wulfrik and his fellow creatures, which they did, almost instantly, killing two dogs. The rest were ordered to fire, on the frontal offensive.

A couple of Wulfdaeden Blackhearts were quickly killed, by Richard's arrows, as enemy bullets, whistled over his head.

He, then heard the screams, of three of his men, as several bullets, ripped into them. At this point, Richard, now chose to abandon his Long Bow and arrows, and grabbed his rifle.

He was quickly, firing twenty rounds a minute, in a desperate attempt, to stop the Blackheart offensive.

One Blackheart was felled, as a bullet nicked, an artery in his neck. He went down, in a spray of blood, spurting through his desperate fingers.

Another went to ground, as two Blackhearts, died either side of him, in a hail of Fantaellen bullets. His first shot fired, from the muddy ground, hit a Fantaellen, clean between the eyes. Reloading, his rifle quickly, the Wulfdaeden Blackheart, then rose to his feet, and went on the attack, once more.

The situation was getting a little desperate. Richard had reached into his ammunition pouch, and realised, he was running out of bullets. He had one in his chamber, and one left in his pouch. Presently, he aimed his rifle, and fired, his penultimate round. One enemy knight went down. He then loaded his final bullet and took aim.

Richard's last bullet blew the brains out of a Blackheart. This caused the last Wulfdaeden, to stop in his tracks, and instinctively, dive to the floor.

Richard now fixed his bayonet, onto his rifle. In quick time, he shouted obscenities while charging towards, the enemy knight. He, then saw, the Wulfdaeden taking aim. Bracing himself, for the impact of a bullet, he closed his eyes, and continued, to charge forward.

The sudden crack of gun fire caused Richard's heart to stop, at once. Nothing. No smash, of a deadly bullet, into his flesh. No pain. And he was still running. Richard opened his eyes, to see the Wulfdaeden, dead on the ground, a bullet lodged, in the top, of his skull.

He, then turned to see Jonti, running away, from behind their vehicle, having just fired his rifle, to save his friend.

Now, with fifteen inches of cold steel, Richard had to take the fight, to Wulfrik and his Wolfdogs, who were charging, and desperately dodging, Fantaellen bullets.

★★★

The energy, around Jonti and the rest of the travellers, was slowly growing. He could feel, the build-up, of the powerful, kinetic energy, that pulsed through the ground beneath, their feet.

Knowing, that they had very little time, before they would be taken into the gateway, Jonti glanced back, to make sure, that they were not being pursued.

He could see Richard, and his last two men, charging with their bayonet's, at Wulfrik and his Wolfdog's.

The fight, had become, a desperate battle, between man and dog. Bayonet, against snarling teeth, and razor-sharp claws.

One grey Wolfdog, cried out, as it was impaled, on a Fantaellen bayonet. Its killer was quickly overcome though, by a white Wolfdog, who ripped the Fantaellen knight to pieces, in a frenzied attack, before it made a sudden rush, at Richard.

Jonti's heart leapt, as Richard killed that creature, with the sudden smash, of his rifle butt, to the skull. Followed, by the lunge, of the cold steel, of his bayonet, deep into its stomach.

Richard, and his last knight, now suddenly dropped their rifles, and produced swords, from their back scabbards. Richard, then appeared to pull out his Gut Knife.

Wulfrik, and the other grey Wolfdog, who had made a strategic retreat, now went on the offensive.

The leader of the Wolfdogs suddenly pulled out of a charge, that he had made at Richard, which caused the knight, to stop in his tracks. The creature, now powerfully lunged left, to join the other Wolfdog, in his assault.

Both Wolfdogs, instinctively evaded the cut and thrust, of the lone Fantaellen knight's sword, and their combined speed and weight, upon impact, instantly threw him to the floor, where they quickly, set about his prone body, and ripped him to pieces. The Fantaellen's screams, soon filled the night air.

Richard charged at the two frenzied creatures.

Wulfrik, barked out a quick order, and the blood soaked, grey Wolfdog, now sped away, towards Jonti and his men.

As, he looked up, into the night sky, Jonti felt a powerful, gust of wind, that suddenly picked up, and turned even stronger, before it whipped through the stones, and encircled them. There was then, an almighty build-up of electric energy, all around them, more powerful, than before.

In the sky above them, a bright white light, now began to manifest.

Jonti, glanced to see the sight of the Wolfdog, charging at them, at breakneck speed. He, then looked past the charging creature, to see Richard swing his sword, and lunge, with his Gut Knife, as Wulfrik pounced upon him. Blood, then shot like a fountain, into the air, as the leader of the Wolfdogs, appeared, to rip out Richard's throat.

As Jonti, briefly closed his eyes in despair, a tear rolled down his cheek.

Then, the last thing, he saw, as he re-opened them, was Wulfrik, leave Richard's body, and start to head towards them.

Jonti's disciplined mind set, now suddenly changed. Having, seen his friend, die so horribly. It would take, an almighty, amount of restraint, not to abandon his mission, and attack Wulfrik. At once, a voice inside his head, dispelled any such thoughts, as it told him, that he would get his chance, one day. Just, not today. Jonti's mind, instantly returned to now.

Yes, I will wait.

The energy of the portal was now at its peak. The travellers had no time to waste.

The grey Wolfdog chose this exact moment, to make his desperate and powerful lunge, towards the light, that engulfed the ground, in front of him. Its jaws were wide open, showing, its blood-soaked fangs, as it flew, through the air.

Upon, landing heavily on its paws, the creature howled in despair. The bright, white light and the pulsing energy, along with all the portal travellers, had disappeared.

Wulfrik, suddenly appeared on the scene, breathless and angry. In an instant, he growled at his underling, before he spat something, onto the ground, in front of him. The bloodied, chewed, chunk of flesh, looked like two human fingers.

'Veron scum!' He hissed.

He, then showed his displeasure, of his underling's failure, by sending the creature away into the night, howling in pain, with a chunk of his ear missing.

Wulfrik himself, then disappeared into the darkness, alone and angry.

The Ring of Stones now fell silent, once more, as the first signs of dawn, began to show their delicate, fresh rays of light, through the dark blanket, of the night.

Chapter Eight

Dawn. No birdsong greeted the new day. Only turmoil, carnage, fire and death, existed in Fantaellen on this new morning.

With, the passing of just a few short hours, nearly all the important coastal fortresses, had fallen into enemy hands. Now, mercilessly, and with a devastating momentum, the Blackhearts were swiftly bringing the country of Fantaellen, to its knees.

Countless Wulfdaeden regiments, had quickly made inroads, deep into the land, of their enemy. Many, towns and villages, were swiftly burned to the ground. Their citizens massacred. An unrelenting chaos, of death and fire, rapidly consumed this once peaceful land. Smoke, flame, and the taste for more Fantaellen blood, drove the Blackhearts, ever forward. And, just as General Grafton had ordered, and his master had wanted, the attack had been swift, and extremely lethal.

Therefore, as the dawn broke, small pockets of retreating, Fantaellen battalions, spread wide across the country, were engaged in a desperate fight.

Now forced, into a defensive action, by the onslaught, of a blood crazed enemy, Robert Scotten's knights, were regrouping, or joining other regiments and battalions, to form a hastily made, defensive line, up and down, Fantaellen.

With, the vast number, of Wulfdaeden Blackhearts, attacking from just about anywhere, and everywhere, many regiments of

Fantaellen knights, had been forced to fight, retreat and regroup, several times. With, the loss of countless men.

Now, with their backs, to the rising sun, and with no choice, but to stand and face a blood drunk enemy, the knights of Fantaellen, made their stand.

In the fields, the woods, and the towns and villages. For, Guinlance and the Motherland. For their families.

To the last man.

★★★

Arami, slowly opened his eyes. Something had awoken him, from his deep sleep.

As his senses awoke, and his eyes adjusted to the darkness, and the feint light of the dawn, which trickled through the gaps, in his curtains, Arami now realised, that he was not dreaming. He had heard it again. A raised voice? A panicked shout? He could not tell. Now, more voices. Yes, it was real. There seemed to be a disturbance, at the front, of the house.

At the foot, of the young boy's bed, his hound Zevarn, suddenly stirred, and was quickly awake. The hound's ears, instantly, and instinctively twitched, as he cocked his huge head, to one side, as he listened.

In the dim light, of his bedroom, the boy could see very little. Nevertheless, he could hear Zevarn making his way, across the wooden floorboards, towards the far side, of the room. Arami, then heard Zevarn sniffing about. This was rapidly followed, by a deep, guttural growling, from his hound.

Arami climbed out of his bed, and fumbled his way across the room, towards his window, and the silhouette, of his hound, who was up, on his hind legs, having pushed his head through the curtains.

'What is it Zevarn?' Arami asked.

The hound barked, then growled, in reply.

When, he reached the window, Arami patted Zevarn's head. Then, he lightly stroked him, in reassurance.

'Good boy,' he whispered. 'There's a good boy.'

Arami's bedroom window, faced out onto the main street, of the village. Consequently, as he pulled back the curtains, he saw a knight on horseback, in a Fantaellen uniform, riding up and down. The rising sun cast a bright light, off the knight's armour, and caused Arami to look away, for a moment.

Arami quickly opened his window, in an attempt, to hear what the knight, was shouting.

On the street, people ran around in a panic, shouting and screaming.

'The Blackhearts! They are coming! Run! Run for your lives!'

Just then, Arami was taken by complete surprise when his bedroom door, suddenly burst open. In the doorway, stood his grandfather.

'Quickly Arami. You must go.' There was panic, in the old man's voice.

The boy stared at his grandfather. He had never seen him, dressed in this way before. He wore, an old, faded uniform, and he had armour on, that had seen better days. Despite his age, shown by his white hair and beard, and his hardened face, Arami's grandfather, was still strong and agile, and the young boy thought, that he did look impressive as he stood in the doorway.

'Come on boy!' His grandfather growled. 'Your mother is waiting for you, downstairs.'

Arami, now called Zevarn's name, and the two of them, swiftly made their way, down the stairs. The faithful hound was just a step behind him.

In the hallway, stood his mother. She was anxiously, looking out of a window, at the chaos on the street. Her attention, instantly turned to her son, when she saw him.

'Arami. Quickly. Come on.' The young boy could see the anxiety and fear, in his mother's face. 'Your Grandfather says that we must leave. We have no time to waste. Here.' She quickly passed her son, a hooded robe, and some trousers. 'Put them on. I've put some food, in the pocket, of the robe. And, put your boots on.'

Arami, could see that his mother, had tied her golden, blonde hair, into a ponytail. She wore a long coat, and her leather, riding boots.

As, he forced his feet, into his boots, and began tying the laces, he could see that his mother, still wore her night gown, under her coat. He was about to ask her why, when a more important question, suddenly sprung into his head.

'Where's father?' He asked.

Arami could see the tears, start to well up in her eyes, as she turned to look at him before she gently grabbed his hand.

'He is at the fortress, near the sea ...' she started to say, before stopping, when she saw the innocence, in her son's eyes.

'Yes, I know mother,' Arami replied, 'I just want him here.'

'Arami.' Her tone had softened. 'We are being invaded. The Wulfdaeden's have attacked us. That is why, we are leaving. Only for a while. Your grandfather has gone to get some men together, to see what is happening. It will be fine.'

'But, what about father?' Arami asked again.

'I don't know Arami. I don't know.' Her voice was now full of despair.

The young boy could see the tears streaming down his mother's face.

At this point, his young heart, felt so heavy, and his mind confused. All, he wanted to do, was comfort his mother.

The two of them, came together and embraced. Whereupon, she stroked, his long blonde hair, and Arami held his mother, as if their lives, depended on it.

'We have to be strong and brave my son.' The truth was, that at this precise moment, she felt anything but.

'We will be fine mother. Father and his knight's will come and save us all. I know they will.'

Presently, two men from the village appeared, from the woods, that surrounded the perimeter dwellings. They had bloodied swords in their hands and looked panicked and breathless.

'You must run!' They shouted. 'Everybody make your way to the hills. Run!'

Arami's mother, quickly ran out of the house, and over to one of the men. He could see her becoming agitated, as they spoke. The two of them talked, for only a moment more. Arami saw the man, shake his head, and his mother cover her face, before crying out, in despair. He, then saw the man, beckoning, towards the hills.

Despite, her obvious anguish, his mother did not need telling again, and she turned quickly on her heels.

'Zevarn,' Arami called out.

His hound was by his side in seconds, and the two were out on the street, almost immediately.

People ran out of their houses, with whatever they could carry. Mother's and father's, guiding their children. Young and old, desperately leaving their world behind them, in an attempt, to escape, the onslaught of an enemy, that would kill them all.

Others looked around in bewilderment, unsure what to do. One old man kissed his wife, and pleaded with his family, to leave. He was frail, and would slow them down, he told them.

Arami watched, a friend and his family, go back into their house, and close the door. He began, to run over to their house, in a desperate attempt, to tell them to leave, when he heard his mother, call his name.

'Arami! Come on. We have to go.' She could see, where her son headed. His safety was her priority.

'But mum. What about my friend, Hugo?'

'Leave them son. They, have made their decision.'

Arami, was soon with his mother. He had tears, in his eyes. 'What about grandfather?' he asked, as she grabbed hold of his arm.

'He gave those two men a message.' His mother's voice wavered for a moment. Then, she continued, 'He said, he would join us soon. Everything was going to be fine. Now we must go. Quickly.'

As the young boy, ran beside his mother, he knew that everything was not fine. He was just conscious, that he had to run. Run away. Run as fast, as his little legs could carry him. It was his job now, to keep his mother safe. With his faithful hound beside him, he knew he had a chance.

★★★

The piercing screams of the tormented and petrified villagers, and the blood curdling cries of hundreds of crazed, demented voices, suddenly engulfed the main street of the village.

The wild, frenzied swarm, of Wulfdaeden Blackhearts charged up the street, desperate for blood. Any villager, unfortunate to still be there, was slaughtered where they stood. Men, women and children, were hacked and chopped to death, by Blackheart swords and axes. The blood ran thick. No one was shown any mercy.

As the main body of Wulfdaeden's, wreaked havoc with their blades, others behind them, with torches, set fire to the buildings.

The villagers, who had sort sanctuary, in their homes, and had repulsed the enemy swords and axes thus far, were quickly surrounded. Anybody, who tried to make a run for their lives, were slaughtered. Within moments, their simple dwellings were set alight, and the remaining occupants, were burned alive.

A Blackheart officer, on a magnificent black steed, was busy shouting out his orders, to his men, as he raced up and down the street. His archers were ordered to go to the west, and hide in the trees, on top of a hill, that surrounded a field, about half a mile away. He then ordered his knights on foot, to carry on pushing forward.

'Show no mercy!' He screamed. 'They must all die! Forward!'

Then, three times in perfect unison, his men raised their swords. Each thrusting action was immediately followed, by hundreds of loud, masculine, crazed grunts.

The thunderous noise from the Blackheart invaders, reverberated around the countryside.

Then, the Wulfdaeden drums began their relentless beating.

Onwards they pushed. With no mercy on their minds. The Wulfdaeden war machine, in full, murderous advance.

★★★

Arami had hold of his mother's wrist, as he pulled her clumsily up the steep hill. She had slowed to almost a walking pace, in an attempt, to gain her breath.

'Come on mother. We can rest, at the top.'

It was now Arami, who had the sense of urgency, about him. He could hear, the faint beat of the drums. They were not Fantaellen drums. Of that, he was sure.

'I can't.' His mother gasped.

'You can,' he told her. 'It's not too far now.'

The hill was steep and long, and they were not even halfway up it. Nor could they see the crest. Arami knew, that they had to keep going. At all costs.

Within, a few more strides, they were forced to stop. His mother had begun coughing, as she gasped for air. She had been ill recently and was slowly on the road to recovery. She looked pale, and tired. So, they had stopped.

The young boy's heart pounded in his small chest, as he now rested. His lungs burnt. He gasped a couple of times, as he struggled to breath. His leg's felt heavy, and he perspired. It had been such an effort to run up the hill. He was exhausted. Arami glanced to see his faithful hound, laying down, and panting, by his side. The hound momentarily looked up at the young boy, before placing its head, on its master's legs, its chest beating hard and fast, and a long pink tongue, dangling out the side of its jaws. Arami stroked his hound, as the two of them recovered.

Zevarn's ears suddenly pricked up. All at once, Arami and his mother, heard the increasing commotion too. The young boy was immediately on his feet. Followed instantly, by Zevarn and his mother. At that moment, as they looked down the hill, they saw the many terrified and desperate villagers, running for their lives, in all directions.

With, the increasing beat, of the Wulfdaeden drums, resonating around the burning land below, and stalking the stragglers,

135

who were being butchered, and left for dead, the situation, suddenly looked desperate.

Arami still an innocent, young boy, now felt very afraid, and alone. He wished that his father were here. He would have known, what to do. He had his mother. He had his hound. But they were his responsibility. The young boy could still see his father, in the doorway, waving goodbye, after telling him, to look after his mother. For, he was now the man of the house, his father had told him.

The despairing screams, of the poor souls, still left in the village, had now almost diminished. And, the thundering, incessant beat of the Wulfdaeden drum's, appeared to be getting closer.

A sudden crashing noise, at the foot of the hill, as a burning building collapsed inwards, gave the primal, survival instinct of Arami and his mother, a sudden jolt.

'Come on. We have to keep moving,' his mother gasped.

Mother and son suddenly had a new burst of energy, as once again, they began to negotiate, the steepness of the hill in front of them. Up ahead of them, was Zevarn, who bounded enthusiastically, up the gradient.

Intuitively, the hound suddenly stopped, to smell the air. Arami could see, that something had startled him, as Zevarn had slowly made his way towards a wooded area to his right. Almost at once, the hound placed his nose in the grass, and slowly approached some trees. Then, as he quickly lifted his head, Zevarn's ears pricked up, in advance, of a sudden sprint, to another smaller crop of trees, to his left. Arami could see, that his faithful hound, was spooked by something.

Zevarn growled, and barked out a warning, as his master approached him.

'What is it boy?' Arami asked.

'Run!' His mother shouted at once, just as two giant, Blackheart knights, stepped out from the cover of the trees, either side of her son and his hound.

Arami appeared to be frozen to the spot, as he stared at the two Wulfdaeden's. Both knights, looked at each other, before a deranged smile, filled their faces. They began to approach, the child in front of them, who now had his growling hound, at his side.

'Come on Arami!' His mother shouted, as she ran towards him. 'We have got to run!'

Both Blackhearts, now had an evil, horrifying smile of anticipation, on their faces, as they unsheathed their enormous sword's.

'Run!' His mother screamed, once again, as she went to grab her son's wrist.

Arami, was directly roused from his daydream, and straight away, he broke free from the hand, that had a grip, of his wrist. In a flash, he turned to run, towards the trees, to his right.

His mother, who had tried to drag her son with her, had turned to run back down the hill. She had taken, very few strides, when she glanced over her shoulder, she saw Arami, heading in the opposite direction.

'No.' She gasped.

She tried to call his name and was suddenly grabbed from behind. Whereupon a giant hand was abruptly placed over her mouth. Immediately, looking up, she saw the dark, evil eyes, of her Blackheart assailant, staring at her, as she felt his strong grip, tighten. As she fought hard, to break free, she was lifted off her feet, and carried away.

There was now utter confusion and desperation, as one Blackheart ran after Arami, who nearly made it to the trees, before being grabbed.

Zevarn, had charged at the other Blackheart, and had hold of his ankle. The giant of a man, yelped, and instantly fell to the floor, with the hound attached to his leg. Zevarn, now pulled and wrenched at flesh and bone, as the Blackheart screamed in agony, desperately flashing his sword around, to try and maim or kill the hound.

Next, in an incredible flash of speed and agility, the hound let go, and instantly grabbed the man's throat. At once, there was a blood curdling scream, followed by a choking sound from the Blackheart. Zevarn, finally let go, as the giant of a man choked on the blood, that filled his lungs, as he bled out.

The crazed hound, now charged at the Blackheart, that had grabbed Arami. The young boy punched and kicked his assailant, who in turn, laughed at the boy, and his futile efforts to hurt him.

The Wulfdaeden knight, suddenly let out an instantaneous scream, and he immediately let go of Arami, when Zevarn athletically leapt at him, and grabbed his sword arm.

Impulsively, the young boy ran towards his mother, who had kicked her attacker, forcing him to drop her, back on her feet.

'No Arami! You must run!' She gasped, as she tried to dig her heels into the ground, and break free, from the iron grip, of the Wulfdaeden.

'Come on you.' He growled, as he tightened his grip, on her, even more.

Arami, now watched helplessly, as his mother fought desperately, to free herself. The urge to run at her captor and kill him, was very strong. But it was as if there was an invisible wall, in front of him. For, he had come to a sudden halt as soon as he had tried to run. He could not explain it, at that moment. Tears of frustration welled up in his eyes. He felt such anger.

'No!' He screamed at his mother's attacker.

'Run Arami!' She yelled. 'You must live my son! Run! Run!'

His mother gasped, as she was lifted off her feet once more, and forcefully dragged away.

Tears of frustration and desperation now streamed down her son's face, as he watched his mother being taken, then disappear from view, at the bottom of the hill.

'Why?' He sobbed, as he felt the invisible wall, slowly vanish, and the words of his mother, echo around his head. He wanted to run down the hill and rescue his mother. It was the right thing to do. He, then remembered the look, on his mother's face, just a few moments earlier, when she was being dragged away. It was a look; he had never seen before.

'Why?' He sobbed, once more. His anger remained, and the tears of frustration, continued to roll down his face.

The loud bark and deep growl from Zevarn, instantly grabbed Arami's attention. He turned to see his hound, chewing and pulling on a Blackheart's arm. The enemy knight screamed in agony. On the ground, Arami spotted the Wulfdaeden's sword.

He immediately ran towards the weapon and straight away, he bent down, and went to pick it up. He struggled briefly before getting a firm grip on the hilt. Then, rather clumsily, with both hands, Arami lifted it up, to waist height.

Now, with an anger, he had never felt before, coursing through his veins, the young boy made his way over to the Blackheart, being ripped apart by his trusted hound.

With a piercing whistle, Zevarn was called off. The Blackheart screamed, as the hound, let his grip go, and blood spurted into the air, from an opened vein in his arm.

As the giant of a Blackheart, struggled to his feet, he became aware of Arami, who stood in front of him. His own bloodied sword, in the boy's small hand's. The pitiful sight, of a puny child, standing there and holding his heavy sword, caused the Wulfdaeden to laugh out loud, through his pain.

'You'll, never lift up that sword boy!' He snarled. 'You're not strong enough.'

Arami screamed at the Blackheart, then he raised the sword above his head and charged with all the strength, he could muster.

The Blackheart in turn, screamed at the young boy, spittle, flying from his mouth. Then, he watched in astonishment, as Arami, was quickly on him, and had made a lunge, with the heavy weapon, before he felt the thrust of the cold steel, of his own sword, cut through his black armour, and into his stomach.

Startled, the Blackheart fell backwards, pulling desperately at his own blade, that now protruded from his guts.

As, he lay dying, Arami knelt beside the Blackheart, looked him in the eyes, and smiled.

'Yes. I am strong enough, Wulfdaeden,' he hissed, in his young voice, filled with emotion and tempered by angered tears. 'I may only be a young boy, but I have the heart of my father. The heart of a lion. Now go to hell.' Arami stared deep, into the eyes of his enemy, before getting to his feet, and pushing down on the blade, with such force, that the action caused him to stumble forward, onto the body of his enemy, as the sword went deeper, into flesh.

The innocence of a young child had now gone, forever. Arami changed, in that moment of anger, frustration and an unknown strength, that had come, from deep within. He was ready to kill again. He now had one thought on his mind. His mother.

Arami whistled for his hound. Zevarn, was obediently by his master's side, in moments, and the two of them, were soon charging towards the commotion, that earlier, they had run from.

With his heart pounding in his small chest, Arami ran blindly, with an anger and courage, that he had never known. All, he wanted to do, was rescue his mother.

Zevarn, who was a few steps in front of Arami, abruptly came to a halt, on the hill. His teeth were bared, and he barked and growled.

'What is it boy?' Arami gasped. He could see nothing. Zevarn seemed to be agitated at something, though.

As he attempted, to run past his hound, Arami was suddenly thrown from his feet, by an unseen force. He, immediately landed painfully, with a bone crunching thud, on the ground.

Zevarn, was still barking and growling, when Arami came round. Dazed and feeling a little stunned, he lay where he was, looking up at the sky. Slowly sitting up, as his vision became clearer, he could see a thin mist, that had begun to grow in front of Zevarn. The hound continued his growl, from deep within his throat.

Arami gingerly climbed to his feet, as he watched the mist grow. Astonished, he observed, as it firstly, took the form of a human, that quickly grew in stature, to the size of a large man. The mist remained transparent, throughout.

'If, you go after your mother, you will be killed,' said a voice, in front of them.

Arami was frozen to the spot, where he stood. The voice had come from the mist.

Zevarn had now stopped growling, and he lay on the floor, looking up in anticipation. It was as if, the hound knew the voice.

Arami, thought he recognised it too. The firm, masculine tone, so familiar to him. Could it be? He wondered.

'Now, is not your time, Arami.' The voice continued, 'You must live. Remember what you see and what you feel today. For, you will get your chance, to avenge it all. But not today. Now run Arami, run.' The voice grew weaker, as the mist began to dissipate. 'Run.' Within a moment, the mist had completely gone.

Now, battling with his conscience, and his instinct, Arami hesitated.

Now, is not your time.

His inner voice repeated the words, as Arami fought the urge, to ignore the mist, and carry on, running down the hill.

Angered, confused and feeling hopeless, Arami whistled for his hound, and the two turned to run back up the hill. Away, from the screams and the commotion. The young boy still felt such anger within him, and the tears of despair, once again filled his eyes. He did not know why; he ran away. The very idea of it, shamed him. All the feelings that he felt at this point were new to him. His innocence seemingly evaporated inside. Maybe, he could find some Fantaellen knights, that he could bring back, and rescue his mother and the villagers. Yes. That is what he would do, he told himself.

They had been running for a long while when they finally reached the top of the steep hill. Arami looked around cautiously. The area looked familiar to him. He could see some trees, that he knew. They overlooked a deep, narrow gorge, about a mile from his village. Within the gorge, was a tributary of the main river of Fantaellen. This particular part of Tre Rive Liefe (The River of Life), was the main source of water, for many of the villages, located along its banks, and beyond.

Arami, suddenly heard the distant and faint echoes of terrified screams and children crying, mixed with deep male voices, also being carried on the wind. Startled and greatly alarmed, by the sudden cacophony of noise, vibrating around the steep sides of the gorge, the young boy decided to find a hidden vantage point, so that he could take a look.

Quickly, and staying as low, as he could, Arami made his way, to a clearing in the trees, just a short distance, from the edge of the gorge. There, he lay down, with Zevarn beside him.

A picture, of true terror and horror, now gradually revealed itself, as Arami, took it all in. Like a bad dream, the story had been set in motion, and it played out now, in front of his young eyes.

People from his village, were being pushed and shoved by hand and sword, into the centre of the gorge, near to the water's edge. Frantically, Arami looked for his mother. He could not see her. Tightly, he held his hound, as he watched and observed the events developing in front of him. As some people protested, and others tried to run, they were dealt with swiftly, and without mercy. Arami, saw a boy who he had grown up with, hacked to death, as he tried to run.

Arami, again searched for a glimpse of his mother. Where was she? He asked himself.

Maybe, she had escaped her captor?

He could not see her. There, were just too many people, crammed together, into such a narrow space, on the floor of the gorge.

Then, a deep voice, suddenly boomed out from somewhere, below. Arami, quickly realised, that it was an order. Swiftly, high up on the top of the ridge, on the opposite side, appeared hundreds of archers, from the trees. Their arrows alight. Arami, watched in desperation, as the Blackheart archers pulled back their bow strings, and pointed their weapons, down into the gorge.

What, followed next, seemed to take place in slow motion as Arami caught a brief glimpse of his mother, by the water's edge, and then the order to unleash the volley of the remorseless, deadly arrow storm was given.

'Loose!'

The hissing and whistling whoosh, of hundreds of Wulfdaeden fire arrows, headed down, at deadly speed, into the gorge. This suddenly caused Arami to climb to his feet, and scream.

'No! No!'

Everything still seemed to be going in slow motion, as he ran, to the edge of the gorge. Arami, reached out his hands, in hopelessness and despair, in a futile attempt, to stop what unfolded before his eyes.

His subsequent, wretched shriek of distress and anguish was drowned out, by the screams of the helpless people below, as the fire arrows, found their targets. Arami fell to his knees, closed his eyes and wept uncontrollably.

The ground and the shallow waters of the gorge was strewn, with lifeless bodies everywhere. Those, that still moved or even twitched, were hunted down, and soon put to the sword.

Arami, peered over the ledge, once again. His stomach turned, as he saw the carnage below. In despair, he looked around, in the forlorn hope, that his mother was still alive. He could not see her.

He watched, as the Wulfdaeden knights, clambered over the dead bodies, to kill any survivors. A young child, who had an arrow in his chest, tried to get to his feet, but was soon stabbed in the stomach, by a Wulfdaeden blade. His body, then kicked and was rolled into the water by his attacker.

Man, woman or child, were finished off, where they lay. There, was no discrimination. No mercy.

Arami saw her. His mother. She was dead. Her body was prone, on a rock, near the water's edge. Her, arms were spread wide, her head tilted upwards, her eyes open wide, staring into the sky. A fire arrow, protruding from her chest.

Arami, cried out in a pain, that he had never known before. Tears of anger, grief, despair and frustration, filled his eyes. He wanted to kill them all. Every Wulfdaeden, in that gorge.

It was at that point, at this place, at this time, that a young boy, named Arami Corder, swore to rid the land of all Wulfdaeden's. His determination, would be driven by grief, anger and revenge. Not just for his family, but for all the people, whose blood turned the waters of Tre Rive Leife, red on that day. This would be the young boy's catalyst.

Before, leaving the gorge that day, he swore this, on his life.

Chapter Nine

On the brow of Ingress Hill, stood a single figure.

'Oh! My God.' He cried out loud, as his eyes scanned the panorama, of the land below.

How did this happen?

Jonti Quixall, could only stand and stare in disbelief. He could not believe it. His second country was ablaze. Everywhere he looked, he could see large areas of flames and smoke, filling the night sky, as far as the eye could see.

'Guinlance is still ours.' Geremi had now joined his friend. He showed no emotion, as he continued, 'Half a battalion, from Guinlance, are waiting for us, about a mile away. One of their scouts has just arrived.'

Jonti nodded but remained silent.

'It's bad Jonti. From what I've been told, the enemy has overwhelmed us, with its sheer numbers and the ferocity of their attack. And, it is not known, how long it will be before Guinlance is attacked. The Blackhearts, are now moving to surround the capital.'

Jonti still said nothing. He didn't know what to say. He was horrified at the enormity of the situation. He felt sick to his stomach, and his mind raced away, with panicked, irrational thoughts.

A silence existed between both men, while they surveyed the land, beyond the hill. Left alone, in their own thoughts, the two friends wondered about their next move.

Jonti did not look at Geremi, as he spoke suddenly, 'We cannot take the twins to Guinlance. It is too dangerous.'

'Yes. Agreed,' replied Geremi quietly, with an air of inevitable acceptance, in his voice.

'Are, they still sleeping?' enquired Jonti.

'Yes. The portal trip, has not awoken them.'

'Good. It's probably best. And the prisoner?'

'We had to sedate her again.'

'Fine. She'll be out for a few hours more.'

'Where, can we take them Jonti?' Geremi's tone had changed. And, the concern showed in his voice, as he continued, 'The countryside, is overrun with enemy knights.'

Jonti, did not answer his friend and second in command. Instead, he quickly turned, and began to make his way down the hill.

Geremi, followed silently and obediently. He knew that Jonti, would know what to do. He trusted his friend, and captain, implicitly. They had been ordered to take the twins to Guinlance, immediately upon arrival. Clearly, from what they had seen, and the small amount of intelligence, that they had received, going to Guinlance was too dangerous.

Jonti began to speak quietly, as he motioned for Geremi to come closer. 'I have sent the scout and his battalion back to Guinlance, with a message for Robert Scotten. We will take the twins somewhere safe. Somewhere, where no one, will hopefully find them.'

At that moment, Jonti felt that it was prudent to whisper his idea, into Geremi's ear.

His friend smiled and nodded in agreement.

'Tell none of our men, my friend. We keep this, strictly between us.'

'Of course.'

'Good.' Jonti patted his friend on the back. 'God willing, we will keep the twins safe. For, they appear to be our only hope, in these dark times.'

Geremi nodded in agreement, once more.

It wasn't long, before the riders in the silver armour, and the purple robes, of the deceased king's royal battalion of knights, made their way across the countryside of their invaded land.

Jonti knew, that each man would be ready to defend the twins, to the death. To the last man. The two small children were the future of their country. They had to be kept alive at all costs.

Dark and desperate times were engulfing Fantaellen. Nevertheless, at that moment, as the young knight, and his men raced towards a safe haven, Jonti promptly felt a sense of hope. He would hold onto that he told himself.

Jonti understood that one day the twins could be their saviour. Their light. In these dark and desperate times.

A man needed hope.

★★★

In the night sky, the two full moons, were swiftly covered by storm clouds, that had suddenly gathered, to envelope them. The heavens, then suddenly erupted, into a symphony of deafening thunder, and blinding sheets of lighting.

The rain came down, hard and fast. The night sky continued to rumble, and explode, in a fierce show of anger and power.

Jonti urged his steed forward, as the Fantaellen weather, threw everything at him and his men.

★★★

A small, lone figure, a creature of the shadows, closely tracked the riders, as they raced away, into the night. His eyes strained to see, through the ferocity of the rain, but the riders remained, in his steely eyed view. He shuddered briefly and cursed the weather, before he made his way down the steep, and rather slippery bank of Ingress hill.

Rubbing the rain from his face, Normauss the troll, sneezed and impetuously dragged his nose across his sleeve, leaving a blob of green mucus, attached to the material. For a brief moment more, he watched the riders.

Where are you going? It's not Guinlance.

His, subsequent action, based on his thoughts and instinct, was still to pursue and observe. Normauss, is physically fit and a quick runner. He can run for hours at a very impressive pace. Those, Fantaellen mountain troll genes of his, had kept him, within eye view, of his intended target, thus far.

I see you, Jonti Quixall.

With as much haste, as his little legs could carry him, the troll continued to track the riders, who seemed to be heading north.

North. Of course.

'I know, where you're going!' he suddenly shouted, breathlessly. 'And I know it is a short cut.'

The troll, then suddenly exploded with excitement. So much so, that he caught his breath, in his throat, before coughing and spluttering, to regain, his composure. This was instantly followed by an enormous, loud sneeze. The mucus was then instinctively despatched, onto his sleeve, once more. Normauss had a smile on his face, that went from ear, to ear. He was, so pleased, with himself. After all, he is the best tracker, in Portaellen.

And, as the rain continued to fall, and the thunder rumbled through the clouds, the white forks of lighting, lit the troll's way. North.

★★★

The guards on the city walls of Guinlance, could only stand and watch all day, as the presence of the enemy camp in the distance, had slowly increased in size, just beyond the tree line of Guinlance Wood.

The camp, that had been firstly made up of a small number of battalions, had grown in size, throughout the day, into a large force. The amassing enemy had slowly fuelled a fear across the walls, that had escalated, over the passing hours.

The thundering noise, of some sort of machinery, that rumbled across the landscape, around dusk, did little to quell the trepidation, either.

As night had fallen, the men on the city walls, had begun to lose count of the Wulfdaeden campfires. The orange, red and blue flames, and the hastily erected tents, were now visible, as far as the eye, could see.

A sudden thunderstorm, and rain like icy needles, had subsequently made their guard duty, for the last hour or so, miserable and almost unbearable. The enemy took a strange delight, in taunting them, as the freezing rain fell, and the sky erupted with a powerful roar, followed by a lighting show of violent intent. The dancing shadows, of the crazed Wulfdaeden's, lit by the two full moons, danced, mocked and ridiculed the Fantaellen knights, on the battlements, who could only watch, in disbelief.

When, the storm had ceased, the men on the city walls, were now kept alert, by periodic mass volleys of Wulfdaeden arrows, fired from the tree cover of Guinlance Wood. In the first deadly wave, several Fantaellen's were killed, as the silent, deadly storm, hit the ramparts, and tore through them, with no mercy.

The officers on watch duty, had come amongst their men to calm them.

'Keep your head down boys and use your shields.' Came the order.

'They mean, to scare us,' shouted another. 'It'll take more than that. Right boys?'

His words were instantly answered with a defiant roar, from the battlements.

One officer, who stood alone, swore under his breath, as he gazed out, over the ramparts.

'Sweet Jesus.' He slowly muttered to himself, as he took it all in. This was the first time today, that he had been up on the wall.

Surely, this was not the whole, entire, Wulfdaeden army, camped outside the city walls?

He, was only a young man, believed to have been promoted to an officer, through connections of his father's. Never, had he been in battle. Never, had he seen a sight like this.

Nervously, the young officer played with the hilt of his sword. He suddenly felt, unready, inadequate, and sick to the stomach.

'Magnificent. Isn't it?' He had been joined, by another officer. An older man.

'Yeah,' came the young officer's, muted reply. 'I suppose.'

'Don't worry,' the older officer, could hear the younger man's trepidation, in his voice. 'We will hold them. They won't break, the city walls of Guinlance.'

From behind them, in the courtyard below, came a sudden order.

'Archers! Make ready!'

Both, officers now turned to see, scores of bowmen, nocking their bow string to the notch, in their arrow, before pointing their weapon into the air, and pulling back, the string of their Long Bows, level with their chin. With, their finely tuned string, at maximum tension, the Fantaellen Long Bow men, now waited for the order. An eerie silence, now briefly existed, until the order, finally came.

'Loose!'

In no time at all, the deadly volley, released from Guinlance, had ripped through the first few ranks of enemy archers, who had dared to break from the cover of the woods. The finest bow men of Guinlance, having fired their arrows, from the best bow, in all Portaellen, had sent their response.

The second wave had just darkened the stormy skies, above the Fantaellen capital. The message was clear, unified and deadly.

The walls of Guinlance, will repel you. Our arrows will cut you down. You will never take the heart of Fantaellen. Ever.

★★★

General Grafton slowly pulled open his tent flap. Bending slightly, to bring his tall, wide frame, through the entrance, he was soon standing in front of his two heavily armed bodyguards, that were on sentry duty, outside. Both knights, instantly snapped to attention. Their general saluted them, before giving a growled order, for his black steed, to be bought to him.

The general, had decided, to show his presence, to his army. He wanted them to know, that he was with them. To give them the heart, and the fortitude, for the attack on Guinlance. Every Wulfdaeden, should know their general's face, he had told himself. The face of courage and war. He would do this, in his full Wulfdaeden armour. With no helmet, and most importantly, on his own.

At a steady pace, the general made his way past the vast rows, of his army's tents. Upon, his scarred face, he wore a look of defiance and determination. He was sat silently, upon his magnificent black steed, his constant expression fixed in place, as he nodded to his knight's, and all manner of strange looking creature allies, as they stopped talking and stared, or desisted from doing whatever task, that they carried out. He did not need to say anything, as he continued his way, along the vast lines of tents. His mere presence was enough to say, what needed to be said.

The camp quickly fell into a ghostly silence, as their general made his way deeper still, into the heart of his army's, hastily erected encampment.

The people of Wulfdaeden, and its army, who had never seen their general before, had their heads filled, with the tales of him, being a giant. He is described, as being between seven feet and eight feet tall. It is claimed that he is as wide as a valley, and as strong as one hundred men. If, General Grafton were to lead the army, on the battlefield, it is said, that victory was assured.

As, he reached the outskirts of the camp, the general swiftly turned his steed around, to face the infinite rows of tents. At that moment, General Grafton, looked beyond his army, and stared for some length of time, towards the prize; Guinlance.

In awe, he studied the magnificent structure before him. For, it was indeed a sight to behold. This was the first time, he had seen it, other than, drawn by an artist, or as a place, on a map. Briefly, it held a sense of wonderment to him, as he saw the power of Guinlance.

Those city walls are long, the general noted. They run the length of the mile wide, Guinlance Hill. In the distance, stood proud and defiant, was Guinlance Castle. General Grafton was confident that the Fantaellen's, would not have the knights, to defend every inch of the city wall, the first outer wall, and the castle. The Fantaellen army, had been weakened substantially, defending its coastline, and fighting a defensive battle, in the fields and towns. Yes, his army would have to run the gauntlet of the city streets, and then attack the first outer wall, before reaching the base of Guinlance Hill. Yes, many of his men and creatures, would be killed, in the name of the cause. He also knew, that despite the defenders depleted numbers, the real resistance, would come from the castle walls. The huge walls of Guinlance Castle were their last line of defence. What, was that annoying saying, that the Fantaellen's had? He asked himself.

Oh! Yes. To the last man.

The general, had acquired a weapon, since the invasion, to hopefully weaken the walls and gain an advantage. And, as proved so far, the sheer numbers within his army, combined with an iron will to win at all costs, would drive his knights and creatures forward.

To eventual victory.

General Grafton's army, of knight's and creatures, now awaited his orders. Silently, they stood, in their thousands. The whole encampment, waiting. Their courage being fed, by the presence of their general.

Then, as if it were ordered to, one of the full moons, in the dark, night sky, slowly crept around the back of the general, to fill the panorama, behind him, with its huge, milky white presence. His black steed then reacted, by rearing up onto its hind legs. General Grafton, now silhouetted against the bright moon, drew his Wulfdaeden sword, lifted it into the air and screamed his defiance, towards Guinlance.

Instantaneously, thousands of Blackheart knights, and the allied creature battalions, raised their swords, and weapons, to the night sky, and roared their defiance towards Guinlance. The cries, and the chorus of hate, rang out towards the Fantaellen capital, loud and true.

General Grafton's, stone cold heart, filled with a joyous evil, as the blood pumped through his rotten veins. He was about, to lead his master's great army to victory. The greatest victory, in Wulfdaeden history. For, no general of a Blackheart army, had ever taken, or sacked Guinlance.

I, General Cedric Grafton, would be the first, he told himself, as he rode his magnificent black steed, back through the rows of his army's tents, whilst acknowledging the cheers and the adulation of his knight's and creatures, with a nod.

The time to smash the dwindling Fantaellen resistance, and to force, a final capitulation, upon its people, was here. Their assault, on the last great bastion, of Fantaellen defiance, was now imminent. His orders were ready to be given, and a city and its castle, was at their mercy.

The Gods will reward our bravery, with victory. The general, was sure of this.

★★★

With, the last few hours of darkness left, General Grafton ordered the trebuchets forward. These were the same weapons, that had sent, a number of his ships to the bottom of the Stoirim Sea, in the early hours of their assault, upon the Fantaellen coastline. Rather than demolish them, the general had noted their value, and had given the order, not to destroy them, if possible. His engineers had then been ordered inland, and tasked with using them, to their full, lethal potential.

General Grafton dismounted his steed, and he stood watching, as two dozen, Fantaellen trebuchets, slowly thundered forward. Pulled by hundreds of men and ropes.

Then, just beyond Guinlance Wood, they were strategically positioned. Whereupon, the engineers, immediately walked away and left the giant, menacing, wooden structures, in full view, of the city walls, of the Fantaellen capital.

With, a wry smile on his face, General Grafton, stared at the trebuchets. He had rarely seen them in action, up until, the attacks on his ships. He was ultimately impressed, after seeing their capabilities, their effectiveness and their potential, at first hand.

Now, looking beyond the trebuchets, the general could imagine, the panic on the city walls, that these structures, now caused. The evil pulsed through his veins, as he became excited, at the thought of smashing down, the walls of Guinlance, with the enemies, very own weapon.

Having, shown his first-hand, it was now time, to put part two of the assault upon the Fantaellen capital, into place. Firstly, he had his orders to give.

While marching back to his tent, General Grafton called for one of his most trusted officers, to join him.

Once inside, the officer listened closely, as he was given his orders.

'So, we have the trebuchets, in position,' the general began. 'We, can bring the creature battalions forward.'

'Yes Sire.'

'Are they ready?' The general enquired.

'They are,' came the tentative reply.

Sensing, something wasn't right, General Grafton looked directly at his officer. His icy stare obviously unsettled his subordinate, who shifted his weight nervously, from one foot to the other, whilst unable, to look his general, in the eye.

'Well?' growled the general, impatiently.

'It was quickly sorted out, Sire. One of the centrolls, had a bit too much wine, to drink.'

'Why the hell! Were they given wine?'

The officer did not answer.

'Well!'

'It was just the one centroll, Sire. He had sneaked into the stores and stolen it.'

'And?'

'Well Sire, the drunker he got, the more he wanted to cause havoc. It wasn't long, before he started on a group of rock men.'

'Ramazen, Zada and Yetus.' The general cursed. Sensing more, he stared at the officer, in disbelief. 'And?'

'Well, there was a mass brawl, because the gigahominums, joined in too. It took a regiment, to bring back order. We, have arrested and caged, the offending centroll.'

The general, could only shake his head in disbelief. He was so angry.

General Grafton slammed his fists on the table in front of him, and let out a cry of anger, before screaming at his officer, to order four battalions of knights to the front.

'In front of them, put the creature battalions. At their head, put that idiot centroll. He is about to get the best hangover cure. He will lead the charge, with no weapons.'

'Sire!'

'And tell the idiot, of the glory of the Forlorn Hope that is his chance for redemption. Now go. At Sunrise, and on my signal, the attack is to begin.'

★★★

The four battalions of Blackheart knights, in full Wulfdaeden black armour, marched with impetus, through the camp. At their head were three smaller battalions of creatures. It was their presence, that bought the camp to a virtual standstill, as the column thundered through, the endless rows of tents.

Many Portaellen, had never seen, the creatures from the segregated, wild, islands around Wulfdaeden. Even when, they were commissioned into service, the creatures, were kept away, from the main body, of the Wulfdaeden army. There had always been, tales told of their existence. The stories increasing from town to town, until the description of them, had been exaggerated, tenfold.

With the early signs of a sunrise, on the horizon, the Wulfdaeden army, could now see, that the tales told, held some credence.

These, creatures from the Islands, that marched for the Blackheart cause, sent a shiver down the spine, of all that now saw them.

This was just the reaction, that General Grafton, had wanted. Not, just for the enemy, but for his own men. What better way, to give his knight's a boost of confidence, than to see their new allies, paraded for all to see.

Even the general himself, was captivated, by their disciplined display of marching.

I am a genius. They are magnificent.

The evil, rapidly pumped through his heart, as he marvelled at the size of the gigahominums, that marched at the rear of the column.

The creatures, known as the Gigahoms, live on a small unnamed island, just off the western coast of Wulfdaeden. They are massive in stature, averaging at least eight feet in height. They are immensely strong and powerful. With the tops of their shoulders, the equivalent in length, of three large men. They, in turn support a neck, as wide as a tree trunk, and a head, the size and shape, of a small boulder. Inside, that huge head, is a small brain, which gives them, very limited intelligence. They possess, fantastic hearing and sight, but they have no tongue. Despite, their size and strength, the creatures, from the unnamed island, are subservient. This pleased the general.

In front, of the gigahominums, marched the rock men. They are men, made of Granite. Legend has it, that they are descended from a god, banished to a small, rocky island, that stood alone, fighting the brutal elements, of the Stoirim Sea. To adapt to the conditions, that he found himself in, the god embraced the granite rock, so much so, that he became granite. Then, one day, he was joined by a goddess, who had also been banished. She too, quickly adapted to the brutal conditions, of the island.

The rock men and women are known as the rock people of Granite Island. They varied in colour. The majority are black, or grey in colour, or a combination of both. Pure white rock people are very rare, but not extinct, and are said to have, magical powers, because of their rarity.

The rock men are tough and strong, in nature. They possess, a high pain threshold. And they are very hard to kill. Their only fear was extreme heat.

At the front of the column, led by one of their own, in his large iron chains, were the centrolls. They are a proud race of creatures, from an island, at the very northern tip of Wulfdaeden. Predominantly, bad tempered creatures, they are tough and thrive on conflict. Their history is sketchy at best, and open to many exaggerated legends and dark tales, of their inception. They have the head, arms and torso of a troll, and the body and legs of a horse.

These, commissioned creatures, made up General Grafton's, creature battalion's and he was very proud, to call them his own.

The suns rose, with more momentum and energy, in the skies above Guinlance, as four Blackhearts battalions, and three smaller creature battalions neared their intended position.

The trebuchets were ready, with an enormous rock, in each sling, put in place, by the teams of engineers.

Archers, from the city walls of Guinlance, had made a nuisance of themselves, by pinning down the engineers, as they went about arming their trebuchets. Several, Wulfdaeden bodies, now lay around, the enormous structures.

In response, the Blackheart archers, hidden in the trees of Guinlance Wood, broke cover, to rapidly send their response.

The arrow storms, from either side, eventually dissipated, as the officers ordered their archers, to save their arrows.

As, the suns filled the sky of a new morning, a sinister silence, and standoff existed.

It would not last for long.

★★★

The Wulfdaeden engineer's, who held the lever arms, awaited the final order, to unleash the missiles from their trebuchet's. A blanket of dark, angry looking clouds had just enveloped the early morning suns, as they had met each other, in the morning sky.

Watching, the messenger ride away, the officer in charge, cleared his throat.

Then, in English, laced with a strong French accent, the Wulfdaeden officer, roared out his orders, to his Anglo French and English, engineers.

'Make ready!'

The officer now drew his Blackheart sword and held it above his head.

A volley of arrows, from the city walls of Guinlance, suddenly filled the darkening sky. A few screams did ring out, along the trebuchet line, as some of the engineers were hit, by rogue arrows.

The officer was dead. He had been hit, right between the eyes. His body lay prone, on the ground, his pupils fixed and staring, the arrow jutted from his head, blood splattered across his ashen face.

Confusion now reigned along the trebuchet line, as the engineers looked for leadership. The Fantaellen arrows, had spooked them. They knew what to do. They just needed telling, when to do it.

A loud panicked cry, suddenly went out, from somewhere, down the line, to alert them of more incoming arrows. A few engineers quickly abandoned their posts.

They were soon forced back into position, by a large figure of a man, in full Wulfdaeden war armour. He bellowed at them, to get back into position, or die at the hand of his sword.

General Grafton, walked towards the Fantaellen arrows, as they filled the sky. A few feet, from the trebuchet line, he suddenly stopped, turned and held, his sword above his head.

As the arrows, landed around him, he screamed out his order, to the engineers.

'Release!'

Two dozen holding pins, were instantly freed from their lever arms, and the counterweights swung round, to launch the rocks from their sling's.

General Grafton's evil laugh rang out, as every one of the projectiles, then smashed into the city walls, of Guinlance.

He watched in excited anticipation, as the engineers, made their trebuchet's ready, for his next order.

From the trees of Guinlance Wood, a company of archers, were ordered to break cover and take shelter behind a row of Blackheart shields, that were placed in a crude line, for protection. At their rear, several small fire pits had been dug, and were alight.

With, the trebuchet's ready, and the archer's fire arrows lit, the general's order, was now eagerly awaited.

Upon, that order, the next release from hell was unleashed on Guinlance.

General Grafton, watched in awe, while a heavy bombardment of projectiles, were released, quickly backed up with a volley of fire arrows.

Barrage after barrage of rocks, now relentlessly battered Guinlance, and its walls. And, with volley after volley of Wulfdaeden fire arrows, released into the city, to set it alight, the evil now pumped uncontrollably through the general's veins.

He was exultant. His joy frenzied, as he ordered the attack, to become even more intense.

'Do, not relent men!' He screamed. 'Give them no favour. Smash down their walls!'

The Wulfdaeden engineers and the archers, showed their enemy no quarter. Driven, by the constant orders from their general, the merciless attack, was repeatedly sent towards, its intended target.

Hell was truly unleashed.

★★★

The Fantaellen archers, on the ramparts of the city walls of Guinlance, were pinned down, along its length and breadth, by repeated volleys of enemy arrows, and the enormous projectiles, as they smashed into the walls, and the city beyond.

It had quickly become, a maelstrom of hurtling rocks, and deadly accurate arrows, that had forced them, to retreat and hide, behind hastily made shield defences. Powerless, to send their arrows, over the wall, the Fantaellen archers, quickly became ineffective. Leaving their attackers, with the ability, to send their rocks and arrows, with no loss of life.

The attack, remained relentless, for a considerable amount of time. Multitudes of missiles smashed into the wall. Whilst many, crashed down amongst the archers, uncharacteristically cowering, beneath their shields, from the constant volleys of Wulfdaeden arrows. Countless men were crushed to death.

Confusion and fear reigned, as the Blackheart arrow storm had suddenly increased its intensity. Screams filled the air, when a great volley of fire arrows, smashed into the desperate lines of Fantaellen archers, on the ramparts. Hundreds, of bodies now lay across the wall, as the officers tried to gain control, by hurriedly getting their orders out to their men.

An instant, second volley of fire arrows followed, which flew over the ramparts, and reigned down, into the city streets. The screams, of the fleeing, despairing civilians, were rapidly heard. As men, women and children, were mercilessly slaughtered, amongst the narrow passageways, between the burning and crushed buildings.

A battalion of knights, located at the north end of the city, urged civilians, to make their way towards Guinlance Hill, and ultimately, the safety of Guinlance Castle.

Once, the majority of civilians had been cleared from the streets, the knights took charge. Mayhem, certain death, and destruction existed around them, as projectiles pulverized anything and anyone, in their path. And, fire arrows streamed into the city, from the darkened sky.

Other, Fantaellen battalions, who had earlier, entered the city streets, had made shield walls, where their officers, had ordered them to. The engineers were then called forward, from the safety of the castle. Their job was to get the trebuchets armed and ready, as soon as possible. The huge structures had been abandoned in the streets, when the Wulfdaeden attack, had begun. Several were ultimately damaged. With, at least two, rendered useless, having crashed to the ground, when the Wulfdaeden missiles, hurtled into them.

With the unrelenting fury, of the Wulfdaeden attack, going on around them, a number of small companies of Fantaellen knights, slowly made their way, through the streets, in a shield wall formation. With, the outer knight's shields, facing outwards, and held, around head height. The men in the middle, also held their shield's above their heads. The men at the front, the eyes of the shield wall. Executing their manoeuvre, was slow and cumbersome, but it would hopefully keep more men alive, as they made their way forward, through the Wulfdaeden barrage. Onwards, they pushed, through the burning and demolished streets of their city, and past the smashed and smouldering bodies, of the dead.

A shrill, horrified cry suddenly went out from the city walls.

The young Fantaellen officer, straining to hear, what he feared he had heard, threw his shield to one side, and climbed to his feet. A cold fear now quickly gripped him, as he finally acknowledged the cry.

Looking out over the walls of the city, he saw them.

Ramazen! No!

His heart instantly sank, and he felt sick to his stomach.

'Rock men!' He screamed, at the top of his voice. 'Make ready!'

The air was now filled, with a high pitched, piercing scream, as the next barrage, from the trebuchets, hurtled towards the city walls of Guinlance.

The rock men of the Granite Isle had been released.

Chapter Ten

The First Battle of Guinlance Hill

The next wave of rock men were already hurtling towards the Fantaellen capital, when General Grafton ordered his archers to increase the ferocity, of their fire arrows. Very little reply was forthcoming from the enemy, which enabled his archers to send repeated volleys of deadly arrows, towards Guinlance.

With the enemy archers, firmly pinned down, the general now gave the order, for the centrolls and the gigahominums, to be pushed forward. They were directed to stand in line, in front of the trebuchets. Finally, the four battalions of Blackheart knights, marched forward, to stand behind the creature battalions. Now, came the drums.

The sound of the Wulfdaeden war drums, being hit with such fervour and vigour, began to drive the centrolls and the gigahominums, into a fever pitched frenzy. The battalions of Blackhearts behind them, watched in astonishment, as the madness grew slowly, until not one creature remained calm. Rogue, centrolls took it in turns to charge forward mockingly, towards the enemy city walls, some choosing to turn about face, and show their rear ends, with the occasional noise of flatulence, greeted with raucous laughter from their battalion line.

The gigahominums, unable to cry out, stayed in line, stomping their huge feet on the ground, creating a thundering noise, that competed with the beat of the Wulfdaeden war drums. In the air, they held up their long, muscular arms, whilst thrusting their enormous, straight bladed swords, vertically into the air, in perfect unison.

The tremendous noise, of drums and heavy foot stomping, created an uproarious din, so loud and intimidating, which increased in deliverance, as it carried on. And, from the rear of the Wulfdaeden columns, the archers continued, their unceasing volleys, of arrows.

General Grafton waited patiently, to give his orders to attack. The noise of the war drums and the frenzied chorus from his creature battalions, was tremendous, he thought. Evil, pumped through his veins, as he watched with pride.

A crescendo of cheers, suddenly went up from the line of centrolls. The gigahominums quickly joined in by jumping up and down feverishly. A cry then went out, from the Wulfdaeden line, and General Grafton's black heart, leapt with joy.

Several rock men, could be seen, smashing their way through, desperate lines of Fantaellen knights, on the city walls.

He could now give the order, he told himself.

★★★

The young Fantaellen officer, awoke, and cried out for his mother. Never, had he known such pain and sudden fear. He had suddenly woken from a strange, dream like state, where his archers flew through the air, as enemy fire arrows, hit home, with deadly accuracy. Mayhem and massacre, continued around him, as he drifted, in and out of consciousness.

When he awoke again, as a bolt of pain shot through him, the young officer realised, that his shattered body, had been thrown into a wall. He quickly remembered that the ground had shook, lifting him off his feet, just moments earlier. Not before, a massive black mass, had come across his line of sight. Then darkness.

Broken and still confused, he struggled to his feet, using the wall, as a prop. He then fumbled, around for his sword. His vision was blurred, and blood ran down his face, from a head wound.

Despite, the terrible noise of battle, going on around him, he could hear a faint voice, calling out to him. Looking down at his feet, the young officer saw a crumpled, bloodied body of a fellow officer. His face was smashed in, and unrecognisable, and his body contorted into a twisted, smashed state. And yet, his mouth still moved.

The young officer recognised the fellow, by the band of jewellery around his shattered right arm.

'Henry!' He shouted, before he knelt, next to his friend. He couldn't make out, what Henry tried to say, until, what were his final few breath's. Whilst, holding his shattered, bloodied hand, his friend spoke softly, almost faint, as he struggled to speak.

'Matthew, tell my father.' His weak voice, began to die away, before he started to choke, on a large amount of blood, that suddenly spewed out of the shattered, mangled hole, that was his mouth.

'I know Henry.' Matthew looked at his friend, and nodded, as the life drained out of him, and the last breath, left his shattered body.

The sound of the enemy horns blaring out, bought Matthew suddenly back to reality. Getting, to his feet gingerly, he now looked around, at the chaos, turmoil and destruction, that continued around him.

Briefly, looking over a wall, and into the city, he could see the rock men of Granite Island, and their huge stone clubs, flailing through the air, as they were being held back, by several battalions of knights. As the huge, solid creatures, slowly smashed their way forward, through the burning streets, the Fantaellen blades and arrows, were having very little impact, on the bodies of the rock men, as they pushed forward. Matthew could see that they were being roared on, by a rock man, a colour unlike, its fellow creatures. He was a stunning, array of colours, including brilliant white, gold, grey and jet black.

He looks truly fierce, and yet beautiful, Matthew thought to himself, as he screamed at his fellow creatures, in a tongue, unknown to the young officer.

Matthew now wished the battalions in the city streets, the best of luck, against such a tough enemy. He had more pressing issues to deal with. Adrenalin, now pulsed through his shattered body, and his pain was quickly forgotten.

The enemy arrow storm had now stopped.

'Archers! To me!' He bellowed.

He was joined by a number of his archers. Swiftly, he then got his orders out to them. Upon hearing the screams of the enemy, as their charge began, he briskly finished up, by telling his men, that he trusted them, to do their duty, and that they had to hold, the city walls, at all costs. He grabbed a bow and arrow. The earlier fear had left him. Adrenalin pumped through his body. This was his first battle. He prayed; it would not be his last.

★★★

The sight of the rock men, on the walls of Guinlance, had roused General Grafton's battalions, and given them a newfound steel, for what, was to come.

With, the sound of the Blackheart horns, resonating around the enemy populated land, that surrounded Guinlance, the battalions of centrolls and gigahominums, charged forward. At their rear, came the more controlled march of four battalions of Blackhearts, to the beat of their war drums.

The centroll, on the Forlorn Hope, had no weapons. His muscled, four legs carried him forward. His heart pounded in his chest, as he screamed a high pitch, war cry. Forward he ran, as fast as he could.

The creature had made a decent amount of ground, when a lone, Fantaellen arrow, smashed into his chest, and pierced his heart. The centroll, was dead before he hit the floor. His Forlorn Hope was now over.

The archers, on the city walls of Guinlance, having been pinned down for so long, and having many of their numbers killed, now made their arrows count.

The Fantaellen response, had begun. Deadly and unrelenting they came. The arrows of the Fantaellen archers, rained down on the ranks of Blackheart knights and creatures, killing or maiming many.

The orders, being barked out, from the city walls, by a raw, young Fantaellen officer.

★★★

Wait. Wait. Matthew told himself, as he fought the urge, to order his archers, to fire too soon. This volley would be deadlier, at a closer range, he reasoned. Silently, the young officer, held his arm in the air.

Wait.

The screams of the enemy were getting nearer.

Now!

'Loose!' Matthew, promptly screamed, at the top of his lung's.

Just as the order, had left his mouth, and the Fantaellen arrows had left their bows, Matthew suddenly became distracted, by a huge catastrophic noise, from the city below.

The ground below his feet still shook, as he had turned to run towards, the nearest steps. Running past his archers, he quickly ordered one of his men, to take charge, briefly telling him to keep, the archers firing, at controlled, regular intervals.

The courtyard below, was now thick with confusion, chaos, screaming and blood. Matthew, stood for a moment, taking it all in, as he watched, the events unfold, below.

The city gates lay shattered on the ground. Several rock men were wildly smashing their heavy clubs, into Fantaellen shield walls, that were desperately trying to push them back. Rock men were suddenly everywhere.

'Christ,' Matthew said to himself. 'This is bad.'

There, were only so many blows, from the heavy weapons, of the rock men, that Fantaellen shields, could take. A whole shield wall was suddenly obliterated, in seconds, by a large group of rock men. Several smashed their clubs, hard and lethal, onto the top of the battered shield wall, whilst the others, swiped their clubs, at speed from the side. Mayhem, then ensued, as the survivors and the injured, from the initial blow, stumbled from formation, to be obliterated, with the full force of a rock man's club. Their bodies exploding on impact, their blood and liquidated flesh, flying through the air, to stain the ground, that they had stood on.

Two Fantaellen shield walls, was all that was suddenly left, in the courtyard. Their officers were now desperately barking out their orders, to keep their men, in formation.

'Push!' Came the command. To be greeted, with grunts from his men, as the shield wall, once more took the strain, then pushed, in a desperate attempt, to move forward, towards the shattered, city gates.

'It looks hopeless,' Matthew remarked to himself. 'The gates were gone, and the city, was now wide open to attack.'

Not, that there was much of the city left, he thought to himself, as many of the buildings had been razed, by fire arrows or rocks.

He, and his archers, were probably the last line of defence. And, it seemed, that there were no reinforcements forthcoming, from Guinlance Castle.

Matthew told himself, that if this were his day to die, he would do it, with a bow in his hand, and his men beside him. His orders had been to hold the city walls at all costs, or to the last man. And that was what he was going to do, he told himself, as he grabbed a bow and a bag of arrows.

Then, with defiance in his heart, that now drove him forward, the young Fantaellen officer, looked down, on the charge of his enemy, once more, as they neared, the open void, in his wall.

Drawing, his bow back, he held the tension, perfectly. Affording himself, a glance at the archer, next to him, he winked and smiled, at him.

'For Fantaellen!' He now bellowed.

'We release our arrows!' Came the loud, chorus from his men.

'Loose!' Came the order.

★★★

Fantaellen arrows, now blacked out, both Portaellen suns, as their deadly intent, flew towards the invaders, from across the Stoirim Sea.

Despite many dead, laying around them, the gigahominums, and centrolls, charged forward. The giant gigahominums, picking up the ladders, of their dead comrades, as they ran. The shield walls of the Blackheart battalions behind them, remained controlled and disciplined, as they marched forward.

The war cries of the centrolls, became increased and more excited, when the gates of the city, came crashing down. Dodging and weaving Fantaellen arrows, they charged, their blood up, and their willingness to kill the enemy, at fever pitch.

A centroll, with long black hair, that flowed, as he ran, was the first to enter the city of Guinlance. With his sword in hand, he charged, through the city gates. Shortly, he was joined, by several more of his kind.

Suddenly, the creature reared onto his hind legs, turned his head, and pointed his sword, towards the city streets. His fellow centrolls, immediately roared their delight. Whereupon, an arrow, swiftly flew within a whisper of his long black hair, and landed on the ground, in front of him.

Turning his body, completely around, the centroll looked up at the city walls, to see several archers, hurtling down the stairs. At the top of the stairs, a young Fantaellen archer, his bow, still aimed, his arrow released. Their eyes briefly met, before the creature raced for cover, as more Fantaellen arrows, rained down on him.

★★★

Matthew cursed, at missing his target. He hated to miss. He would not miss again, he promised.

He ordered, every third archer, on the wall, to follow him, and with his bow on his shoulder, and a fresh bag of arrows, Matthew left the city walls, and sped down the steps, towards the centrolls, in the courtyard. His men, right behind him.

Quickly, the young officer organised his men into a line, as the roar of the enemy neared, and the bodies of their fellow Fantaellen knights surrounded them.

Matthew knew that his archers had to be disciplined. His men could fire off at least ten arrows, a minute. Those arrows would be fired together, as a deadly storm, on his orders.

'Archers! Ready!'

Fantaellen bow arms tensed. The enemy roar, increased. The last line of defence of the city wall and gates now awaited their officer's order to release.

'Loose!'

★★★

Fantaellen archers, fired arrow after arrow, with deadly accuracy, into the advancing creatures, and the Blackheart shield walls, outside the city walls.

The centrolls, despite being heavy footed, in their charge, were extremely agile. Numerous, evaded the deadly arrows, as they swerved, their bodies, to avoid being hit. Still, many died, in the hail of Fantaellen arrows, that did not desist, for one moment.

The gigahominums, were not so nimble footed, however. Because of their size, they presented the Fantaellen archers, with a bigger target. Also, they were not intelligent enough, to try and swerve or dive out of the way. Many charged at the city walls, with multiple arrows, protruding from their thick-skinned bodies, that protected, their vital organs.

The Blackheart shield walls, held their discipline. Slowly, they marched in unison, towards their target. They, were protected somewhat, by the creatures out front, but many, still died or were injured, by the Fantaellen arrow storm. Such had been, and still was its ferocity.

A large group of gigahominums, had reached the city walls. As they balanced their ladders, against the rough stonework, they were fired upon, by archers, from the walls. One gigahominum, who had managed to climb, halfway up his ladder, came crashing down, on top of his fellow creatures, when he was hit simultaneously in each eye, by an arrow, after looking up the ladder. He was quickly replaced, by another, who had dozens of arrows, embedded in his body.

There, were now an innumerable number of ladders, filled with hordes of gigahominums, climbing upwards, through the strafe of desperately fired Fantaellen arrows. It was mayhem, and bloody. But still they climbed. Their sheer numbers, and their incapacity to die easily, driving them upward, into the maelstrom of arrows.

Several gigahominums, suddenly reached the top of the city wall. Instinctively, they lashed out, and swung their huge swords, as they jumped from their ladders. Their lust for blood, could now begin.

***

Matthew and his archers had held their ground, with bow and arrow. There, were many dead centrolls, around them. Nevertheless, they were running out of arrows. The young officer drew his sword. They had no shields, for protection. They were bowman.

Above them, on the defensive walls of the city, their fellow archers, fought desperately, to repel the bloodthirsty giants, as more and more of them, jumped from their ladders, and attacked.

The gigahominum swords, were so large and razor sharp, that they easily cut a man in half. Many Fantaellen archers, were being slaughtered this way, in defence of the city walls. Their bloodied, butchered bodies, strewn along the pathways.

Matthew, saw the man, he had put in charge of the wall, fearlessly charge at a gigahominum. As, he bought his blade across, and struck the creature's left side, he was cut in half, by the blade of another, who split him from the top of his skull, downwards, in one clean cut.

The gigahominums had now taken the city walls of Guinlance, which ran thick, with the blood of Fantaellen archers. The resistance of the enemy cut down, with the slashing, deadly blades, of the giant creatures.

★★★

The disciplined defence, of the city of Guinlance, held for as long, as it could. Matthew and his archers, in the courtyard, now broke rank.

Through the city gates, ran more centrolls, and Blackhearts, their blades, flailing above their heads. From the city walls, the blood drunk, gigahominums charged down the steps, and into the courtyard. From, the rear of the remaining archers, came the other centrolls, previously forced into hiding by Fantaellen arrows, and led by the centroll, with the long, black, flowing hair.

Lastly, the battalions of Blackheart knights, broke from the cover of their shield walls. It was now every man and creature, for themselves.

The courtyard now echoed with the screams of men and creatures. The clashing of blades and armour, and the noise of slaughter and death.

The Fantaellen archers, fought bravely, despite the overwhelming odds. There, would be no reinforcements, to come and aid them. The leaders, choosing to retreat, their main body of knights, back to the castle walls, upon Guinlance Hill.

Matthew had spotted, the centroll, from earlier. His lust for battle, was up. He had already had his first kill, in open combat, when he had gutted a centroll, just moments prior. Now, the centroll, had spotted him, too. Their eyes met, once more.

The centroll and Matthew, charged at each other, at full speed, as the battle continued around them. It was as if, they were both invisible to anyone else, apart from each other.

The young Fantaellen officer, lunged first. He missed. The centroll, then threw out his sword, in a controlled lunge, that also missed, before quickly turning on his hooves, and moving behind Matthew, and then whipping his blade, to strike him on the lower part of his back. The young knight screamed out in pain, before stumbling forward.

Momentarily, unsteady on his feet, Matthew managed, to turn to face his attacker. Pain, seared through his back, as he now tried to compose himself.

The centroll charged once more, his four legs pushing him forward at speed. As the two, were about to clash, Matthew moved to his left, and bought his blade across the body of the centroll, who, as the blade sliced across his stomach, howled out in pain. His, two front legs, suddenly buckled, and the creature, then slumped forward.

Matthew now ceased the opportunity and went in for the kill. Bringing his blade across the back of the centroll's neck, with all the strength he could muster, the young Fantaellen officer, took the creature's head, clean off its neck.

With no further thought, of that kill, and an overwhelming enemy around him, Matthew charged forward, as the blood poured from the wound, on his back.

Around him, the battle raged on, whilst the young Fantaellen archer, and officer, ran head on, into the chaos, and death, his bloodied sword, in hand.

★★★

General Grafton's creature and Blackheart battalions had finally overwhelmed their enemy, in the streets. Their sheer numbers and lack of fear had driven them forward, towards the city walls of Guinlance.

The Fantaellen knights in the shield walls and deadly archers on the city walls, had all been massacred. Their bodies lay everywhere, their blood soaking the ground.

The streets, of the city were ablaze. Guinlance was on its knees.

The only thing, that now stood in the way of General Grafton, securing the total surrender, or annihilation of Fantaellen, was its last remaining, beacon of hope.

He was so close, to executing his master's orders, he could now taste it.

For the moment, the general was content, to see the red, black and silver heart Tri Lance banners and flags, of Wulfdaeden, being marched through the city gates of Guinlance, for the first time in history.

In the distance, Guinlance Castle, atop, the steep and treacherous Guinlance Hill, towering over the burning buildings, of its once proud city. The last beacon of hope, for Fantaellen. And its last line of defence. Standing strong, and defiant. The beating heart of Fantaellen.

Chapter Eleven

Guinlance Castle, the beating heart of Fantaellen, has stood, proud and strong, for centuries. A show of engineering brilliance. A symbol of respectful governance, power and hope. Never before, have its walls been breached.

The castle is built on Guinlance Hill. A near vertical, natural structure, of rough grassland, a mile wide, and itself, surrounded, by impregnable rock formations, that seem to go up to the sky. The entrance, leading up to the castle, has been cut into the hill. It was purposefully built, to be long and narrow, to be met at the end, by the first outer wall, always manned, by archers and crossbowmen. Beyond that wall, stands the main entrance, into the castle. The vast, wide drawbridge, that when down, covers a man made, sheer drop, into a deep, dark pit, full of deadly spikes, made from Fantaellen oak. This, line of defence, covers the entire length of the wall.

Now, under imminent attack, from the enemy from across the sea, the magnificent and deadly, yet beautiful structure, stands defiant and alone. The seemingly last symbol, of Fantaellen hope.

★★★

A small number of rock men, their best free climbers, had begun the first part of their attack. They were aided by the long, coarse grass of Guinlance Hill, which they used, to pull themselves up, the vertical climb, with relative ease. Over their shoulders, they carried a rope, that would be secured into the hill, for the rest of their battalion, to ascend, as quickly as possible, and secure their ladders, at the top of the main outer wall.

Fantaellen arrows, had been fired, from the ramparts, down onto the free climbing rock men, who had taken the defenders on the ramparts, by surprise, as they climbed up, over then down, the impregnable rocks. They were spotted, as they began their next climb, up the grassy hill. The Fantaellen arrows, had thus far, made no impact.

Now, with their ropes secured, the free climbing rock men, descended, as the defender's arrows, eventually dissipated.

The Fantaellen officers, had quickly realised, that they needed to use a different tactic, to repel the attackers, from Granite Island. In a matter of minutes, the orders to the ramparts, were quickly changed. Fires were now lit, and vats of oil ordered forward.

At the bottom of Guinlance Hill, multitudes of rock men, had now joined the free climbers, and had begun to ascend their ropes.

★★★

The rhythmic, military beat, of the Blackheart drums, had started up. Battalions of Wulfdaeden knights and creatures, suddenly bustled into line, ready to march forward.

The archers and the crossbowmen, on the ramparts, along the first outer wall, were hurriedly ordered to make ready their weapons.

The war drums of the Blackhearts instantaneously stopped. The perfect, military lines of knights and creatures now fell silent. A breeze, blew through the Wulfdaeden banners and flags, the only sound to be heard.

'Forward!' Came the confident order.

'For Wulfdaeden!' Declared, a different, and deeper voice, from the rear of the Blackheart rank and file.

Disciplined lines, of knights and creatures, slowly and in perfect time, began their march towards their intended target, of breach.

General Grafton had thrown his dice. This was his next move. Mounted at the rear, on his black steed, Napoleon Victory's most trusted general, urged his knights and creatures forward, with further encouragements, of power and glory.

The beating heart of Fantaellen, was now under attack.

★★★

Deadly fingers instinctively twitched on Fantaellen bow strings and crossbow triggers. The officers, along the wall, calmly urged their men, to hold steady.

'Hold your fire. Keep your aim.' This was repeated, all down the line. Patiently, the highly skilled killers, waited.

Forward, the Wulfdaeden lines, continued their march, in measured time, down the long and narrow entrance. Even the usually excitable gigahominums, kept their discipline, as their officer's, strode beside them.

Watching their resolute steps, with pride, General Grafton stroked the mane of his black steed. Never, had he seen anything so magnificent, he remarked to one of his men, who in turn, congratulated his general.

Then, abruptly turning his ride, with a quick rotation of its body and a signal on the rein, General Grafton, raced his steed, back down the burning streets of Guinlance city, his bodyguards, in proximity. The next part of his attack would follow shortly. For that to happen, he would need his engineers.

★★★

The captured siege weaponry was now ordered forward, by General Grafton. He liked their destructiveness, they made his black heart, beat with desire. He had seen their effectiveness, in causing the damage on the city walls and streets of Guinlance. The general knew, that to take the castle, he would need something else, as throwing his battalions at the walls, would end in probable defeat.

The Fantaellen's would not give up the castle easily, he had told his officer's. In his mind, this would be the setting, of the pure hearts last stand. They had left the city walls, with very little firepower, on its ramparts, and the defence of the city gate, had been, at best, futile. Before retreating, to the safety, of the castle walls, Guinlance Castle would be the place, where they would, put their main body of knight's. Their country was on its knees. Occupied by an enemy, superior in numbers and skill. With the best officers in Portaellen, leading them. He had wanted to finish his brief, with that statement, as he needed to build up the confidence, in his subordinate officer's, but he was suddenly interrupted, by a Blackheart knight, who had appeared, before them.

'Sir! News from the attack, on the hill.'

'Go on man!' Demanded the general.

The Blackheart messenger cleared his throat and continued. Nervous, in the company, of the general and his officer's, the young man stuttered momentarily, before regaining his composure, and carrying on.

'The enemy, have started using burning oil, on the rock men, sir!'

General Grafton, stared at the young Blackheart, for a moment, before turning to one of his officer's.

'Get more archers, further to the front.' Came his order.

'Yes sir.'

'They must protect, the rock men, with their Long Bows.'

'Sir!'

The officer then hurried away, quickly calling his junior officer's, to his side. Fervently, he passed his orders, to his men, before running off, to ready the rest of his battalion.

General Grafton briefed his engineers, on what he wanted. This was going to be a siege, he told them. The attack on the walls, from his battalions needed to happen. With support from, their newly gained siege weapon, the trebuchet. The engineers were then quickly dismissed, with their orders, still fresh.

There was another way, that an attack, could be mounted. And, a coded message, had been dispatched, some time ago. The strike at the enemy, would take some careful planning, and the general knew, that it would take time to initiate it.

General Grafton, afforded himself a smile, as the picture, of his master, being crowned on the Throne of Portaellen, and becoming the Sovereign of the Portal World, filled his black heart, with joy. There, stood at his master's side, would be his most trusted friend, and general of his armies. General Cedric Grafton.

★★★

The piercing screams of the burning rock men, dying at the bottom, of the castle wall, drove forward, the aggressive attack, of their fellow creatures. They had gained, a foot hold, at the top of the hill, and they tried to bring their ladders forward, before the Fantaellen's, could pour their next batch of oil, upon them. Despite, their vulnerability, the creatures from Granite Island, showed great courage, as they charged up their ropes.

Their courage was subsequently rewarded, as Wulfdaeden arrows, fired from quite some distance away, pinned down the Fantaellen knights, who made ready, the deadly vats of oil. The enemy archers, on the ramparts of the castle, who had lit their fire arrows, ready to burn the rock men once more, now had to fire their arrows, down upon the Wulfdaeden archers, who had come, to their aid. The rock men now had some cover, as they ran at the wall.

As they reached the flatter, top part of the hill, some twenty feet or so, from the bottom of the castle wall, they were faced with a burning barrier of oil, the flames of which, were spread across, a vast distance. For a moment, their attack stalled, as the sight of the deadly wall of fire, and the screams and the smell of the burning bodies, of their fellow creatures, startled them.

One rock man, who stumbled around, in front of the castle wall, screaming in agony, and completely engulfed in fire and flame, suddenly ran back through the fire wall, past his fellow creatures, still alight, and down the grassy bank, before falling, then rolling down the steep hill. The rock men, on the ropes, coming up the hill, quickly swung to avoid him, as he rolled at speed, past them. At the bottom, of Guinlance Hill, still alight and smouldering, he was put out of his misery, his screams, finally silenced.

The rock men, who had climbed the hill, on the west side, had found a gap, in the Fantaellen fire wall. The message, was quickly sent down the line, for the ladders, to be bought over, and for the attack on the wall, to come from there. With many Fantaellen archers, pinned down, or shooting their arrows into the city streets below, the rock men, began to race along the top of the hill, unhindered, towards the opening in the fire wall.

Once, through the other side of the flames the men from Granite Island ran freely at the high walls of Guinlance Castle, ladders in tow and their guttural war cries, driving them forward, to glory.

★★★

'Loose!' Screamed the Fantaellen officer, at the top of his lungs. In his chest, his heart pounded, as his archers and crossbowmen, fired their deadly arrows and bolts, at the invaders, from across the Stoirim Sea. 'Go on.' He muttered to himself, as the sky filled with the lethal load.

He was a seasoned officer and in his third decade of service. He loved nothing more, than to watch his men firing with accuracy and deadly intent. It still, made his heartbeat fast, and the hairs on the back of his neck stand up. Even though, many of his archers and crossbowmen, were still in their teens, he knew that not one of them, would let him down. He trusted them implicitly.

Stroking, his greying beard, the officer watched intently, wishing that he could fire his bow, as he used to. He had lost his index and middle finger, of his right hand, cut off, whilst in captivity, as a young man, in a Wulfdaeden gaol. A place of hell, that he had eventually escaped from.

His men, affectionately called him lucky Joe, due to the fact, that he had escaped, from a Wulfdaeden gaol. Something, that not many men, could say. To his face, they called him Sir.

Their first arrow storm had killed several Blackhearts, who had been too slow, to form up or join the hurried shield walls, that had been urgently ordered by their panicked officers. The long and narrowing entrance way, to Guinlance Castle, had forced the Blackheart lines, to reform, as they drew close to the first outer wall. Their lines, that had quickly formed into shield walls, were no more than twenty men, in length across, which then made the depth, of their shield walls very deep.

Barrage after barrage of Fantaellen arrows and crossbow bolts, now reigned down, on the shield walls of the Wulfdaeden and the creature battalions. Many bowmen found gaps in the hastily made defences, and the screams, of the dying and injured, rang out from the ranks, as blood sprayed the air and soaked the ground.

Then, came General Grafton's immediate reply. Defiant, Blackheart cheers rang out, as missile upon missile from the trebuchets, promptly flew over the ranks of pinned down Wulfdaeden's and creature battalions. The din and roar increased, when a number of the huge rocks, hurtled over the first outer wall, and came crashing down, within the castle grounds. Furthermore, the ground immediately shook, as other missiles, strategically smashed into the thick stone walls, of Guinlance Castle, in the hope of weakening, its structure and its foundations.

The barrage and the ensuing impact, of the enormous stone boulders, upon the first outer wall, and the main outer wall, now continued relentlessly, and showed very little sign, of coming to an end.

The men, upon the ramparts of both walls, and the knights and civilians, hidden within the confides of the distant castle, would have never experienced, anything as destructive as this, before.

Guinlance Castle was under siege, by an enemy and a general, who was prepared, to smash it to the ground, over time, to bring about, its final capitulation.

★★★

Getting to his feet, a little dazed and confused, Joseph looked around hurriedly. He watched, as another missile, flew over him, and headed for the main outer wall, behind them. There was blood and bodies, all around him.

Momentarily, he looked down at one of his archers, who was crushed underneath a section of the wall, that had been smashed to pieces. His whole lower body, was beneath the stonework, only his head, chest and arms showed. The young archer was still alive, but he began to cough up blood, as the life left his crushed body. Within, a matter of moments, the young man passed away, with Joseph comforting him, as chaos reigned, around them.

We still have to defend this wall. At all costs.

Joseph's senses had now kicked in, as another missile, impacted against the wall, farther along.

'Archers and bolt men.' That was his nickname, for his crossbowmen. 'On me!' He ordered.

Presently, he was joined by three dozen, able bodied men. Shortly after, more answered the call. He quickly barked out his orders, before sending them, to their defensive positions.

Their wall may have been battered. Their will tested; he had told his men. But it was up to them, to hold the wall. He, then watched his archers and bolt men, ready themselves, with yet more Wulfdaeden missiles still flying at them, his own orders ringing in his ears. Around him, the crashing noise, of impacted missiles, and the screams of his fellow countrymen, did not affect his nerve.

Now! His inner voice demanded.

Joseph licked his dry lips and took one last glance at his men.

'For Fantaellen!' He screamed; his sword thrust out in front of him. 'Loose!'

In that split second, Joseph's voice disappeared into a wall of noise. Behind him, a tremendous crash, had created mayhem and carnage, that had drowned out his order. It had not mattered however, as his young bowmen, had seen his sword raised, then lowered, and dutifully carried out his order.

They then charged. The Blackheart and the creature battalions, suddenly broke rank buoyed, by the trebuchet missiles, that were seemingly smashing down, the castle walls. Wave upon wave of knights and creatures, now charged at the first outer wall.

Joseph kept his men firing, as quickly as they could, down onto the hordes, in the narrow passageway. At one point, they fired more than twenty arrows, a minute. With the same number of crossbow bolts, being released. His men, now began to wreak havoc and death on the waves of knights, centrolls and gigahominums, that charged at their wall. The accuracy, of their firing, combined with the speed of how quickly they reloaded, now proved deadly.

Very soon, the bodies of countless attackers, began to litter the ground below. Several times, the enemy shield walls quickly reformed, to then break rank once more, and launch another assault.

Hours passed, as the intensity of the Wulfdaeden attacks, showed no signs of abating. Siege missiles continued to batter, the castle walls. Guinlance Castle remained defiant. Around its first outer wall, the vast numbers of bodies of enemy knights and creatures, were strewn across the killing ground.

★★★

With the going down of the suns, on another Portaellen day, General Grafton suddenly ordered his battalions back to camp, to regroup. Countless numbers of his knights were dead. Many of his creature battalions, decimated, which included the rock men, who had suffered great losses, in the fires, on Guinlance Hill. Neither attack, had really bought him any success. Even so, it had been reported, that his siege weapons, had weakened the walls of Guinlance Castle, which did please him.

He never thought that it was going to be easy. As he had told his officers, this was always going to be a siege. Those walls would not come down easily, if at all. Now it was time to regroup. And wait.

Guinlance Castle will fall. Fantaellen will be brought to its knees. These thoughts would bring him solace, as he waited, for dawn, and the return, of a coded message.

★★★

Joseph and his men were exhausted. They had managed to repel, the crazed enemy for hours, with their arrows and bolts. Whilst the ground around them, had shook on countless occasions, as Wulfdaeden missiles, had smashed their wall, and the great wall behind them. Both had stood firm, nonetheless.

Upon, the enemy retreat, he had allowed his young archers and crossbowmen, the chance to taunt the Blackhearts. This was done, in the customary way, by a right-handed gesture, and then raising their index finger and middle finger, in a V sign.

The seasoned officer was proud of his young men. They had held the line. The enemy had been sent from the battlefield; defeated. But, he knew, that they would be back; Better and stronger.

The Wulfdaeden invasion had stalled, he told his men. Tomorrow, they would attack again. Tomorrow, he and his men, would have to hold the wall, once more.

'So, eat, drink and get some rest boys. For, on the morrow, we will have to be even better, than we were today.'

★★★

Robert Scotten had mixed emotions, as exhaustion, abruptly overcame him. From, the balcony, of the Royal Quarters of Guinlance Castle, he and Henri had watched, the Wulfdaeden attack, being repelled, by the thick, stone walls, and the skill of the men, on the ramparts. His plan, had worked, thus far. But, at what cost?

As night-time quickly approached, Henri had become relieved, that the attack of the enemy had begun to diminish. He too felt exhausted. It had been a terrible few days. He had tried to support his friend, who carried the weight of the country, on his shoulders. The burden of being the Guardian of Fantaellen, must have been so great for Robert. Therefore, Henri had tried to be with him, and offer his support, as much as possible.

Hearing, of the merciless attack of the Blackhearts, on the army and the people, in the towns and villages, had horrified them both. At, the first sight of the enemy, at the city walls of Guinlance, this had prompted Robert, to decide on a defensive strategy. Knowing full well, that the thick stone walls, would deter the invader. Giving them time, to plan their next move.

They now used, the time that they had, to go over their plan, and finalise it, as the battlefield, remained silent, in the darkness, of the night.

'You look tired Robert.' Henri put his hand on his friend's shoulder. 'Why don't you get some rest?' he continued.

'You, too Henri.' Came, the weary reply. He smiled at his friend, to show that he was grateful for his support and concern. 'I, just need to make sure, our exhausted archers and crossbowmen, get their food and water.'

'I'll do that,' offered Henri.

'Thanks, my friend. Use the water from the well, in the barracks, for the fighting men. Use the water from the main well, for all civilians and court staff. Make sure, that the food and the water is distributed, as best you can. Give, the fighting men more, to keep up their strength.'

'Yes Robert. I will.'

'I will leave you to organise, the care for the injured, Henri.'

'Yes. No problem. Now, go get some rest.'

Henri marched off with purpose. Taking two bodyguards with him, the royal physician, charged down the corridors, of Guinlance Castle, and out into the courtyard, towards the barracks.

Wearily, the Guardian of Fantaellen, trudged towards his chambers. At, his flank, his bodyguards, following obediently. He did feel exhausted, but his mind still raced. Such was the burden. Thoughts, ideas, eating away at his mind. His next move, and the next move of the enemy, played in his mind's eye.

Not long now, he told himself. Death or glory. Those were his last thoughts, as he slowly succumbed to his exhaustion.

★★★

Henri had been in a deep sleep, when the door to his chambers, suddenly burst open. As, he wearily pulled himself up, his eyes slowly adjusted to the darkness, and he cursed his ageing body. He heard footsteps approaching, and then became aware of the shadow of a large knight, who stood at the bottom of his bed.

'Sorry, to disturb you sir.' The knight spoke with a deep voice, that had a panicked tone.

'What is it?' Henri sighed.

'Our Guardian needs to see you. Straight away.'

Hurriedly, Henri put on some clothes. He, then recognised the knight, as Wilfred, the captain of the royal bodyguard.

The captain was a giant of a man. He was from Africa. He had discovered his Dual Blood lineage, completely by accident, when running from a gang, near the Ring of Stones. Upon, arriving in Fantaellen, confused, dazed and without any clothing, Wilfred had been found by a patrol, and bought back to Guinlance Castle.

After being questioned, by Robert Scotten, he was placed in the ranks of the Fantaellen army. He had quickly proven his bravery in battle, and in the odd skirmish with the Wulfdaeden's. Robert took a personal interest, in the man's welfare, as he had seen something in him, from their first meeting. Over the subsequent years, Wilfred rose through the ranks. After, King Stefan's death, Robert had promoted him, to the highest captaincy, within the Fantaellen army. Wilfred was also the personal bodyguard, to the Guardian of Portaellen.

The guards, outside Henri's bed chamber, snapped to attention, as he and Wilfred, quickly made their way, out the doorway, and down the dimly lit corridor. Behind them, the guards followed.

The Royal Physician, promptly saw, that there were no sentries on duty, as they walked the corridors.

That's strange.

'Where, are the rest of the sentries?' he suddenly asked, Wilfred.

Wilfred did not answer. The silence from the captain, now fuelled his concern.

Upon, arriving at Robert's chambers, Henri stood stoically, his hands behind his back. Wilfred, then slammed his huge fist, onto the ornate, wooden door. Directly, a reply came.

'Enter.'

Wilfred pushed open the heavy doors and proceeded to enter the guardian's chamber. Behind him, Henri followed, as the two guards, closed the doors behind them.

Robert was dressed in full battle armour. He had his back to Henri and Wilfred, as they entered his chambers. When, he turned to face them, he sighed. His face looked grave and agitated.

'Why, are you dressed like that?' Henri enquired.

There, was no instant reply, as Robert, just stared at Henri. He appeared to be, extremely troubled, and Henri had never, seen his friend, looking so distressed.

'Our men are dropping like flies,' Robert, suddenly declared.

'What?'

'Our knights are dropping dead. All along the castle walls.'

'How many?' enquired Henri.

'Not sure,' Robert uttered. 'Hundreds, we think.'

'Oh Christ!' Henri exclaimed, as he approached his friend, whose face had now turned ashen.

'The men were fed and given water, some hours ago,' Robert declared, as he turned his back on his friend. 'We have lost a lot of men. It, must be the food or water, or both.'

At this point, Robert did not seem, to be making any sense, to Henri. The physician put it down to exhaustion, and he let his friend continue, as he watched his facial expressions rapidly change, along with his general demeanour.

'We do have men in reserve, from our east wall. They seem to be fine. But it's only a few hundred knights.'

Henri suddenly spoke up. 'Did they eat or drink, the same food and water, as the other men?'

Robert, turned to face his friend once again, and then he glanced at Wilfred.

'No,' started Wilfred. 'They, have a different well, and food stores.'

'I need to get to that well and food store,' stated Henri, as he now saw, what his friend, was trying to say.

'No problem,' said Robert.

Wilfred, who grew impatient, suddenly interrupted them.

'We don't have much time left, sir,' he remarked.

'Yes Wilfred. I know.'

Robert continued, as his friend, listened intently. All, the time he spoke, he stared at Henri, as if gauging his reaction.

'There is only so long, that the fifty-foot-high walls, and the thirty foot deep stonewalls, will hold back our enemy, Henri.' Robert moved closer to his friend, as he looked to finish, his conversation. The royal physician could see guilt, in his friend's face, as he carried on. 'Our numbers, are so low now.'

A sudden realisation overcame Henri. He knew, what his friend tried to say. He nodded his head and stopped Robert in mid-sentence, as he spoke, in a calm tone, to reassure his friend.

'You do not need to justify to me, the reason for your actions. You do this for Fantaellen, my friend. You must live, for our future. So, you can pass on the wisdom and the knowledge, to the one true blood. The future king or queen of Fantaellen.' Henri smiled.

'Thank you, Henri. And, for the future Sovereign of Portaellen, I do this.'

As Robert, said these words, Henri, saw a strange look in his friend's eye. One, he had not seen before. He would put it down, to the emotion of the moment, he told himself.

Henri quickly realised, that it was the best decision, for Portaellen and for Fantaellen. The guardian had to stay safe. There, was a distinct possibility, that Guinlance Castle, could now fall into enemy hands, for the first time in history. There was only so long, that the depleted knights and archers, would be able to hold back, the Blackheart onslaught.

'Goodbye my friend,' Robert started. 'You make sure that if the worst happens, that you have an escape plan.'

'I will.'

Henri, smiled at his friend, once again. He had no intention of leaving the castle, he would be needed, to tend to the wounded.

As, the two men stared at each other, Henri, suddenly saw no emotion, in his friend's eyes. They seemed dead and devoid of anything. He had never seen that before in the eyes of a man so passionate about his country.

Henri suddenly felt uncomfortable, with the tense, strange atmosphere, and he needed, to get out of the room.

'Dawn is fast approaching,' he remarked. 'You, need to go, my friend.'

It wasn't long, before Henri and Robert parted, after an awkward farewell.

The Guardian of Portaellen, now strode down the corridor, with purpose. At his side, his most trusted bodyguard. Wilfred listened, as orders were given. Time was moving fast. The future of their country, and the world of Portaellen, depended on an escape plan.

While, Henri made haste, towards the barracks, he felt an uneasy sense of impending defeat. Yesterday, the walls of Guinlance Castle, had held the enemy. Overnight, it seemed, that the same enemy, had struck, a devastating blow from within.

The royal physician, needed to find out, how that blow had been delivered. He had his own ideas. If, it was the poison, that he thought it was, then there would be no trace of it, in the food or the water. If, that was the case, then he just needed to find a body, to confirm it.

He would head to the mortuary, he told himself.

★★★

General Grafton had hoped that the attack had been carried out, by now. He had been eager to receive news, of its success. None had come yet. His eagerness had extended to the body littered battlefield, around the castle.

For, the last two hours, his battalions of knights and creatures, had stood in columns, in complete darkness, facing the walls.

Where, is that coded reply?

An officer suddenly approached the general and he went on to explain, that there had been a lot of commotion heard and seen, on the ramparts, and that he had received reports all night, that a lot of bodies had been spotted, being dragged away.

The general, immediately laughed out loud, before raising his sword in the air, with delight, at the news.

Within minutes, he rode up and down his columns of knights and creatures, declaring that the castle and Fantaellen, would soon be theirs.

Thus, as the two suns of Portaellen, began to rise on another day, the next phase, of the Wulfdaeden assault on Guinlance Castle, commenced. The ground, once more shuddered, as the Blackheart sieged weaponry, launched its power, at the castle walls.

★★★

Henri gasped, at the smell of rotting corpses, as he reached the mortuary. It, was here, that the extent of the enemies' attack, now became apparent.

The bodies of the dead were everywhere. The orderlies tried their best, to give some dignity, to the dead. There, were just too many corpses. The back door, to the mortuary, had been opened, and the trail of bodies, now extended outside.

Henri was promptly given a mask, by a sympathetic orderly, when the smell of death, became too overwhelming. He was taken, to a back room, where the orderlies, had left a body, for him to examine.

'It won't take me long to find, what I need to find,' Henri, told the orderly, as he left the physician, to carry out, his examination.

Henri slowly pulled away the sheet, that covered the knight's face. He opened the mouth of the dead knight, and gently pulled out his tongue. It was black. Henri said nothing. He then replaced the sheet, over the dead man's face.

He walked silently out the room, and out of the mortuary, into the courtyard, just as the ground around him, shook. In, the distance, towards the castle walls, he heard the screams of Fantaellen knights, as another Wulfdaeden missile slammed into the main wall.

Somewhere out there, he told himself, amongst the fighting men of Fantaellen, was a killer. A mass murderer. An assassin, with blackened fingers.

★★★

Roared on, by their general, the Blackhearts threw everything that they had, at the walls of Guinlance Castle, as the daylight from the two suns, slowly increased. Just, like the day before, it was a two-pronged attack, with the rock men climbing their ropes, and the main assault, attacking the first outer wall, that guarded the main entrance. Bodies were added to the dead of the previous day, as the knights on the ramparts, continued to let loose, their arrows and bolts, with a disciplined show, of speed and accuracy.

Despite, their depleted numbers, the archers and the cross-bowmen of Fantaellen, still managed to create, an arrow and bolt storm, that proved to be deadly.

Joseph kept his men firing at disciplined intervals. His, voice shouted out his orders, as the roar of battle, continued around them. His, voice had croaked, several times, as exhaustion, flirted with him. He had not slept. He had managed to have some food and water, from the officer's quarters, before deciding to get some rest. Yet, before he could finish his meal, he had been called back to the ramparts, to find a majority of his men, dead or dying.

So, on this new morning, Joseph stood on the ramparts, with a handful of his original men, and a small number of reserves, that had been placed, under his leadership. At his feet lay several loaded crossbows, that he fired with his left hand, then loaded, himself.

As, a missile smashed into the wall, several feet below him, Joseph fired a bolt into a gigahominum, that roared aggressively at his fellow creatures, as they neared the bottom of the wall, with a ladder. The gigahominum, then pulled the bolt from his chest, snapped it in two, and he began to climb the ladder.

All, along their wall, Joseph could now see the ladders being placed, into position. Despite the best efforts of he and his men, he knew that the sheer numbers of the enemy, attacking the wall, would soon overwhelm them.

The giant gigahominums, were the first up the ladders. Their huge bodies, clambered up the steps, protected by a large shield, that the first creature, carried above his head, to shelter him and the others, below him, from arrows and bolts.

Fantaellen bolts and arrows, continued to rain down, into the tight mass of knights and centrolls, charging behind the gigahominums. Temporary shield walls were now made hastily, before Wulfdaeden archers, could return fire.

The pathway, up to the entrance of the first outer wall, was now a concentration of Wulfdaeden aggression. The battalions of Blackhearts and creatures were desperate to smash their way into the castle. The ground around them, was littered with their dead, and the smell of blood and decaying corpses, overwhelming.

Along, the line of ladders, the first gigahominums, breached the ramparts. From the last step, they jumped, landing with a heavy thud, into the line of Fantaellen bowmen. With relative ease, many Fantaellen's were gutted, by a giant sword, where they stood.

The ladders, now began to fill, with Blackheart knights, as they broke from their shield walls. With, Fantaellen arrow and bolt storms, now slowly diminishing.

Joseph fired a bolt, into the massive forehead, of a gigahominum, as it appeared, at the top of the ladder. The giant creature, a surprised look in his eye, as the life left him, then fell from the ladder. His enormous carcass now came crashing down into a mass of Blackhearts, below.

Along, the ramparts, the giants, overwhelmed the bow men, many of whom, had run out of arrows and bolts, and were now engaged in hand-to-hand combat, with the enemy. The overwhelming, numbers of creatures and their sheer size and power, enabled them to quickly cut and slash, their way along the ramparts.

The wily, old Joseph had fired his last bolt. It had been dispatched into a Blackheart, who died instantly. Now, throwing his crossbow to the ground, he drew his sword, and ran towards, two of his men, who were being overwhelmed, by the enemy creatures.

Slashing his blade, across the stomach, of a gigahominum, gave one of his men, time to retreat. Joseph continued his frenzied attack, as he slashed and stabbed his sword, into the creature, who cried out in pain and agony, as his blood spurted up and covered, his assailant. Eventually, the creature died, in a melee of unrelenting cuts and thrusts, from Joseph.

Many, Fantaellen's were dead on the ramparts. Joseph looked around him in despair. The enemy just kept coming. And Joseph, he kept killing. That was all, he could do.

With, another gigahominum slaughtered, Joseph moved onto his next attack. His blade dripped with the blood, of many creatures, and his body was battered. With a quick glance, around him, Joseph suddenly realised, that he was the last man. The bearded warrior smiled to himself.

Time to die!

The signal, of the capitulation, of the first outer wall, was given to General Grafton, with the severed head of a Fantaellen knight. The Blackheart held up the bloodied head, by its grey hair, for all to see. The lifeless eyes, open wide, and blood dripping from a greying beard.

★★★

A small band of men, in purple hooded robes, rowed silently, from a secret entrance, below Guinlance Castle. The oars of the two boats, moved quietly through the water, as they made their way towards, a bank.

On the bank, were a dozen men. They too, were dressed in purple robes, their hoods covered their faces. Silently, they had waited, with their tethered steeds. All eyes scanned the immediate and furthest reaches of the landscape, around them. They quickly readied their steeds, when the boats were spotted, heading their way.

Robert Scotten had cursed their delay. They were supposed to have left, in the last few hours of darkness, but there had been a security scare, when one of the royal bodyguard's, had been found dead with his throat cut.

Arriving on the riverbank, the hooded men, quickly mounted their steed's. Robert, saw the fresh mound of earth, and said nothing. His order had been carried out. At speed, they then rode, along the track, that followed the natural path of the river.

A few miles later, they headed away from the river, and turned north. Riding, away from Guinlance Castle, that became a distant landmark, as they rode, Robert could still hear, the noise of war, as the enemy attack intensified.

From a tree line, to the west of them, the purple hooded riders, were spotted by a Blackheart patrol. From their position, the patrol watched, as the riders negotiated a hill, before riding off and over the crest.

'Are we to engage them sir?' asked, one of the Blackhearts.

'No,' came the officer's reply. 'They, are to be left, alone.'

The purple hooded riders continued to make great haste. Their magnificent white steeds swallowed up the ground, below their hooves, as they headed to their secret location.

★★★

A disciplined line of Blackhearts, snapped to attention, as a rowing boat, rode the last few waves, and the breakers bought the vessel to a halt, in the sand of the shallows.

Almost immediately, a figure in a black hooded robe, disembarked from the boat, and made his way up the shore, towards the line of Blackhearts, in the distance. As, he strode, he was flanked either side, by knights in Blackheart armour, armed with crossbows.

The wind, continually whistled through the rocks, that jutted out into the sea, as the Wulfdaeden banners now danced, proudly, in the air.

The hooded figure, briefly bent down, to touch the sand, not before looking up, to see a seabird, soaring high above, in the cloudless sky. His hood suddenly fell away from his head, and the scar faced figure, smiled to himself, as he cupped some sand in his hand. He turned to one of his bodyguards and laughed out loud.

'Home, sweet home.' Napoleon Victory declared, as he threw the sand into the air.

Chapter Twelve

Characteristically, the Majestic Wood now came to life, as the riders neared its edge. The oaks and their cousins, the beech trees, spoke quietly, as the message proceeded through the branches, carried on the wind, to their king.

Oakengarne, is the oldest tree, in the wood. He is several hundred years old. If asked, he will say two hundred, next birthday. He has counted backwards, for many decades. He is strong and wise, and has provided many lost and frightened souls, shade and shelter from harm.

Oakengarne is the grandest tree, in the grandest wood. He stands alone, encircled by his seed and kin. The king of Majestic Wood.

The riders were weary. They had pushed their steeds hard. Their steeds in turn, had grown heavy footed, so they had slowed the pace, in desperation of them making it to the safe place. One man knew that it was imperative, that they made it to the shelter of Majestic Wood. This was the safest place, in Fantaellen. A place, known for its sanctuary. A haven, where a person or a creature, of pure heart and blood, was welcomed, and protected.

Jonti felt such relief, at the sight of the treeline. Their ride had been hard, through torrential rain and sleet. Unable, to stop for shelter, they had kept going, pushing their steeds, to the limit. No food, no sleep, for he or his knight's.

As they crossed the boundary into the wood, the ceremony of entrance, could begin. First Jonti, then his men, following his actions, raised their arms in the air.

Jonti spoke, in a raised voice. 'We, call upon the oaks and beeches, of Majestic Wood, to recognise us, as pure of heart and blood.' He dismounted his steed, and proceeded to stride forward, walking his mount, behind him. His knights followed suit, leaving the unconscious twins and their aunt, still securely mounted, on their rides.

The branches of the trees, began to sway, in a gentle breeze. Jonti could feel, the pleasant current of air, cooling his face. He welcomed it.

Going deeper into the wood, Jonti continued to talk to the trees, telling them, how grateful they were for the shelter and the comfort, they now gave him and his men. He knew, the deeper that they entered, where the older, wiser, stronger trees, were situated, that their captive, would become a concern. The oaks, deeper in the wood, were the king's guard. They fully encircled him, but not so much, as to take his light.

The gentle breeze had now gone. It had been replaced, by a small gust of wind, that increased in power, by the second. Jonti, had to speak now. He knew that the old oaks, could sense evil, in their midst.

'Oh! Wise oaks of Majestic Wood, I bring a precious delivery, for you to take care of. I also have someone, who was once of pure blood. Third in line, to the Throne of Fantaellen, and the sovereignty of our world. She was turned, with the poison of evil. I pray, that you can see beyond her present state, so she can be saved.'

As Jonti finished speaking, he caught a glimpse of the light of the two suns, streaming through the branches of the old oaks. It was a beautiful sight. So, calming after the arduous journey, that they had endured. The wind, had now completely dropped, and sweet birdsong, emanated from the trees.

Deeper, they walked into the wood, carefully negotiating the raised roots around them. The beautiful sunlight still streamed through the branches, with no sign of it disappearing, the further they walked.

Coming to a flatter, grassy part of the wood, Jonti suddenly recognised, where they were. They were close now, he told himself. There ahead of them, was the circle of oaks. The king's guard. Their branch's lowered, to shield their king.

'Oh! King's guard!' Jonti suddenly shouted. 'We ask permission, to enter your circle. We seek an audience, with the one whose roots are deepest and furthest. The one, true father oak, of Majestic Wood.'

Jonti now fell to his knees and bowed his head. There, he remained for a short while, in silence, before getting to his feet, he drew his sword, and laid it upon the ground.

'I come in peace. I am your servant, Jonti Quixall.'

The branches of the oaks now began to slowly lift. As they did, Jonti gasped. He had never seen a sight so beautiful. It took his breath away.

Oakengarne, looked so exalted, as Jonti stared in wonderment. The great oak stood strong and alone. The light that shone brightly through his branches, gave him an air of supremacy, and a glow of supreme dominance and superiority. His trunk, so wide and thick, supporting the branches, that went on forever, into the sky.

He truly is the King of Majestic Wood.

'Oakengarne, is Majestic Wood.' Jonti whispered in reply, to the voice in his head.

Jonti, had spoken to Oakengarne, on several occasions, to seek his advice. He had always thought of him, as a wise, thoughtful and peace-loving king. He had also seen, the other side of the oak. For, when required, Oakengarne could be strong and deadly, to protect everything that he held dear, and anybody who had sought shelter with him.

'Come forward, Master Quixall!' A deep voice cried out. 'It is nice to see you.'

Jonti and Oakengarne, now spoke for a few moments together, just like old friends would, when neither had seen each other, for a while. The light of the two suns, shone so brilliantly, through the great oak's branches, bringing a serenity and warmth, to their conversation, despite the urgency of the visit.

'I noticed some new additions, to the family, on the way in.' Jonti winked, which made Oakengarne laugh heartily, before he proudly announced, that there would be more to follow. Jonti then smiled.

'You know, the family trait Jonti.' The great oak, suddenly began to laugh to himself, as he said the words, 'Good, strong acorns!'

The two friends laughed out loud together, with Oakengarne's deep guffawing, reverberating through the branches of the wood, and beyond.

As, the oak's laughter slowly died down, the conversation, now turned to more serious matters. Jonti, moved closer to his friend, and his voice changed, as he began to tell him of the grave situation, that their country, and their world, now found itself in.

Oakengarne, remained still and silent, as he listened, to everything his friend told him.

When Jonti had finished speaking, the great oak began to express, his utter horror, at the situation.

'The sovereign, dead!' He began. 'That brings me, great pain and distress.'

'I am so sorry, your Majesty.'

Jonti had now become, more formal in his language and tone, as he felt that it was appropriate, given his news did concern, another king.

'I know that you and King Stefan, were good friends.' Jonti's tone now softened, as he could sense the oak's distress. The air around the tree, had now become thicker, and the sunlight slowly dissipated, as his branches moved, in a swaying motion.

'I had known him, since he was born,' Oakengarne suddenly said. 'His father bought him to see me, the day that he was born. The joy. The hope.' The oak's voice, began to tail off into the wind, that now whistled through his branches.

Jonti took a step back, and beckoned his men, to bring forward the two steeds, with the twins mounted on them.

'Great Oak. I bring you something precious, to keep an eye on for me. Our new joy. Our new hope.'

Oakengarne remained silent, as if taking everything in. Jonti knew, that the oak used his senses to assess the situation.

'The children are twins,' Oakengarne, suddenly said.

'Yes, your Majesty.' Came Jonti's formal reply.

'Their blood is extremely pure. Like, that of a sovereign.'

'Yes, your Majesty.'

'Mmmmm. What of the evil heart?' Oakengarne asked.

'She is King Stefan's sister. Turned by the enemy, whilst put in charge of the twin's welfare, by her brother.'

'I have never met her.' Oakengarne stated.

'Yes. That's right Your Majesty.'

'Jonti. Stop being so formal.' The King of the Oaks mocked.

'Sorry, Sire.' Jonti composed himself and carried on once more. 'She, was born two years, after King Stefan and his brother.'

'Do not! Mention him!' Boomed Oakengarne suddenly, as his lower branches thrashed about, in obvious disdain, at the very mention, of the king's brother.

Jonti, had been taken aback, by the Great Oak's sudden outburst, but had quickly regained his composure, before swiftly continuing, as if nothing had been said.

'I thought, we could see if Tryne, could save her? After all, she is the twin's aunt. Their blood.'

Jonti waited patiently, for the Great Oak's answer. The knight was desperate, for the twins, to be kept safe. He knew, that right now, the safest place for them, would be here, with the King of the Oaks. That would then, give him the time, to assess the situation in Fantaellen, he had reasoned.

'Come forward and enter young knight and seek sanctuary for your precious load.'

'Thank you, my friend,' Jonti replied, gratefully.

With, his command and consent now given, and sanctuary for the precious twins, granted, The King of the Oaks, promptly fell silent.

The hollow, into Oakengarne's inner sanctum, slowly began to reveal, its entrance. Within moments, it appeared to the weary travellers.

'Enter.' Beckoned, a warm and gentle voice.

The entrance into Oakengarne, loomed large and well lit, as Jonti entered. The young knight briefly turned to see that no one, had followed him. He smiled warmly at Geremi, who had Maddie in his arms, before beckoning the young knight and the rest of his men to follow him, as he disappeared from their sight, into the bowels of the Great Oak.

The torches, on the earth wall, flickered, as the last man entered, carrying Josh. Instantly, the entrance behind him, began to close, causing a brief vacuum. Geremi watched, as a moist membrane engulfed the hollow, before the diminished sunlight, from outside, totally disappeared, when the solid bark of Oakengarne, sealed them in.

The wooden steps, that took them down, into the innards of the oak, seemed to go on forever. They were built into a wall of earth, then stone, that descended into the dimly lit darkness, below them. The steps were wide and well-constructed, with a rail either side. Down they spiralled, into the depths of the unknown, taking the visitors, deeper within.

The staircase had moved out from the earth wall, and had taken them outwards, and towards a large wooden platform, that had a rail, around it, with further stairs, leading down.

Jonti, who had stayed ahead of everyone, waited on the platform, for the rest to catch up. Geremi joined him. A wind howled, in the darkness, above them, as both men, looked over the rail.

Silently, they stared into the dimly lit abyss below. The staircase, their only means of progress, seemed to disappear into a dark void, for it to reappear further down, lit by the distant flames of torches.

'Come on', said Jonti. 'Shouldn't be long now.' He remembered, the platform from his last visit, his first visit. It shouldn't be long now, he told himself.

Down, deeper they travelled, the staircase spiralling further still, into the bowels of Oakengarne. All around them, the roots of the great tree, thick, strong and entwined with the earth, the stone and the staircase.

Jonti, could now see the last few steps, as the staircase, spiralled round in a sharp turn, to reach the firm ground, of the lit passageways and caverns of Oakengarne. The very hidden, inner sanctum of the King of the Oaks. They had made it. Sanctuary.

★★★

A little time had passed, since the weary travellers, had reached the passageways and caverns. They had been allocated, a small cave, and Jonti had made sure, that the twins, were safe and comfortable. Jonti, then placed a guard, outside the cave.

He, and his most trusted friend, and second in command stood within the doorway of their cave, discussing their situation.

In the long corridor outside, all sorts of people passed by, men, women and children, all desperate looking. Also, many knights in Fantaellen armour, and the purple robes of their army, filled the long corridors. A look of defeat and despair, on their faces.

The two friends, stared in astonishment, at the sight of their fellow Fantaellen's. There, were so many.

'Jesus.' Geremi whispered.

'At least, they are now safe, young knight.' The voice, spoken from the shadows, in front of them, took Jonti and Geremi by surprise.

Out from the shadows, stepped a troll. A troll, with a huge, long beard, and a chubby, red face. Jonti recognised him, straight away.

'Hello Theo.'

'Hello Jonti.'

The two, stood looking at each other, for a moment, before Jonti eventually approached the troll.

'Good, to see you my friend.' Jonti offered the troll, his hand.

'Yes. You too, young knight.' Theo walked forward, and the two friends shook hands.

Theo and Jonti began to briefly discuss the current situation, in Fantaellen. Geremi listened intently, before being introduced, by his captain and friend.

'Theo. This, is my best friend, and second in command, Geremi Hammam.'

'Pleased, to meet you, young knight.' Theo approached Geremi, and the two shook hands.

'Theo is a tracker, from the Fantaellen Mountains, Jonti began to explain. 'The best in Portaellen. I would not be surprised, if he hasn't been tracking us.'

'Been, tracking you?' Theo mocked, which he followed up with, a wink at Geremi. 'Of course, I have. Hence, that's why I knew, you were here. Also, half the Wulfdaeden spy network, were on my trail. I needed a place to hide out, for a little while. You know, stay low for a little time.'

Theo the troll, was indeed a brilliant tracker, who King Stefan had employed, to do the dirty work, within the shadows. He and his fellow trolls, which there were many, lived in the harsh conditions of the Fantaellen Mountains. They, were very rarely bothered by visitors, or intruders alike, because of the invariably unliveable conditions, of their chosen home. In the deep of winter, no one entered or left, the mountains, as death was inevitable. That was unless, your name was Theo, the most fearless tracker of his kind. For only he and his brother, knew the trails in and out, of the range. And, to mention his brother's name in front of him, would mean, your throat being slit. So, no one did.

'The Great Oak, has asked, for you to bring the evil heart, to the main chamber,' Theo suddenly stated.

'Right,' began Jonti. 'Geremi. You stay with the twins,' he ordered.

'Yes sir.'

'No. Oakengarne wants them there too. He says, that their purest of heart's, will help in the cleansing and ridding of the evil poison, from their aunt's heart.'

In, no time at all, they made their way down the long corridor, with Theo guiding them. Jonti carried Josh, and Geremi carried Maddie, with their aunt being carried, by two knights, in the groundsheet, she slumbered on.

The corridor, seemed to go on forever, until they came to a room, that Theo told them to enter.

The room was cold. A wind whistled through it, and the flames of a fire and the countless torches on the walls danced, creating shadows, all around them.

Theo turned and beckoned for aunt Grimshaw to be placed on a grand, ornately carved table, in the middle of the room. This was the only object, in the vast, cold and airy room.

The troll left. He had briefly smiled at Jonti, before leaving. An uncomfortable silence now existed, as nobody moved. The wind whistled, and the chill remained.

'Welcome, sanctuary seekers!'

Jonti, instantly recognised the voice, of Oakengarne.

At the same time, Josh and Maddie, suddenly sat up, wide awake. Their eyes quickly scanned their surroundings. Bewilderment and fear quickly overcame them. Maddie began to shake, Josh just stared. Then, each twin glanced at each other, then at Jonti, then Geremi, before seeing their aunt, prostrate on the table.

Maddie, her eyes wide in fear, screamed. As, she tried to stand, her legs gave way, and she collapsed to the floor. Geremi moved quickly, to comfort her.

Josh however, seemed to be in a trance, as he stared at Jonti. The young knight slowly approached the boy, so as not to spook him. As he tried to stand; Josh collapsed to the ground. Jonti slowly picked him up and held him.

Maddie, who had now turned hysterical, was hyperventilating, and struggled to breath. Geremi remained calm and slowly bought her into his body, to comfort her.

'It's all right,' he whispered. 'Everything, will be fine.'

A sudden noise, in the corner of the room, grabbed everybody's attention. They watched, as a doorway gradually opened, and a pair of beautiful, sparkling, pure, sky blue eyes, pierced the darkness of the doorway. Then, the most brilliant golden horn, was seen, as the four-legged creature entered the room. Its pure white body, carried on the most graceful four legs. The creature walked so softly, that it made no noise.

Everyone stared in amazement. It was so beautiful. So pure and emanating such peace.

'Her name is Tryne.' Oakengarne declared. 'She is the last known, free Unicorn of Portaellen. She can sense the purity, in the room. Look.' Jonti could see Tryne looking at the twins, then slowly approaching. 'She, can also sense the evil, that is present too.'

Maddie had stopped crying, and her breathing had become normal. She continued to stare at the unicorn, as it approached. Even holding out her hand, in readiness.

As Tryne came closer, Maddie broke free from Geremi, and stood, swaying slightly at first, before she steadied herself, and approached the unicorn, with slow, unsure steps.

Josh followed his sister, his approach cautious at first, with his hand, also held out. Both twins together, now put their hands, on Tryne's mane, warily stroking it at first, before moving in closer, to stroke her head. The Unicorn's beautiful eyes remained fixed on the twins, as they stroked and caressed her head.

'She is beautiful.' Maddie had spoken her first words. Her twin brother smiled at her.

'She is,' he replied, softly.

Maddie looked over at her aunt, for a very brief moment. What, she did next, nobody saw coming. But the little girl knew that it was the right thing to do.

Slowly, she made her way, over to her aunt. She glanced back once at Tryne, who tentatively, made small, silent steps to follow her. As, she reached the ornate wooden table, she looked down at her aunt, before holding her hand.

Tryne joined her, and the two of them, looked at each other, for the shortest of moments.

Jonti approached, and spoke softly to Maddie, he encouraged her to remove her hand, from her aunt's. She did so, almost immediately. She then took a few small steps back.

Tryne, now moved round to the other side of the table. For a moment, she hesitated, before she touched the chest of Aunt

Grimshaw. The unicorn aimed for the heart. Her horn did not need to pierce, flesh and bone. Just, touch the heart. Her power, her purity, would do the rest.

Tryne's horn suddenly began to light up. Her eyes were closed, her head shook slightly, as her power and magic, began to work their way, into the infected body. Aunt Grimshaw remained perfectly still.

Then, in an instant, her body began to violently shake. Aunt Grimshaw began to chant strange words, in a deep, tortured voice. Nobody could make out, what she said, as the words rolled from her tongue, before dying down, and giving way, to a piercing scream, that shot out of her gaping mouth.

A dark, sinister mist, now proceeded to float up, and out of her body, towards the dark shadows of the room. Hurriedly, it turned, to show a contorted, evil face of a bearded man. As if in defiance, the mist let out a scream, that shattered, several glasses, in the room. It then disappeared, as if it had never been there.

In a violent spasm, Aunt Grimshaw's body contorted, into a rigid, deformed form. Tryne backed away. Her work was done. Maddie ran round, to comfort the unicorn, who appeared troubled and drained.

Aunt Grimshaw now fell silent, she was barely breathing. Her body now relaxed. Her arms spread either side of her.

Josh stepped cautiously towards the table. Briefly, the young boy stared at his aunt. She looked so tranquil. Her face had even pinkened, and she immediately, looked younger. She also had a smile on her face. This was the aunt, that Josh suddenly remembered, from way back, when they had first arrived, into her care.

'She will rest now,' Jonti whispered, as he put his arm, around the boy. 'She is cleansed.'

★★★

The rock men had finally made a breakthrough, along a small section of the main outer wall. The Fantaellen bowmen, had managed to pin them down for a while, when the enemy had reached the flatter, top part of the hill, but unlike the day before, there were less fire arrows, and no fiery blaze, to greet them. Up their ladder's, the hordes of Granite Island warriors duly climbed. Their blood curdling screams, drove them upwards, with such speed and agility, that they had suddenly overwhelmed the enemy. Along the ramparts, they now charged instinctively slashing, hacking and killing with no feelings. Their blades, carving a path, along the battlements, as Fantaellen blood soaked the ground, once more.

They had now tasted blood. They liked it. Blood drunk, and wanting more, the warriors of Granite Island screamed their war cry, charged forward, and killed, without feeling.

★★★

The sky was filled with Fantaellen arrows, that rained down on the enemy, like a storm of defiance. The attack on the main entrance, of Guinlance Castle had begun, with hundreds of Wulfdaeden's, gigahominums and centrolls, dying in the initial volleys. These bodies slowed, the subsequent surge, of the knights and the creatures, who followed.

From the two towers that stood at opposite ends of the main outer wall and overlooking the carnage below, an order quickly went out. Countless crossbow bolts were now systematically fired, into the faltering charge, of the enemy. Within seconds, the deadly bolts, flensed through skin, and penetrated flesh. Large numbers of enemy knights and creatures were killed or maimed, in an instant.

The Wulfdaeden reply, was ready, to be released. The engineers awaited their general's order's. Timing was everything in battle, he believed.

Just, a moment longer.

General Grafton ordered his engineers, to fire rapid and constant barrages, aimed at ceasing, the Fantaellen arrows and bolts. A storm of missiles, immediately flew from the trebuchets, that had been bought forward earlier, to a position, near the first outer wall. The onslaught of the hurtling rocks, quickly succeeded in pinning down the archers and the crossbowmen on the ramparts, of the walls and towers. Enabling his attack on the ground, to immediately regain its momentum, once more.

Scores of gigahominums, now ran forward in pairs, carrying long wooden beams. Whilst, dodging the barrage of crossbow bolts and arrows, some of the creatures managed to lay their boards, across the deep chasm, just in front of the main entrance, of the main outer wall. Many others, either thrown off balance, or hit by the bolts and arrows, from the enemy ramparts, fell into the sheer drop beneath them. Every one of them, instantly crashing down, upon the hundreds of deadly wooden spikes, in the depths, below. The screams of the dying soon diminished.

With the missiles, still smashing into the castle and its wall's, the charge was suddenly sounded.

So, they came.

General Grafton's knight's and creatures now charged the wall, as if their lives depended on it. Their scream's reverberated and cut through the air, as they ran.

With, the sound of the resurrected Blackheart charge, the Fantaellen bowmen, once more, took to standing on the ramparts, to fire their weapons en masse, as the unceasing bombardment, of enemy missiles, killed many, and continued to shake the very foundations, of the castle.

When the ladders, reached the wall, the climb into the unknown began. Countless ladders were now filled with Blackheart knights and gigahominums, who tried to scale the wall, as quickly, as they could. The ladders had been custom built, to climb, the steep, high, vertical walls of Guinlance Castle.

Still, many enemy knights and creatures, that attempted to cross the wooden beams, to gain a foothold, on the narrow ground at the main entrance, were being quickly cut down, by crossbowmen, as they waited to get onto a run, of a ladder. The concentrated line of fire, shot through the narrow, arrow loops, on the walls, high above the raised drawbridge, had sent many, into the deadly depths of the chasm.

Desperate, Fantaellen archers and crossbowmen, continued to fire at anything that moved. They were, quickly running out of arrows and bolts, and their weakened numbers, made it difficult for them, to keep up the momentum, as the enemy, continued to climb further up their ladder's.

Hordes of Blackhearts and gigahominums, suddenly breached the top of the wall, at various points, and stages, along its vast length. Quickly, they began to charge along the ramparts, towards startled Fantaellen archers and crossbowmen. Almost, at once, many defenders, were slaughtered, thereupon.

Several missiles suddenly smashed into the east tower of Guinlance Castle. Instantaneously, the tower shook, with the impact. A large crack quickly shot up the tower's stonework, before the rampart, swiftly fell away from the foundations, taking the bowmen with it. Their screams of terror were eventually drowned out, as the rest of the tower suddenly exploded, and came crashing down, within a tremendous tumult of noise, stonework, rubble and blinding dust.

The falling stonework and debris, that had scattered over a large area of the castle grounds and ramparts, consequently crushed and disintegrated, anything beneath it.

All, along the wall, the Wulfdaeden's and their creature allies, had now broken the main resistance on the ramparts, and streamed down the steps, into the castle courtyard and grounds.

They were instantly met, with a charge from a large number of Fantaellen knights. A clash of steel now ensued, as the Fantaellens fought desperately, to repel the Blackheart and creature swarms.

The formidable numbers of the invaders were soon overwhelming their enemy. Many Pure Hearts died, trying to defend their ground, and more importantly, the raised drawbridge.

The Fantaellen's, now launched another counterattack. This time, with greater numbers. At their head, Wilfred, his sword raised high and the blood pumping through his heart.

'For Fantaellen!' He screamed, as he lead the way.

With one swipe, Wilfred killed a Wulfdaeden, who had dared to charge at him. Before, the gutted Wulfdaeden had hit the ground,

Wilfred had taken the arm of a gigahominum, then plunged his blade into a Blackheart, who had lunged at him.

'Come on!' He screamed.

Onwards he went, his men following behind, slashing, cutting and stabbing their way, through the Blackheart hordes.

Many enemy knights and creatures died in their charge.

'We must hold, the main entrance.' He told his men.

The captain of the royal guard, and his men, made it to the main entrance. His sword was soaked with blood, and there were countless bodies around them. His heartbeat so fast in his chest, as he surveyed, the situation. There were still skirmishes, going on above him, on the ramparts, and Fantaellen's were dying, everywhere.

He and his men had repelled a Blackheart attack, at the main entrance. For now, they held it.

'Sergeant!' Wilfred cried out.

A breathless young knight joined him.

'Yes sir?'

'Have the men form a shield wall, here in front of the main entrance.'

'Yes sir.'

A desperate cry suddenly went out, as the sergeant turned to carry out his captain's order.

'Arrows!'

A storm of Wulfdaeden arrows, quickly cut through Wilfred's men, as he watched helplessly. Not one man, was spared.

Wilfred ran over to his sergeant, who had a Blackheart arrow, buried deep in his chest. He watched, as the life left, the young knight's body, as he clawed, at the black arrow.

The main gate! They cannot take it>!

The captain of the royal guard now sprang into action. He grabbed his sword, and a discarded shield, before turning to face the crazed hordes, of the enemy.

'Come on!' He cried, as he held out his arms. 'What? You scared?'

The last thing Wilfred saw, as a swarm of enemy knights, descended on the main entrance, were the last battalions of Fantaellen regiment's, forming up to receive the enemy, in what he believed, would be a last defence.

The captain of the royal guard died defending the main entrance, and the ropes and gears of the drawbridge. His body was brutally cut into pieces, then thrown at the lines of Fantaellen knights, who had formed up, in readiness.

The thick, high walls of the castle had failed to repel, the invaders thus far. Now, it was the fate of the several depleted regiments, to defend Guinlance Castle, the people and the creatures that remained, the Throne of Fantaellen, and more importantly, the throne of the Sovereign of Portaellen. Everything, that made up the very fabric, of their world.

When, the drawbridge, came crashing down, the sound thundered through the courtyard. As the dust settled, the screams of the charging rock men, centrolls and Blackhearts, sent a shiver down the spine of the Fantaellen knights, formed up into their lines.

An officer presently drew his sword. His numbers had been swelled, with the injured from the infirmary, and any able-bodied men, or young boy, able to wield a sword, or carry a lance.

'Shield wall!' He screamed, before catching the eye of someone, he knew. He smiled at him.

Henri nervously returned a smile.

Hundreds of Fantaellen shields, now smashed into the earth. 'Present! Lances!'

Hundreds of lances were instantly thrust forward.

The shield wall now braced itself for the impact.

It was coming. In the form of hundreds of demented, blood drunk, enemy knights and creatures, who were just a heartbeat away, from taking their castle, their country, the throne of a king, and a sovereign.

★★★

Jonti Quixall, had left the twins, in the charge of his second in command. It was decided that they would be safer, in the sanctuary of Majestic Wood and with Oakengarne. That had been the plan,

209

as soon as he had found out about the attack on Guinlance. Now, with the children safe, he could move around, with a bit more freedom. He needed to assess the situation, around the country and find out, first-hand, what was happening at the capital. He knew that things were bad. He just needed to know, how bad. At least now, he could operate in more dangerous surroundings, without having to think about anybody else's welfare.

Alone, the young knight rode out of the Majestic Wood, as the shadows lengthened, and the two suns, came down, on their horizon, to signal the end of another day.

The oaks and the beeches whispered their farewells on a breeze, as Jonti's steed, bolted out of the wood.

In great earnest, Jonti pushed his steed, towards the sunsets. For, as beautiful and enchanting, the blaze of golden sunlight was, his focus was beyond that horizon.

★★★

In an area, just outside of the Majestic Wood, where the newest saplings grew, lurked a lone figure, in a hooded cloak. He was a creature of the shadows. Silently, and patiently, he waited unable to enter the wood, for fear of being spotted, or found, not to be of pure heart.

When, he saw Jonti riding out of the wood, he congratulated himself, on his tracking skills. He knew that his initial hunch would have been right. The young knight had put the children, within the sanctuary of the King of the Oaks.

'Oakengarne.' As, he had said the name outload, he did so, in a mocking tone. 'Ha!' He exclaimed, 'Pathetic.'

What, Jonti Quixall now did, was not his concern. As a creature of the shadows, he would report back his intelligence, to others. Hopefully, his information would gain him, some credence with his master.

It was time to report back. The twins were going nowhere.

As fast, as his short, stubby legs could carry him, Napoleon Victory's, number one spy, as he called himself, left his hiding place.

It was time, for Normauss the troll, to shine.

PART II

THE DARK EPOCH

Chapter Thirteen

Untold numbers of refugees filled the open wheat fields, around Guinlance and beyond. Forced into running for their lives, from the ferocious onslaught of the Blackheart invasion, pockets of men, women and children, from the same towns and villages, had joined other groups, who they had encountered en route. Nobody knew, where they were heading, for most had left in haste, with only the clothes they had on, and with whatever they could carry. Food, water and any type of weapons, taking preference.

Cloud cover, over the two full moons of the night, now provided the fleeing, with an element of concealment. Yet still they feared an unexpected attack, from anywhere. Whilst the horizon, at their backs, glowed with an orange hue. The deadly consequence, of the fires from the many burning towns and village, that had been raised, by the merciless enemy.

The noise of war and battle from the capital, had all but abated. Images of looting, killing and blood drunk lunacy, now filled their heads, as the noises of the darkness, played with tired, and desperate minds.

A small group of men, dressed in the armour and blood-soaked robes of Fantaellen knights, had suddenly startled a small group of refugees, when they had appeared, armed with swords and crossbows.

A man, carrying a heavy ladened sack, and dressed in a purple hooded robe, stepped forward from the trees. He tried to calm their fears, as he explained, who he was, and where, they were from. Placing the sack on the ground, the man now walked towards the startled refugees. His face was covered in sweat and blood, and his robes were ripped. They could see that he had no sword, at his side. And so, he posed no imminent threat.

Henri had dropped his sword, when he had run from the fury and death, of the shield wall, in the courtyard. The blood on his face, was that of the men either side of him, within the wall. He too, was now a refugee. A royal physician, who had barely escaped, with his life, from the slaughter and subsequent capitulation, of Guinlance and its castle.

Henri had noticed a small boy, who seemed to be alone. He carried a bloodied sword. Beside him, walked a strong, black hound, his head almost wolf shaped. Henri approached the hound, who growled when the physician held out his hand, to stroke him.

'He doesn't like strangers.' The boy stated abruptly.

'What's his name?' Henri enquired, as he slowly pulled his hand away.

'Zevarn.' Came, the reluctant reply.

'A good, strong name.' Henri remarked.

'Yes. It means warrior, in the old language.'

'I see,' said Henri, as he now stared at the bloodied sword, that the boy carried in his small hands. 'And the sword?'

'Taken, from the body of a Blackheart, who I killed.'

'Right. It's, a nice sword.'

'It is,' agreed the boy. 'And it's mine.'

'I have no doubt of that. So, what is the name of the young boy, who owns such a fine sword?'

The young boy looked up at Henri. The royal physician, could see a burning flame of desire and strength, never seen before in the eyes, of someone so young. It sent a chill, down his spine.

'My name is Arami Corder,' the young boy said, with an unbridled pride.

Jonti, rode his steed Braern, hard. He knew that his mount, could take it. He needed to get to Guinlance, as fast as he could. However, he had cautiously chosen his route, as he needed to stay aware of any enemy movement, along the way. Strangely, he had seen none, thus far.

What, Jonti did see, were small groups of men, women and children, just wandering through the fields. The nearer he got to the capital, the more he began to see. He had stopped at one point, to speak to a small band of children, who were totally alone. They told him, that they had fled their village, on the north coast. Everybody had been killed, and they had only got away, because they were near, the underground tunnels, that they had used to escape, when the attack came.

Jonti told them, to head east, to a wood, called the Majestic Wood. He reassured them, that they would be safe there. Before riding away, the young knight, gave them some food, from his satchel.

After riding hard, for about an hour, Jonti came to a clearing, that looked out, onto a large wheat field. There he stayed for a moment, staring into the darkness, in disbelief, at the sight before him. He could not believe, what he saw.

Where, have all these people come from?

With a gentle kick, into Braern's hide, the young knight, made his way towards a group of men. They wore the armour, of the Fantaellen army, and one of them, had a purple hooded robe on. The hood concealed his face.

Approaching them with care, Jonti saw the look of defeat, in their eyes. Their armour was covered in blood, their heads were down, as they trudged through the wheat.

The man in the hooded robe, lifted his hood off, and walked towards Jonti. The young knight, suddenly recognised, the bloodied face.

'Henri?' He was instantly, taken aback, by the appearance, of the man before him.

'Master Quixall.'

'What happened?' Jonti asked.

The royal physician, tried to compose himself, as he stared at Jonti, desperately looking for the words to begin, as tears welled up in his eyes. His voice faltered slightly, as he began.

'They came at us.' Henri stopped, as his voice, suddenly broke.

'It's fine my friend. Take your time.'

Jonti offered Henri some water who drank deeply before continuing. This time, his voice did not waver as he began.

'They came at us, in the main courtyard, of the castle. They, had stormed the walls, overwhelmed the archers and crossbowmen, and had taken down the drawbridge. More than half of our men had been poisoned, the night before, when drinking from the well in the barracks. So, our numbers, were severely depleted. Anybody, who could wield a sword, or carry a lance, were called to the shield wall. I included. We held them back, for as long as we could, but there were just too many of them. The giant creatures, with huge swords, cut swathes, through our shield walls. Fantaellen knights died, in their hundreds, and their blood soaked the ground. The men either side of me, were cut to shreds, by Blackheart blades. So, I ran, as the wall collapsed.' Henri now looked at Jonti. He had a look of guilt, in his eyes. Tears ran down his face.

'You did the right thing,' Jonti said reassuringly.

'I am not a warrior,' Henri sobbed. 'So, I ran, as fast as I could. Towards the royal gardens. Up, the hill I went. The noise, of the charging enemy, behind me, drove me forward. Eventually, I made it to the castle. My first thought was for the crown of Fantaellen. So, I made my way towards, the throne room. Out the windows, I could see, the enemy, as they charged up the hill, slaughtering everybody, as they ran towards the castle. Once, I arrived in the throne room, I grabbed the crown, the orb and the sceptre. I knew, I had very little time. So, I then made my way to a secret door, in the throne room, and down the secret passageways, I ran. Eventually, coming out on the jetty, upon the moat, whereupon I rowed for the shore.'

Henri passed Jonti the sack. It weighed heavy, in his hands.

'The poison?' Jonti enquired, as he secured the sack, on Braern.

'They had someone, on the inside. They must have had. Because up until that point, we had held them. The walls of Guinlance Castle would never been breached. We killed hundreds of them, around the walls. Their general, just kept throwing his knights and creatures, at us, and we just kept repelling them. Even when, their missiles were thrown at us. Robert was confident, that the castle walls would hold. They just kept coming. Those crazed, blood drunk, heathen hordes of Blackheart killers.' His voice faltered, as he finished. 'We were overwhelmed once they breached the ramparts. We, could not hold them back.'

Jonti could hear the pain, in the physician's voice.

'What happened, to Robert?' he asked.

'It was thought best, that he should leave Guinlance, before an attempt, on his life was made, by whatever assassin, lurked in the shadows. He, and his men, escaped to a secret location, before the walls fell. I pray, that he is safe.'

The two men continued to discuss, the dire situation, that they now found themselves in.

It was shortly agreed that the desperate refugees, from the wheat fields around Guinlance, and further afield, would be offered the shelter, of the King of the Oaks.

Jonti felt sick, to the pit of his stomach. He felt so helpless. He reasoned with himself, that his time to spill Wulfdaeden blood would come. This night was not the night for that. Tonight, was about the safety of the refugees.

The Fantaellen capital, and its castle, had fallen. His country was on its knees. And, Jonti Quixall had just been informed, that Napoleon Victory, had been seen, on Fantaellen soil. For the first time, since his brother had exiled him.

★★★

The air was thick, with the smell of death. The smouldering fires, all over the once peaceful country of Fantaellen, created a thick smoke, that threatened to engulf, the two suns, as they ascended, the early morning sky.

All over Guinlance and its castle, the Blackheart drums of victory, had resonated throughout the shattered walls, since the first moment of its capitulation, and the last drop of Fantaellen blood, had been spilt.

The mass clearance of the innumerable number of bodies, within and around the walls of Guinlance had continued throughout the night. Mass graves had been dug near the Wulfdaeden camp, and out in the fields beyond. The task had been enormous, and was still being carried out, with the first light of the new day.

Word had reached General Grafton, that his master, had been seen, just a few miles from Guinlance. The general had organised a display of victory, for his friend and master. He had been giving out his orders, to his officers all night. Since first light, he had overseen the final preparations, before riding the route, his master would take. Making sure that everything, was to his own satisfaction.

In the courtyard of Guinlance Castle, the general remained, waiting, mounted on his black steed. Surrounded by his officers, and numerous lines of drummers, he looked around and smiled, at the countless Fantaellen bodies, purposefully left scattered around, to hopefully heighten the pleasure of his master, as he rode over the drawbridge, and into the courtyard.

General Grafton now ordered the prisoners to be bought out. Blindfolded, the four Fantaellen knights, stumbled. Their feet and their hands bound. They were abruptly shoved onto their knees. The drums now instantly fell silent, upon the orders of their general.

In the courtyard, an eerie silence now existed, as a cold, harsh wind, whipped through, the open quadrangle, as the red banners and flags of Wulfdaeden, danced.

High, in the sky above, circling the highest towers of the castle, hundreds of scavenger birds flew, desperate for a taste of rotting, bloated flesh.

★★★

The Wulfdaeden army, camped in and around the fields of Guinlance, suddenly came to life, whilst a hurried message was quickly passed down, the incalculable rows of pitched tents.

Riders had been seen.

The officers, around the camp, ordered all their men and creatures, to stand to attention, outside their tents, in full battle armour, and in complete silence. Any failure to comply, would result in instant death.

Over the brow of the hill, they came. Two dozen Blackheart riders, on magnificent black steeds. They wore the armour of the Imperial Guard. The gold plate, of their chest armour, with the silver emblem of the three lances, shining brilliantly, as they rode. In the centre rode a giant of a man, his black hood up, concealing his face.

'That's him.' Came the whispers, as the riders entered the camp.

The sound of Wulfdaeden horns, and the slow melodic beat, of the drums of victory, signalled their appearance. Officers saluted their passing. The riders, looking staunchly forward, as their black steed's, steadily carried them onwards, towards the castle.

Leaving, the camp behind, the riders headed towards the ruined, city walls. After negotiating the rubble, the debris, and the burnt out, smouldering buildings of the city, they were greeted by the chorus of hundreds of Blackheart drums, at the entrance of the narrowing passageway, that led to the smashed, first outer wall.

Countless lines of drummers, and knights, stood down both sides of the passageway. The beat of the drums was deafening, as it resounded around, the man-made entrance, into the castle.

Along the first outer wall huge spikes had been thrust into the soil. On them, were placed the heads, of several Fantaellen archers and crossbowmen. Their headless bodies were then strung up, by their feet, from the arch way of the entrance.

Riding, towards the drawbridge into the castle, the riders were ceremoniously greeted with the sight of hundreds of Wulfdaeden lances, raised in salute, of their arrival.

As, their hooves thundered over the drawbridge, the riders raced through the enormous archway, to then make a sudden and dramatic entrance, into the courtyard.

Their entrance was heralded, with the furious beat of Wulfdaeden drums, as General Grafton, dismounted his steed. His officers and knights, then sprang to attention. Then, on their general's signal, the drums suddenly fell silent.

The giant of a man dismounted his magnificent black steed and walking over to the general, he removed his black hood. General Grafton smiled, and held open his arms. He hoped, his master was pleased.

Napoleon Victory was, indeed, joyous. His evil heart had never felt such joy and happiness. Looking around, at the Fantaellen bodies, strewn around the courtyard, he experienced a feeling of elation, and laughed, uncontrollably when he saw a large, black carrion bird, land on a corpse, and begin to peck at the lifeless eyes.

The laughter stopped suddenly, as the two friends embraced. General Grafton craved acceptance, for what he had achieved. As they parted, he looked at his friend, who smiled at him.

Rubbing his scarred face, Napoleon Victory stared at the prisoners, kneeling before him.

'Are, they for me?' He asked.

'Yes Sire. We thought, we'd let you decide if they were to be turned or executed.'

'Mmmm. Kill the first and the third one. Turn the other two.'

General Grafton, then gave the signal, and the two ordered to be executed, had their throats cut, there and then.

'You, have done well my friend.' Victory stated, as he watched the two Fantaellen knights choke on their blood, as the cuts across their throats, simultaneously opened up. The two knights collapsed on to the ground, gasping for air, as the blood now haemorrhaged from their wound, which soon covered the earth beneath them, in a thick, red river. Napoleon Victory watched them die, before he ordered their heads to be taken, from their lifeless bodies, and displayed next to their countrymen, along the first outer wall.

His order was instantly executed.

General Grafton, now spoke to his master and friend, as the two walked together.

'There, are still small pockets of resistance, Sire. And, we are still awaiting intelligence, on the whereabouts of your niece and nephew.'

Napoleon Victory, spoke almost immediately, as his general, waited for a response.

'Fantaellen, is broken General,' Victory stated, 'And, my friend, we stand within the walls, of the last great symbol of hope and defiance. My father always told me, of the importance of Guinlance. When, my brother exiled me from my homeland, I swore that I would take it back. Well! Here I am, brother!'

As he said this, he looked up at the sky, and mockingly, he threw a kiss, skywards.

The man, born Michael Grimshaw, was now back in Fantaellen, for the first time, since being exiled. This was his birth right. He, had waited, so long, for this moment. Fantaellen, was now his.

Chapter Fourteen

Josh and Maddie had slept well. It had been a natural sleep, too. Not one delivered, by a tissue, over the mouth. Rather, a sleep born out of sheer exhaustion. Whilst, they had slept, Geremi Hammam, had stood on guard duty, outside their cave.

Oakengarne had asked for the twins, to be bought over to the Peace Room once he had learned of their waking. The room was where tranquillity existed, deep in the depths of the King of the Oaks. Located, far within his roots and soil.

As they walked, the children stayed silent, looking around at everything, that was going on around them. The people and strange looking creatures, going about their business, held a fascination, for them both. Indeed, the interesting and mesmerising creatures, had them staring, not out of rudeness, but by the sheer fact, that they were spellbound. Never, having seen anything, like them, before.

Geremi smiled to himself, as he watched the children, cautiously looking at creatures, who were not strange to him. And those he took for granted, as always being around.

Along the passageways, and within the doorways and cavernous rooms, leading off the torch lit walkways, many creatures of Portaellen origin lurked. Including trollogres, mono optis, trolls, and the nasty vermin, known as thrats.

The trolls, of which there were many, seemed to be huddled in the shadows. They stood away from their distant related, cross breed ilk, the trollogres, who were taller, and wider in stature.

A chubby, red faced troll, with a long beard, had smiled at Geremi and the twins, as they had passed.

'Hello Theo.' Geremi called, as they carried on.

The troll winked at the two children, as they passed. Maddie turned her head and smiled, whereas Josh seemed to be someplace else, as there was no reaction, from the boy.

As well as the people, the trolls and the other creatures, there were many animals, such as deer, birds, foxes, rabbits, squirrels, and all manner of countryside creatures. Even domestic animals, including dogs and cats. All, driven away from their natural surroundings, by fear. Whether, human or creature, they had all sought the sanctuary, of Oakengarne.

The look in Maddie's eyes, had suddenly, become very intense. It was if she was staring at something beyond, their surroundings. Geremi, then saw, a deep, confused, frightened look, develop in her eyes. A look of shock, like that, when you suddenly know, of the presence of an unknown fear, located ahead of you. Then, as if she had come back to their surroundings, Maddie would look up at the young knight. Whereupon, her normal look of innocence, returned. This happened a couple of times.

The young knight tried small talk, to pass the time, as they walked. The children stayed silent. Geremi persevered, in a gentle way, to reassure them, of their new surroundings. Even more so, when several small, black creatures, ran past them in the shadows, nearest to the ground. They were thrats. Three headed rats, that were not the disease carrier, of old. Nevertheless, they were nasty, and would give you a vicious bite, if one of their heads, felt threatened.

'Look up children. See.' Geremi swiftly pointed upwards, to quickly change the subject. 'The roots of Oakengarne, go on forever. They are his roots of life. They keep the Great Oak, alive. They, keep his heart pumping.'

The children, gaped at the sight, above their heads, of the hundreds of thick roots, ascending into the lofty, dark heights, of Oakengarne. They did indeed, provide, the great tree, with the moisture and nutrients, that he needed. As well as, a firm and stable support, for his enormous trunk and branches.

Maddie, suddenly gasped, when a small furry creature, with an eye, in the middle of its head, grabbed hold of her hand. It had come from out of nowhere and had startled her. She was frozen, to the spot. A look, of complete fear, upon her face.

'Don't worry Maddie. It is harmless.' The next few words just fell out of Geremi's mouth, as they eventually, continued, their walk. 'Well, lucky for us, they are, now harmless.' His voice had trailed off, as he finished speaking. Geremi, suddenly wished, that he had not said the last bit, out loud. What, was he thinking? He looked for a reaction, from either child.

I don't think they heard me. Phew!

The small creature was a mono opti. That was a name, given to them, by Oakengarne. Over the years, they had stowed away on Wulfdaeden ships, and had arrived in Fantaellen, in swarms. Originally, they were called Flesh Goblins, and were renowned for taking the flesh off the bone, of anything, dead or alive. Many, of the vicious creatures were killed, the rest were cleansed, and sold to rich Fantaellen's, as cute and cuddly pets.

Geremi kept his eye on Maddie, as she stroked the mono opti, who was presently joined, by several more of its kind, also looking for attention and affection. The little girl smiled, as the creatures, wrestled for the merest of attention, as they jumped up and down, in excitement.

'Come on Maddie,' called out Geremi. 'We have got to go.'

The young knight shooed the lively, energetic creatures away with the gentle push of his hands. The excited mono optis, in due course obliged, and were soon gone. Back, into the shadows.

'Goodbye,' called Maddie.

When, they reached the Peace Room, the children were told to take a seat, at a huge, elaborate, wooden table. On the table, a banquet, of fruits, nuts, seeds, and bread, was laid out. With ornate, hand carved jugs of water, at opposite ends of the table. Before he left them, Geremi told them that they could eat and drink.

'You must be hungry?' he said.

As, he went to leave the room, Geremi saw the look of fear, in the children's faces. He smiled at them warmly.

'It's all right. I will be outside. Oakengarne, will be with you shortly. His voice will be all around you. Do not be scared. Now eat.'

The two children did not need telling twice. They had never seen, most of the food on the table before, never mind tasted it. They were hungry, and everything looked so tempting. They both, walked around the table, first tasting, then placing, whatever they liked, upon the wooden plate, in their hand. Soon, both had a full plate, and were greedily consuming, their food, as fast as they could.

The Peace Room was vast. The earth walls had mirrors upon them, at intervals. The floor had a lush moss covering, that was soft and cushioned, when walked on. In the roots above, beautiful white doves, were nested. In addition, a highly decorated, candle lit chandelier, hung down from a thick root, located in the ceiling. They were suddenly joined, by an elderly man with greying hair, who sat in the corner and began to play a huge, golden harp. The melodic, gentle music now resonated throughout the room. The air, appeared cleaner, fresher and cooler, because of several tunnels, built into the ceiling, that went up to the surface. A welcome calmness existed, within its walls, which showed why, the room had been given, its name.

The old man on the harp, suddenly stopped playing, as if on cue. He stood up, and left the room, not before, bowing before the children.

'He recognises royalty.' Came, a sudden voice from above them. Josh and Maddie instantly looked up.

'No, need to look up children. I am all around you. Please, carry on eating and drinking. We need, to build your strength up.' There was an immediate silence, as the children continued to eat.

'I will formally introduce myself, to you both now. My name is Oakengarne. I am the King of the Oaks. You, have been bought to me, for sanctuary.'

'Are, we at the bottom, of our aunt's garden?' Josh spluttered, as he spoke with his mouth still full.

'Dear child.' Oakengarne's voice had an obvious tone of irritation, as he continued. 'Have you not been taught, to not speak, with your mouth full?'

Josh finished chewing his food, before answering.

'Yes. Sorry sir. We were normally beaten around the head, for it. It feels different here. I just forgot myself, for a moment. Sorry.'

'Same principals, of manners apply here young Josh. Though, I promise you, on my beating, wooden heart, that no one, will lay a finger on you, or your sister, whilst you are within, my sanctuary.'

Oakengarne let the two children have their fill, of the wonderful food, and clear, cool water, whilst he enquired how they were feeling. He wanted, to put them at ease. To make them, feel as comfortable, as possible.

'So, how old are you both?' he enquired.

'We, are nine,' replied Josh.

'Who, is the eldest?'

'Josh is,' Maddie said quietly.

'By five minutes,' Josh stated proudly.

'Our mother died when we were babies,' Maddie stated.

'So, sorry.'

Oakengarne knew the truth, of their mother's death. She had died, giving birth, to the twins. Her last breath left her body, as she gave birth to her daughter.

At this point, Oakengarne chose to stay quiet, and let the children speak. He knew that they had more to say.

'And our father is away exploring.' Josh had walked into the middle of the room, to look around, at all the mirrors. 'We haven't seen him since we were six. Our aunt has been telling us for a while, that he was dead. Ever since she changed. She used to be, so nice.'

'But, we know, that he is still alive,' Maddie, suddenly said.

'Yes, he is,' piped up Josh.

'He is just exploring,' continued Maddie. 'He will come and take us home soon. Wherever that is?'

Oakengarne, continued with the gentle questioning. He could see that the two children knew nothing, of their current situation, and the fate, of their mother and their father. Which meant, that they also knew nothing, of their importance and their destiny. The children seemed so naive. He needed to do this gently, he decided.

He began in, the best way, he knew how. With, the one thing, that all children loved.

'I am going to tell you both, a story,' the Great Oak, started.

'Oh! How wonderful,' exclaimed Josh.

'Is it, a good story?' enquired Maddie.

'It's a true story,' replied Oakengarne. 'About, two brothers.'

'Oh! Great!' exclaimed Josh, in excitement, his mouth still full. 'Sorry.' He, then spluttered.

The Peace Room suddenly fell silent, and the light from the chandelier began to diminish. The children looked up, to see a wisp of smoke, from several candles, as if they had just been blown out.

'Our story begins, in a world, that you are not familiar with,' started Oakengarne.

Josh and Maddie looked at each other. They, both liked stories. Especially ones, about distant lands. It had been a long time since they had heard a story. Any, kind of story. Their aunt had stopped telling them stories. Which, they were both glad about, as her tales, had become very dark and scary, over time.

'It is a tale of two brothers. Stefan and Michael. They were twins.'

'Like us!' shouted Maddie, instantly.

Oakengarne said nothing, before carrying on with his story.

'They both lived in a country, called Fantaellen. It was a peaceful country, in a world called Portaellen. The two boys were Dual Bloods.'

'What, are Dual Bloods?' asked Josh.

Oakengarne did not reply. Choosing to carry on with his story.

'Their mother and their father were the king and queen of Fantaellen, which made the two boys, the Princes of Fantaellen. Their father was very proud of his son's, as they grew into strong and intelligent young men. They showed great skill with a sword, both having been trained, by the best swordsmen, in the country. The king, became especially proud, of his eldest son, Stefan, who was only five minutes older than his twin brother, because, he showed great potential, to fulfil, his destiny.'

The Peace Room now fell silent, as the light decreased once more, until, just several candles, remained lit. Maddie, felt a shiver, go through her.

'Stefan's destiny was suddenly thrust upon him, when their father, suddenly died, and their mother, shortly thereafter, from a suspected broken heart. Their first-born son, his blood being the purest, was now the king of Fantaellen, and the Sovereign of Portaellen.'

The children listened intently, as Oakengarne told them, how the country rallied around the new king, after the death of his father. The country had been so peaceful. Times were good, for the people. The new king, also fell in love, with a beautiful girl, called Emily, who was the daughter, of one of his general's. The two were quickly married.

'A couple, of years later, children followed. Twins,' continued Oakengarne. 'Sadly, Emily died in childbirth. Just managing to give life, to their daughter, before taking her last breath.'

'Stop!' shouted Maddie. 'This story is now making me sad. I want to leave. Where is Geremi?'

'It's all right.' The young knight had entered the room. 'I am here.' Geremi put his arm around Maddie. 'You need to hear, what Oakengarne is telling you,' he said gently.

'All right,' Maddie replied, as she composed herself.

Oakengarne, continued once more. 'The two brothers began to argue. A lot.'

The King of the Oaks, began to spin a tale, which involved an argument, about who was the king, and King Stefan banishing his twin, from the country.

The truth though, was probably, a lot darker and sinister. For, many dark rumours, had come from the court of Guinlance Castle. Too nasty and evil, to even contemplate. Oakengarne, treated them, for what they were, rumours. He had prayed though, to the gods, that they were not true. And he vowed, to never speak of them. This day would be no exception.

Once, King Stefan did come to the Majestic Wood, in the dead of night, to seek council from Oakengarne, on the issue of his brother. The king had told the Great Oak, that his twin brother had been captured and turned, whilst on a mission, in Wulfdaeden.

One night, Michael had crept into the king's chambers, with the intent of killing him. A member of the king's guard, who had been close to Michael, had heard about the planned attack on the king, and had warned him. As Michael, had entered the king's chamber, with a knife in his hand, he was captured, and detained.

The fate, of his twin, lay in the king's hand's. Deciding not to execute his twin brother, out of love for him, the king exiled him, from Fantaellen. He would not have the blood of his twin, on his hands, he had said.

It was rumoured, that Michael had managed to get to Wulfdaeden, in a small boat. A miracle, given the unforgiving currents, crashing waves and the winds of the Stoirim Sea. Once there, it was rumoured, that he had joined the Wulfdaeden army, before working his way through the ranks, and becoming a prominent general.

Within weeks, news filtered through of the mysterious death of the major general, who had reportedly promoted Michael, through the ranks. This suddenly pushed him into the reckoning, to become the supreme leader of the Wulfdaeden Army.

Intelligence had reached King Stefan, that the entire Wulfdaeden army, its officer's and its men had rallied around Michael, when he announced, who he really was, and his birth given lineage. At this point, he announced, his change of name, to Napoleon Victory, and that he would begin his plans to invade Fantaellen, kill his twin, the king, and bring the country to its knees. He would then, place himself on the Throne of Portaellen, which would make him the sovereign of their world.

The intelligence had placed the Fantaellen army, on high alert, and had seen, a doubling of the guard, around the king and sovereign.

So, Oakengarne continued, with his spun tale, for several minutes, which had contained, a large element of truth, to it. The children had remained silent, as he had carried on.

'Michael rowed across the Stoirim Sea, in a small boat. He managed to get to a country called Wulfdaeden, where he became a great warrior. Eventually, he was promoted through the ranks of the army, before becoming its supreme leader, years later. In the meantime, King Stefan became ill. He then died, some days later, from a fever.'

The King of the Oaks fell silent once more. It was an uncomfortable silence. A silence, where the person who had spoken did not know what to say, at that point.

'What happened, to the king's children?' asked Josh.

'They are …' Geremi, instantly stopped, as he corrected himself. 'They were safe. The king had ordered that his children, shall be taken to a safe place.'

'Yes,' continued Oakengarne, 'The king, placed his dear children, into the safe keeping of his sister. Unfortunately, Michael, who had changed his name to Napoleon Victory, bought a vast army of knights and creatures to the shores of Fantaellen. It, wasn't long after the death of his brother, that he had invaded Fantaellen, and bought the country to its knees.'

As if by magic, the candlelight slowly increased in the Peace Room. The heaviness in the atmosphere now lifted, as one by one, each unlit candle, relit by itself. The two children, watched in disbelief, and in awe of what they saw.

'The story, you have been told,' began Oakengarne, once more, his voice very calm and soothing. 'Is a true story. It is a tale, not to scare you, but to help you understand your being here. In, this place. Josh and Maddie Grimshaw are your names.

Your father's name was Stefan. Your mother's name Emily. Your uncle is Michael. Your aunt, is in the other room, recovering.'

Maddie and Josh, were now on their feet, holding each other.

'What, are you saying?' Maddie screamed. 'I don't understand. We are Josh and Maddie Grimshaw. We know that. Our aunt is in the other room. Our mother died when we were four. Father put us in the care of our aunt. He's on his travels exploring. He's coming back for us.' Maddie was now hysterical. 'I, don't understand. Josh?' Maddie looked at her brother, who could say nothing.

All Josh could do, was look at Geremi. He didn't understand, what they were being told either. Geremi, now moved in closer to the twins, and he gathered the two children together, before speaking.

'We, are here, in the sanctity of Oakengarne, in Fantaellen. Which is a country, in the portal world of Portaellen. You two, are what we call Dual Bloods. This enables you, to travel between the portals here in this world, and earth. You both, are very special children. You just don't realise it yet.' The young knight now smiled warmly at them.

'And our father?' asked Josh.

'Well. He did tell you the truth. He was an explorer. He loved nothing better, than going through the portals, between Portaellen and Earth. Then, destiny came calling, when his father, and then his mother passed away. For, he was destined, to be a king. The King of Fantaellen. The Sovereign of Portaellen. The world, that we are currently in. He kept all of this, from you, to keep you safe. Everything, that Oakengarne has told you, is true. Our Country, Fantaellen, has been invaded. Your uncle has bought it to its knees. It, is also very important, that we keep you both safe.'

'So, our father is dead?' Maddie was crying, the tears streamed down her face, as she looked, to her tearful brother, for comfort.

'Yes. He is.' Geremi replied softly.

The young knight now gently ushered the two distraught children, out of the Peace Room. As, they made their way, slowly down the corridor, Theo the troll, appeared. Seeing the distress, that the children were in, the troll took hold of Josh, as Geremi took care of Maddie.

The talk, about why the two children were in Fantaellen would wait. Geremi could see, that they were understandably too upset, to be given more information, today. Their destiny would still be there tomorrow.

★★★

The smell of death hung so heavy in the air, as the young woman stepped over, the mutilated bodies of the dead. She was dressed in blood stained, black armour, that weighed heavy, on her weary body. Sweat trickled down her brow, and her long black hair, underneath her black helmet, flowed in the wind, that blew, forcefully all around her. Despite, her face not being fully formed, as if it had been erased, from the surface of her head, she was still able to see, everything. Her surroundings were unfamiliar. Yet, she knew, she had been, in a great battle, and she had killed many knights, in the silver armour. For, the sword, that she held in her hands, appeared stained, with the blood of the enemy.

Slowly and cautiously, she now made her way down a rocky path, with snow covered mountains, either side of her, that led her to a ravine, in the distance.

There was something, she had to do. She felt uneasy.

Why?

She knew someone had to die. A voice in her head, told her to turn back. It was a voice, she knew. A warm voice, she had heard, just recently.

Behind her, she suddenly became aware, of a powerful presence. One glance, over her shoulder, confirmed it. Whatever it was, took the form, of a giant figure. Its face unrecognisable, just black and featureless. A man, judging by the tone of his voice, as he now, began to speak to her.

'You, have won, a great victory, my princess. I am so proud of you. Now, go and find the prince. He is alone and defeated. Now, is your chance. Your time, to take your destiny. Take his head.' As, the figure had spoken, it had gradually evolved, into a larger form.

A wind had swiftly whipped up into a frenzy, and it swirled around her, as the young woman, made her way down the blood-soaked pathway, to the ravine.

Instantaneously, she found herself, suddenly standing in a circle of raging flames, that seemed to reach the sky. The heat was tremendous. The flames danced, as a hot wind, blew them into a frenzy. A loud, rhythmic beat of drums, now resonated through-out the circle, as all at once, a faceless figure in a silver helmet and armour appeared, from nowhere.

'He, must die.' Whispered a voice, in her ear. 'Take, his head.'

The young woman hesitated, just for a moment. She had her sword in her hand and had been ready to kill. Something was holding her back.

The person, in the silver armour, seemed hesitant too. Their swords were drawn, and held out in front of them, in readiness to attack.

The two figures now moved around the bright, flamed circle, as if they were weighing up the possibility, of an attack. Probing. Looking for a weakness.

The young woman's heart then missed a beat, as her senses kicked in. She knew, the figure in front of her. She now felt love. She could not kill this person. She, loved them. Warm feelings instantly overwhelmed her, just as she suddenly felt a jolt, like a bolt of electricity, shoot through her body.

The flames, around the circle exploded, and the drums be-came louder and faster, as a hatred, so pure, so strong, swiftly overcame her. The faceless, young woman gripped the hilt of her sword, so tight, and then charged, towards her enemy.

Immediately, the faceless figure in the silver armour, made their charge towards her. Both screamed defiantly at each other, as the circle of flames, once again exploded. The power within the circle, was tremendous, as the evil pulsed through the veins of the young woman.

Both figures, instantly smashed into each other in the centre, as their blades clashed together, causing enormous, bright sparks to fly, all around them.

Upon, pushing each other away, the young woman, regained her composure the quickest, and instantly charged, at her enemy. There was a crunching sound, as armour smashed into armour and their swords, once again clashed.

This time, the young woman went to ground, and swept her legs round, to bring her enemy down. Seeing this, a little too late, the other faceless figure, thrust their sword down, in a desperate lunge, before crashing to the floor, in a heap.

Now, above them, stood the young woman, her sword in both hands, ready for the kill. As, she raised her sword above her head, the faceless figure at her feet, suddenly spoke, and a familiar face transformed, under the silver helmet. A face, she did indeed love.

'Oh God!' She muttered.

'He must die! Take his head!' A voice, behind her called out.

The evil that pumped through her heart was strong. It coursed through her veins, with such power. It had now become, her very life's blood, and had driven her to this moment. This day. Her destiny.

'Take! His! Head!' The voice behind her, now screamed.

'No!' She shouted.

'Now!' Boomed the voice behind her, as the flaming circle suddenly exploded, into a mass of flame and intense heat.

Bringing, her sword down with such an immense force, caused her to scream, as the blade struck flesh and bone, and removed the head of her enemy, in one swift movement.

When, the head stopped rolling, she screamed in terror, upon seeing the now clear face, staring back at her, within the silver helmet.

'Why?' she exclaimed.

The face, that stared back at her, was her face.

The circle exploded one final time, in a maelstrom of fire, flame and tremendous heat, before falling silent, and leaving the lone figure, on her knees, screaming at the sky.

Everything now went dark and silent, as a distant voice called her name. She felt herself drift towards it, slowly at first, until time and motion seemed to speed up, and the voice crept closer. She felt anxiety, and an overwhelming need to wake up.

Maddie suddenly sat upright in bed. Sweat, poured from her, as she stared wide eyed, into the face of Geremi.

'It's all right Maddie. It was just a bad dream.' The young knight wiped her forehead.

In the ceiling, a shadow moved through the roots of Oakengarne, trying to avoid detection. It had the shape, of a human, and was desperately trying to escape the room. Geremi, had seen it, exit Maddie's head, the minute he had burst into the room, having heard, the screams of the little girl. He now knew that she had been having a nightmare, probably implanted, by what he had seen, leave her moments earlier.

Geremi, would have to let Jonti know, that Maddie had possibly been visited, by a Dream Demon. They would visit, their victims regularly. Some believed that they only visited the minds of a host, who had evil traits. This had never been proven. It was just a myth. They were also undetectable. As, they lived in the shadows. The demons had been known, to drive their hosts, to madness. It was also believed that they were also a premonition of the future. This was also unproven. They were also known, to prey, on the vulnerable. This had immediately concerned Geremi, as he had initially comforted, the little girl.

Still, confused and upset, Maddie wept. Her brother had woken too and was doing his best to comfort her.

'It's all right Madd's.' This was a name, for his beloved twin, that he had not used for a while. It made her stop crying, just for a moment, as the tears rolled down her face.

'I love you, Josh,' Maddie whispered, to her twin brother, as the two children embraced.

'I love you too, Madd's,' he replied.

★★★

Normauss the troll, was soaked to his skin. The sky above, remained inky black, and the rain incessant. He, normally hated rain. However, at this moment, the troll, couldn't care less about it. He was in awe. The troll could not believe his eyes. Guinlance, had indeed fallen. The city streets, that he now walked upon, had once been bustling with people and creatures, coming out of, or into the buildings. Those buildings had been smashed and burnt to the ground. There were burnt, decaying, bloated corpses everywhere. The rank, and pungent, sweet, sickening smell of rotting flesh hung heavy in the air.

The troll felt exhilarated. He had to report back to his master. His, report was extremely urgent. He knew the whereabouts of the twins. This was intelligence gold, he reckoned.

There were guards placed, at every entrance into the castle. Up, on the smashed and demolished, high walls of the castle ramparts, were Blackheart archers and sentries. Their duty, to keep their eyes peeled for any Fantaellen attack, that may come. This order had been given, tongue in cheek by their general, to his officer's. No Fantaellen attack, would come, he had said, shortly after, giving his order.

As Normauss approached, the first outer wall of the castle, he looked up at the bloated, headless bodies, hanging by their feet, from the archway of the entrance, before spotting the heads, on the spikes.

His short, stubby legs could not carry him fast enough. He was fit to burst. He just wanted, to give his master, the important information, that he had. The troll, now began to run, as he saw the drawbridge up ahead. Past, the guards on duty he ran, and into the courtyard, where he was greeted by a large Wulfdaeden officer, who, when the troll presented himself, in front of him, nearly burst into laughter.

'And who are you?' Scoffed the officer.

'I am Normauss the troll,' the troll blurted out, breathlessly. 'And, I am here to see, our Master.'

'Don't worry captain. I will deal with this.' Hissed, a voice.

Normauss, turned to see two red eyes, appear from the shadows. Instantly, the troll recognised, the black, wolf shaped head, the pointed ears, and the long snout of Wulfrik.

'Hello, Normauss.' Growled Wulfrik.

'Hello, Wulfrik.' Snarled Normauss, in a short, sharp reply.

Chapter Fifteen

The oaks and the beech trees of the Majestic Wood would never have seen something, so desperate and pitiful, as the sight of Jonti and the hundreds of Fantaellen refugees, when they came into view.

The endless stream of men, women and children, filled the immediate cloudy, grey horizon, led by the young Fantaellen knight. He had dismounted Braern and was slowly walking with an elderly man and woman, whilst two small children, were mounted on his steed.

The civilians had fled from towns and villages around the country, desperate to escape, the invasion and slaughter, with little more, than the clothes on their backs. The rest of the displaced and defeated mass, were made up of around a hundred fighting men, dressed in Fantaellen armour. These men had told tales of escaping battles and skirmishes, all over Fantaellen. Some had injuries, but most were able bodied and carried a sword.

A dark, angry sky had followed them, for the last few hours. With, an incessant, driving rain, soaking every one of them, to the skin.

Jonti, had now left the elderly man and woman with someone, and pushed on ahead, by foot. He had wanted to speak to Oakengarne personally, to see if the Great Oak would grant sanctuary, to such a large group of people. The young knight felt nervous. He, did not want to assume that his friend, would indeed offer his sanctuary. It was a large group of people. Did the Great Oak, have the room? Would having all these desperate people, put the wood in danger? Jonti, suddenly thought about the twins; would having them, in the sanctuary of his friend, put the Great Oak and his wood, in danger too? The young knight did not want to take his friendship with Oakengarne for granted. Mixed emotions, now ran through his head, as he suddenly hesitated, on the edge of the Majestic Wood. For a moment, he remained still, just in front of a bunch, of the newest saplings.

Jonti, took a deep breath and slowly stepped across the boundary line, into the wood. His, heart raced. The young knight, now closed his eyes, raised his arms, and continued forward.

The branches of the trees, began to sway in a gentle breeze, and he could hear whispered voices, around him. Jonti opened his eyes, and he began the Ceremony of Entrance.

'We, call upon the oaks and the beeches, of the Majestic Wood, to recognise us as pure bloods.' Jonti, turned to face the refugees, who stood warily on the edge of the tree line. 'All of us,' he stated.

'You, and your people, are welcome.' Came a voice, unexpectedly from the trees. It startled, the young knight, who swung around, to see where it had come from.

'The Great Oak, has sent me to welcome you once more, master Quixall.'

Jonti now recognised the voice. He smiled to himself, in relief.

Theo the troll, suddenly burst out of a large growth of vegetation, a big grin on his face.

'Hello Jonti.'

'Hello Theo,' replied the young knight. 'Nice, to see you again.'

'I'm sure it is. Come.' Theo, now gestured, for Jonti to follow him. 'And bring those poor people, with you.'

As Theo ran on ahead, the trees in front of him, parted their branches and roots, moving to immediately produce a clearer path, to a flatter, grassy part of the wood. Jonti now beckoned, for the refugees, to be brought forward.

Despite, his own weariness, the young knight, strode forward, with purpose, as Theo ran on ahead. In the distance, he could clearly see, the circle of thick trunks, and enormous branches, that made up the strong circle, of the king's guard.

Upon, reaching the boundary of the circle, Jonti cleared his throat, before speaking. His mouth was dry, and yet, his words, would be clear and true.

'Oh! King's guard! I ask permission, to enter your circle. I seek an audience, with the one, whose roots are deepest and furthest. The one, true oak of the Majestic Wood.'

Jonti, now fell to his knees and bowed his head. For several moments, he remained there, in silence, before getting to his feet, drawing his sword and thrusting it, deep into the soft earth.

'I come in peace and despair. I am your servant, Jonti Quixall.'

The branches of the king's guard, slowly lifted, to reveal the Great Oak. Jonti, now sheathed his sword, and stepped into the circle, past the king's guard.

In front of him, looking as breath-taking, majestic and as regal as ever, was the King of the Oaks. And, sheltering from the rain, underneath his magnificent and strong branches, a smiling Theo, and a concerned looking, Geremi.

'Come forward, master Quixall,' Oakengarne suddenly said.

'Thank you, your Majesty,' replied Jonti.

'All of you. Please, come forward.' Consented, the Great Oak.

Jonti, turned to see the hundreds of refugees, staring in disbelief, on the edge of the king's guard, circle.

'You are all welcome,' Oakengarne's voice, was soft, yet regal. 'Come. You are safe now.'

Slowly and cautiously, several of the refugees, entered the circle. As, one woman shuffled forward, Jonti could see the tears streaming down her face. He smiled softly at her, as she slowly passed him. She carried a small, wrapped bundle, which she clutched to her chest, as she gently rocked it, in her arms. Jonti could see, the face of a small infant, its eyes closed, its face deathly pale, its tiny lips, purple.

'Thank you,' she whispered.

Jonti, could say nothing. His heart broke right there and then. Inside, he cried a thousand tears, for a poor defenceless mother and her baby.

The rest of the procession of refugees, slowly entered the king's circle, and were directed towards, the shelter of his great branches.

Oakengarne, remained silent. He had given his precise instruction, to Theo and Geremi. The latter now approached his friend and captain.

'Where, did you find, these poor people?' Geremi asked. 'And is that Henri?'

The royal physician, approached them, as Jonti began to explain, where he had found the refugees. Geremi listened, as his captain and friend, told him of their arduous journey, through the wheat fields.

'Guinlance, has been taken.' Henri suddenly blurted out. He looked exhausted and defeated.

Geremi, looked at Jonti for validation. Instantly, he saw it in his eyes.

Jonti sighed deeply, as he continued. 'It's true. I could get nowhere near it, but I saw the burning city. Henri here, barely escaped with his life. Guinlance, has been taken.'

'Ramazen!' Geremi cursed 'Our country, is on its knees.'

'However, we still have hope, Geremi. We have the twins. And, while we have them, we have hope for the future.' The outwardly optimistic Jonti, now put his hand on Geremi's shoulder, as he finished, by reminding his sergeant, once more. 'We still, have hope.'

'But our army has been annihilated,' cried Geremi.

'We have to believe, that we will prevail, one day.' Jonti looked deep into his friend's eye's, before continuing, 'These people, here with us now, have got to believe, that we will prevail one day. For, that little boy, and that little girl, that we, we my friend, rescued from right under the nose of evil, are our saviour's. For, those two, we fight on.'

The two friends, now hugged, as the rain thankfully slowed. Then, the two friends parted, and ran to help, the weakest and most vulnerable refugees.

Oakengarne welcomed all the refugees, into his inner sanctum. Down, into his sanctuary they travelled, in a procession of fatigue and defeat. Silently and slowly, the line of men, women and children, made their way, without a thought, a concern, or a care.

Jonti and Geremi watched the line of their fellow Fantaellen's as they entered the Great Oak, in silence. Neither knight, could say anything. There was nothing, that neither of them, could say.

Henri nodded to Jonti, as he entered the sanctuary. The royal physician, looked weary, and close to tears. Jonti smiled, then nodded.

The young knight could not believe that it had come to this. Total annihilation. The sheer ferocity and the enemy's numbers had obviously taken the generals by surprise. They knew that the enemy would come, as the armada, waited for their signal, in the waves of the Stoirim Sea. And yet, the directness, of their attack, had not been anticipated.

Why?

The enemy, with their greater numbers, and the fact, that they were whipped up into a fierce, savage force, that killed and burned, everything, had made them unstoppable. This momentum had driven them forward, quickly and deadly, through the Fantaellen countryside, and on to the capital.

Jonti, now wondered, how his second country, would ever recover, and ultimately rise up, and take back, its rightful land. These thoughts, he would keep to himself. For, somebody had to remain positive.

As he watched, the last of the refugees, enter the inner sanctum, of Oakengarne, the young Knight realised, the enormity, of that task. It was at this point, that he swore, that he would never be defeated, whilst he had, breath in his body. Fantaellen, one day, would once again, belong to the very people, who now sought sanctuary.

Before, they entered the door into Oakengarne, Geremi spoke to his friend, about what he had witnessed, with Maddie earlier. Jonti listened, as Geremi explained what he had seen.

'Are you sure, it was a Dream Demon?' Jonti asked.

'Yes. As soon as I entered the room, I noticed a human shaped shadow, leave her head, and shoot up into the ceiling, amongst the roots. It was desperate to escape.'

'Did Maddie, mention what she had dreamt about?' Jonti now had a concerned expression, upon his face. He seemed worried.

'No. She couldn't,' replied Geremi. 'She was too distressed. I didn't want to upset her anymore. Maybe it's a conversation, we could have, with her later?'

'Yes. Good idea.'

Jonti was concerned. However, the problem could wait for a little while. Dream Demons, despite being a myth, were real. He had seen them before. Whilst, they were dangerous, to their host, it took many visits, to drive a person, or a creature, to madness. Also, a Dream Demon, once detected, would not visit a host, for a while, for fear of detection. There were ways, to stop such spirits, entering the mind. That would mean training a victim, on how to fight off an attack, through positive mind power and meditation. This was something, that they could look at, for the little girl, to help her, as Jonti had heard, that a Dream Demon's persistent visits, could also be a premonition of the future, if a certain path, is followed.

The future for his second country, did look very bleak. Yet, Jonti still had hope, in his heart. Even as, the two young knights, entered Oakengarne, that hope remained. In his hand, Jonti held a sack. In that sack, were the symbolic items, for the rebirth, of Fantaellen. The Orb, the Sceptre and the Crown. Moreover, inside the inner sanctum of the Great Oak were the two most important children, in their world.

One day, we will prevail.

There, was still hope and Oakengarne reminded the young knight of this, when Jonti presented him with the sack, for safe keeping.

The two now spoke, at great length. The Great Oak did not know why, the king's brother, had not killed or had turned, the greatest threat to his claim, to the Throne of Fantaellen, and ultimately, the sovereignty of their world. Michael, as Oakengarne still called him, could have had the twins dealt with, at any time.

The King of the Oaks explained, that he had only met Michael, a few times. He told Jonti, that he had seemed a nice boy, who had grown, strong and brave, but was always seen, as second best, to his older, twin brother. He had heard about the argument, between the brothers, and the subsequent banishment, of Michael. There had been rumours, of all types, and indeed Stefan had visited his confidant in distress, a number of times, to ask his advice, regarding his brother's erratic and concerning behaviour. Oakengarne, did not go into specific details, but he mentioned that he had listened to the king's concerns, and that he had always felt, that he had held back, from telling him, certain things.

Oakengarne, spoke candidly with Jonti, and had advised the young knight to thank the god's above, that Michael had not harmed the twins. Whatever, his reason. He then reminded Jonti, that his rescue mission, had probably saved the lives of the two children, and given their country, and their world, a chance of fighting back.

As Jonti, continued to listen to the King of the Oaks, he had a feeling of hope in his heart. In his stomach, he felt a sudden fire ignite. The fight back, would begin here and now, he told himself.

And James Jonti Quixall, would take that fight, to the enemy.

★★★

Hundreds, of Wulfdaeden Tri Lance banners, were being draped, in readiness, over the vast walls of Guinlance. The Blackheart flag had also been hoisted, up the flagpole, over the royal quarters, and was now proudly, blowing in the wind.

The coronation of a new king and sovereign was just hours away. The whole castle was a hive of activity, with orders being barked out, to servants and knights, alike.

Napoleon Victory and his most trusted general, Cedric Grafton, were in the royal quarters, going over the plans, and the promised, land gains, he had given, to the gigahominums, the rock men and the centrolls. In a corner, Wulfrik sat on his hind legs, his red eyes, scanning the opulent room.

Presently, there was a knock, on the huge, ornate wooden doors. Victory now looked up from his map and growled his disapproval.

'I told them, not to disturb us.' He snapped, 'Come!'

The door was opened by a Wulfdaeden guard, who snapped to attention, as Normauss the troll, entered the room. Wulfrik, subsequently growled, as Normauss, gave the hound a glance of pure loathing.

'Well, if it isn't my trollian friend, Normauss.' Victory, had an irritated look on his face, and his tone was one of sarcasm, as he continued, 'What news do you bring, of the twins?'

Before speaking, Normauss cut a glance to Wulfrik, whose red eyes, stared at the troll. Normauss chuckled to himself, before having his dig, at the hound.

'Sire,' he started, 'as a result, of the failed mission, to bring the twins, into our safe keeping ...'

A growl from the corner of the room, bought a smile, to the troll's face. An awkward silence followed, as the troll milked, the discomfort of the hound, before he carried on.

'Upon, arriving back in Fantaellen, I was able to not only, find the raiding party, that had taken the twins, but I was able, to track their movements.'

'And?' Snapped Victory, who was clearly irritated, by the troll's brash and self-confident, demeanour.

'Sire. I know where the twins are.' Normauss paced the room as if he owned it. He, had his master and his general, held in suspense. And, that stupid hound at this moment, looked like an incompetent idiot. Normauss, was enjoying himself.

'Stand still troll!' Shouted the general. 'You're, making us dizzy.'

'Well!' Demanded Victory, suddenly.

'They have been taken, to the Majestic Wood. I believe, Jonti Quixall is in charge.'

Before Normauss, could say another word, Napoleon Victory, slammed his fist onto the table, in front of him, as a broad smile, came across his evil looking face.

'Oakengarne!' Victory roared. 'They have entrusted, the safety of my niece and nephew, to that arrogant, sanctimonious, deciduous, fake king! Priceless!'

Napoleon Victory, and his general looked at each other, before busting into fits of laughter. The laughter, then became more raucous, as Victory spluttered the Great Oak's name, over and over.

Presently, the two men composed themselves. As they walked over to Normauss; each man placed a hand on the troll. Normauss, immediately felt the grip of his master, tighten. Feeling suddenly uncomfortable, the troll stared at the roaring fire, ahead. An unexpected icy chill, then shot down his spine. Consequently, Normauss shivered, which prompted his master, to release his grip, and gently pat the troll, on the shoulder. Normauss now became, even more weary, of the presence of the two men, behind him.

'Normauss. You have done well,' Victory suddenly said. 'They do say that you Fantaellen mountain trolls, are the best trackers, in our world. Maybe, you Normauss, have gone someway, to prove this. I wonder?' The troll, could now feel his master, tapping his finger's, on his shoulder.

Victory walked away from the troll and began to study his map. He seemed excited, and ebullient, as he suddenly exclaimed. 'Yes!' whilst he tapped his finger, on a certain area, of the map, in an exhilarated manner.

General Grafton had now joined him, and the two men, spoke quietly. It wasn't long, before the general nodded his approval.

'In this room, we allegedly have, the two best trackers in Portaellen. Each, with their own attributes.' Victory paused for a moment, and watched, as both creatures, stared at him. 'You, will both go on ahead together, to the Majestic Wood, as my scouts.'

The look of horror on the troll's face, and the narrowed, red eyes, that stared at Victory from the corner, amused him, as he continued, his orders.

'You will work together.' As he said this, he looked at the troll and the hound individually, 'I want you both, to be my eyes. Make sure, that kid Jonti Quixall, does not move the twins, again. In a few days, you will be joined by General Grafton and a large army. You will then, report back any movements, to him. Do you understand?'

Wulfrik and Normauss said nothing. Both chose, to remain silent.

Inside, Normauss boiled with anger. He hated Wulfrik, with a passion. The troll was sure, that the hound, felt the same way about the mission too. He, could now feel a set of red eyes, burning into his back. Normauss knew, that Wulfrik could, and would, rip his throat out, with very little motivation, or care. He had to be ready, to do the same.

After, a short, uncomfortable moment had passed, both creatures, reluctantly nodded their acceptance, of the given order.

'You two, may leave now,' Victory stated. 'And remember gentlemen,' his tone had now turned sarcastic. 'Play nicely, with each other.'

Neither creature said anything, nor were given any time to respond, as Victory instantly turned to more pressing matters.

'I now, have a ceremony to prepare for. And with this.' Their master, suddenly produced, a heavily soiled cloth bag, from underneath the table. 'Now in my possession, our wonderful world, has a new sovereign, to be crowned.'

'Indeed Sire. It does.' Acknowledged the general.

'Now, go you two,' barked Victory. 'We, have work to do.'

Normauss did not look at Wulfrik, as the two creatures, left the royal quarters, side by side. As, they walked the long corridors, the silence between them remained. Once, they were out into the courtyard, Wulfrik, ran up ahead of the troll, before turning to face him, an evil, burning fire, igniting his pure red eyes. The hound had a low growl, that had settled in his throat, and he now used it, to let the troll know, of his hatred, for him.

Normauss, stared at Wulfrik for a short moment, before swiftly walking towards him, then directly past the hound, which only served, to rile Wulfrik up, further still.

'I'm going, to rip out your throat!' Wulfrik, suddenly roared. Normauss chose, to say nothing to the hound, in reply, to his threat. Instead, he muttered to himself, as he continued walking. 'And I dear Wulfrik, am going to cut your throat, and watch the life, leave your canine body.'

The troll lightly touched the hilt, of the dagger in his belt, as under his breath, he angrily continued to say, his last few words.

'Only one of us, will be coming back to Guinlance. And, that tracker, will not have four legs.' Normauss then spat, a large amount of sputum, onto the ground, before finishing his angered muttering's. 'That, I swear! Dear Wulfrik.'

★★★

The hour had finally come, for those of blackened hearts. The impending coronation, of the new ruler of the portal world, the next king of Fantaellen, the supreme ruler of all the kings and queens; the Sovereign of Portaellen, would very soon ratify, the early days, of the Dark Epoch.

In the courtyard, of Guinlance Castle, a large majority, of the Wulfdaeden army, stood silently waiting, with a resolute discipline.

Whilst, along the vast corridors, leading up to the throne room, hundreds had gathered. The officers had been joined, by the heads of the creature battalion's and their officer's. Every knight and creature stood in silence. The corridors, of the castle, awaited the appearance of their master. The soon to be crowned king of Fantaellen, and Sovereign of Portaellen.

Ever since, he had been a child, Napoleon Victory, (or Michael Grimshaw, the second Prince of Fantaellen, as he was formerly known,) had dreamt of this day. He had wanted it to go according to a plan, that he had fantasised of and nurtured, for many years. Since the moment, that he had rode back into his childhood home, barely two days earlier, the fantasies of his younger days, had played out in his head, once more.

His turned and blackened heart had instantly ignited the dreams of an innocent child, into those of a leader, now filled with pure hatred, for the country of his birth. What, his subjects and army, would witness today, would be the ceremony, that he had demanded of his general's, when he had described every small detail, to them, just days earlier.

When one of his general's had tried to advise against hailing him, before he had been crowned, that same general, was demoted on the spot, and dismissed from the room, under an armed guard, to be tried for treason, at a later date.

With, the rising of the two suns, Victory and General Grafton, had ridden, with their personal bodyguards, to the edge of the Wulfdaeden army encampment. There, they had then waited, for the suns to burn off, the early morning mist.

Napoleon Victory looked magnificent in his Blackheart war armour, with the red and regal, Tri Lance cape, flowing behind him, as he had ridden at speed. Sheathed, at his side, his heavy, ceremonial sword, with his Wulfdaeden initials, etched so beautifully, into the reinforced, pure silver hilt.

It wasn't long, before both suns, had disappeared behind, angry, black storm clouds. As a cold wind grew momentum, the sky rumbled. The Fantaellen heavens, then promptly opened up, with a deluge of freezing rain.

The riders stayed stoically in position, as the wind and rain, now battered them. Lightning, interspersed with deep, rolling thunder, that echoed across the land, showed very little sign of abating.

'Seems, the gods are not happy.' remarked Victory.

'When, are they ever Sire?' replied General Grafton, who had to raise his voice, as a clap of thunder, rumbled overhead.

'It is time,' stated Victory, suddenly.

The riders now formed, into a two-man, wide column, with Napoleon Victory at its head, and his friend and general, Cedric Grafton, by his side.

Slowly, the riders made their way, through the rows, of Wulfdaeden army tents, upon their ride, back towards Guinlance. The thunder and the lightning had halted, and the rain had been replaced, with a sleet, that fell like icy needles. Onwards they rode, as the waiting Blackheart army, greeted its leader, its sire, its master, with a roar, and a chorus.

'Long live the king!'

'Long live the sovereign!'

'Long live the king!'

'Long live the sovereign!'

Thousands of voices, continued to roar their support, for their master, as the riders negotiated, the muddy path, through the endless rows of tents.

Once, out of the encampment, the enormity of the structure of Guinlance Castle, came into their view, once more. Briefly, it took Napoleon Victory's breath away. He had forgotten, how magnificent a structure of engineering brilliance, the castle really was.

On his first ride, back into his childhood home, just a day or so earlier, the magnificence and the construction of the castle, had been lost in his urgency, to ride across the drawbridge, and make his dramatic entrance, into the courtyard.

At this moment the once second Prince of Fantaellen, had decided, to let the sight of his castle, on top of Guinlance Hill, encompass him, as the sleet, slashed across his face.

The riders now gathered more pace, as they entered the burnt-out streets, of the once bustling, and vibrant city of Guinlance. And, it wasn't long, before those streets were behind them, as Victory encouraged his steed, to pick up the pace, as part of his anticipated, dramatic entrance.

Along either side, of the long and narrow pathway, that led to the first outer wall, ceremonial lines of Blackheart knights and creatures, greeted the riders, as if, on cue.

'Long live the king!'

'Long live the sovereign!'

Wulfdaeden banners and flags were now raised in triumph, while the riders gathered more pace, as they raced towards the castle. Down the long pathway, they rode, the voices of his knights and creatures reverberating around Victory, as he stared ahead, through the thick blanket of sleet.

The cheering Blackhearts, on the ramparts of the first outer wall, were treated to the sight of their master, drawing his sword, and raising it, in salute of their support, and the show of countless, red Tri lance banners, adorning the captured walls.

Upon, approaching the vast drawbridge, at the main entrance to the castle, Napoleon Victory's sword remained raised. The icy sleet had been replaced by a driving, unrepentant rain.

When, the hooves of the riders, suddenly thundered onto the drawbridge, the hundreds of Blackheart knights, and creature battalions, in the royal courtyard, instantly snapped to attention, in a disciplined unison, upon the shrill order, of an officer.

The Wulfdaeden war drums, now beat out, their military greeting, quickly and efficiently, as the officer, screamed his next order.

'Swords!'

Thousands of swords were now unsheathed, and raised to the sky, as the rain bounced off the muddy ground, of the courtyard.

'We are the darkness!' Shouted the officer. 'We are Wulfdaeden's! We, are black of heart!'

The reply, from the rank and file of the Wulfdaeden army, was instant, as the drums suddenly ceased, and their master rode into the courtyard, on his magnificent black steed.

'Long live the king!'

'Long live the sovereign!'

'Long Live Wulfdaeden!'

'Long live the king!'

'Long live the sovereign!'

'Long live Wulfdaeden!'

And, so the voices echoed around the courtyard, for quite some time, as their master rode his steed at pace, along the slippery cobbles, his sword raised in the greeting and acknowledgement, of their adulation.

The chanting continued, even when Victory finally sheathed his sword, and dismounted his steed. Then, raising his arm one last time in appreciation, he quickly disappeared through a doorway, surrounded by his personal bodyguards, General Grafton, and his men.

Napoleon Victory, suddenly felt his black heart, miss a beat. He had felt a sudden surge of excitement, when entering the first, of several passageways, that would take him and his specially chosen entourage, through to the main walkway and corridor, that led to the throne room. This was his day. A day, that had taken years of planning, on paper and in his head. A sinister smile now enveloped his scarred face, as he thought about his next move. One, that would make him and his country, invincible. It would be an historical legacy. His, legacy.

Marching down the corridor, towards the throne room, Victory stared ahead, as the lines of his general's, and the officers of his creature battalions, remained silent, with their heads bowed. Behind him, his entourage followed. This was Victory's wish. All part, of his boyhood fantasy.

At the doorway to the throne room, he was greeted by two Blackheart guards, who had their lances, crossed over the doorway. With a guttural order, from an officer, the lances were parted, and Napoleon Victory, then entered the throne room, for the first time, since being exiled.

What, an exhilarating thrill he felt, as he did so. He had purposely chosen, not to go anywhere near, the throne room, since his arrival, to heighten his pleasure, of this exact moment. His first step, into the room. He was not disappointed.

Wulfdaeden drums greeted their leader. Their beat was disciplined and slow, as he entered the marble floored room. Looking up, at the beautiful, stained glass windows, high in the ceiling, Victory could see the angry black clouds, still making their presence known, with all manner of natural elements. Then, to his amazement, one shaft of brilliant white light, suddenly shot through one of the stained-glass windows, before engulfing the two thrones that stood in the centre of the room.

In between the thrones, was an enormous oak table, dark in colour, its thick, strong legs, were carved into intricate looking unicorns, that were reared up, on their hind legs. On the table, a crown so beautiful and magnificent, that it now held the gaze of everybody in the room, as the shaft of light, enhanced the delicate colours of the tiny diamonds, that adorned the gold crown. This was the crown of the Sovereign of Portaellen.

Behind the table, hung an enormous Tri lance banner, its colours so brilliant and vibrant. The red background intensified the emblem in the centre of the banner. Two black hearts, that shrouded a single silver heart. A symbol of evil, swallowing all that is good.

Napoleon Victory approached the Throne of Fantaellen, known as the Thoriron Throne. For a moment he paused, remembering the memory of his father who had sat upon it.

The ancient throne looked magnificent, but it was simple in design. Made, with the strongest metal in the Portal World, known as Thoriron. A metal, so strong, yet so beautiful, with its hue of purest, brilliant silver. Upon, the back of the throne, in each corner, were two unicorns, who stood on their hind legs, holding a crown, between them. On each armrest, the words; Stronivus, Honorous, Courous, ornately etched into the metal.

Victory touched the throne briefly and ran his hand along one of the arms. Once, seeing the words of his past, he cursed their meaning, as a look of utter disdain, came over his face.

The drums had now ceased, in anticipation of their master, placing himself upon the throne. Napoleon Victory took a deep breath, before turning to his men and creatures, as he quickly produced a map, from his pocket, and held it in the air.

'The title of king of Fantaellen, shall no longer exist,' he exclaimed, as he shook the map vigorously. 'I personally would, if I had the power, send Fantaellen to the bottom of the Stoirim Sea.' Victory now paused, for maximum effect. The room remained silent. 'I am many things, but I am not a god. You! My brilliant general's and subjects have destroyed all Fantaellen resistance. As a people, they are finished. Destroyed. So, I will do the next best thing, that I can do, as a mortal man. A man of Wulfdaeden. A Blackheart.' He then paused, for a final time, before finishing his speech, 'From this very second in time, the pathetic name of this country, will be erased in name, from all maps! All maps!'

The throne room suddenly erupted into frenzy of excitement, as their leader's words echoed around the room, and then deeper into the crowds. The heightened exhilaration exploded further, as Victory unexpectedly, tore the map to pieces, and then threw the pieces into the air.

As the delirium and elation slowly diminished, Napoleon Victory produced another map, from his pocket, and held it in the air.

'And, from this day forth,' he suddenly declared. 'Our newly acquired land, will also be known as, Wulfdaeden!'

Holding the new map out towards everyone in the room, he creamed, at the top of his voice, 'This land, is ours!'

The excitement, the delirium and the elation grew once more, amongst the throng of his subjects. Napoleon Victory now had the entire room, in the palm of his hand.

'And, as this land is now ours, I have given some of it, to our allies and friends from the creature battalions.'

Every gigahominum in the room, now stamped their feet in appreciation, as the centrolls and rock men cheered, with delight.

'General Grafton has the details for their general's. I am grateful to all of you creatures, in the execution of our mission. I hope that this gesture, goes some way, to prove that.'

Once, the tumult of excited creatures, had all but died down, Napoleon Victory, continued to address the room, with his next subject.

'So! What of the Thoriron Throne?' Shouted Victory, as he threw his arms in the air in mockery, to encapsulate, what he was about to say.

The throne room soon fell silent, once more.

'Well! I don't want it. It now, has no use. Shall I tell you, what we will do with it?'

Victory's eyes immediately scanned the room, as the question, left his lips. Instantly, he then felt the excitement growing once more, as the pockets of whispers, around the room, slowly grew.

'Destroy it!' Screamed a centroll, suddenly.

The creature was instantly beat about the head, by his officer, as the room, immediately fell into silence.

'The Thoriron Throne,' began Victory, 'will be dug up from its foundations, here in this room and taken to the coast. Where, it will be thrown from the cliffs and into the crashing waves, of the Stoirim Sea. To rot forever!'

Once more, the throne room erupted into a frenzy of excitement and delirium. There, was a lot of cheering and foot stomping, and general elation, as everyone now enjoyed, their master's declaration.

With General Grafton's signal, the drums began their military beat once again. The excitement slowly died down, as the drums signalled, the next stage of their master's inauguration.

Napoleon Victory slowly approached The Diamond Throne the throne of the sovereign made from a substance called Zubacron, (a very strong metal, fused with the strongest diamond, known in Portaellen.) It also has diamonds, the size of a man's hand, all around its structure, that ensures that when you look at it, from any angle, you see hundreds of different subtle, coloured anomalies, depending on the light around it.

As Victory, placed himself upon the throne, and made himself comfortable, General Grafton picked up the sovereign's crown, and proceeded carefully towards his master.

From, behind the thrones, a choir of men, in black robes appeared, and began chanting, in an old Wulfdaeden language.

The drums had now dissipated, and nobody spoke, as the general placed the crown of the sovereign, on his master's head, before taking a step back, and going down on one knee. He then bowed before, the new Supreme Power.

The whole room, at once followed the general's actions. Not a single soul, was left standing, as the ancient chanting, eventually ceased, and a sudden voice from the back of the throne room declared, 'Long live the sovereign!'

Everybody in the room, got to their feet. The sound of deep, masculine voices reverberating around the room, was so loud and clear, as the declaration, was now made.

'Long live the sovereign!'

'Long live the sovereign!'

'Long live the sovereign!'

The chant, went on for several minutes, before Napoleon Victory, the newly crowned Sovereign of Portaellen, finally got up from his throne, and raised his sword, in acknowledgement.

It took quite some time, for the chanting to fully cease. When it had gone completely silent once more, only then, did Victory speak.

'My first order, as the Sovereign of Portaellen, has been passed to General Grafton. We have received intelligence, of the whereabouts of my niece and nephew. The general has the details of the battalions, that will carry out my orders. He is under no illusion, of how this order must be carried out. With fire and Wulfdaeden blades. Those two children must be brought into the fold. Now, that I am the sovereign of our World, there must be a continuation of the bloodline. A pure bloodline.'

The frenzied fever of delirium began to build in the room again, and Victory could feel it. He wanted to fuel it, even more.

'This magnificent throne will also be dug up from these foundations and taken to where it belongs. A place, that will become its home forever. The Diamond Throne of the sovereign will now become a symbol of Wulfdaeden, Blackheart dominance, and placed into stronger, deeper foundations.' Victory could see the excitement growing, yet again, in the faces of his subject's. 'Gentlemen! The Diamond Throne, is going home!' As, he said the last few words, he screamed them. 'To, the Fortress Of Fear!'

Napoleon Victory just stood and watched, as the throne room, erupted into an unquantifiable and deafening excitement. His mission was accomplished. With his words, he had whipped up the entire room, into a frenzy of unprecedented excitement, delirium and exaltation, which he let continue, for as long, as he wanted it to.

The unequalled scenes, of elation and triumph, did eventually cease, with the new sovereign's nod, to his drummers. The first few beats quickly bought the room, to order.

Upon, the satisfactory ending of his crowning, Napoleon Victory beckoned General Grafton over, as the rank and file of his army, finally began to leave the throne room. He needed to make sure, that everything was in place, for his next move.

'Sire.' General Grafton bowed his head, as he approached.

'Are you clear, on what to do about, the Majestic Wood?' Victory asked him.

'Yes Sire.'

'Not a soul or a tree is to live, except the twins.' Victory's eyes, suddenly turned, the deepest, darkest black. 'Burn it! To ashes!' he hissed.

'What, about your sister? Have you decided?' asked the general.

'Only, the twins are to survive Cedric. She failed me.'

The general, instantly nodded his acceptance, of his master's order's.

'Have, you given your orders, to the battalions, looking after our allies?' Victory asked.

'Yes Sire.'

'Good. And remember.' Victory stared deep into his friend's eyes. 'We must have both twins! They must be turned.'

'Yes Sire.'

As General Grafton, left his master and friend, alone in his throne room, to enjoy his newly gained sovereignty, he couldn't help but wonder why, both twins were needed. Surely, with the boy reportedly, being the eldest twin, and so, being the next in line, he would be the one to be turned, and so carry on the succession.

Just yesterday, when the general had questioned, the reasoning behind that decision, Victory had suddenly snapped, and quite firmly stated, that if the boy were to die, they needed a backup plan in place. This had been his only answer. A firm answer, to his friend's question.

The general, did not want to push his friend too much. He felt sure, that there were other reasons behind his thinking. The short burst of irritation and anger had shown this, to the general, and had quickly made way for an uncomfortable silence, as Victory had put up his barriers, to protect, the reasoning for his order.

The general, had accepted the order yesterday. However, as he marched up the long corridors, of Guinlance Castle, towards the courtyard, it had not stopped him from still questioning, the reason why, in his mind.

As, he walked through the doorway, and out into the wet courtyard, General Grafton, was greeted by the sight of two full battalions of Blackheart knights, a hundred or more bowmen and a dozen engineers, with two Trebuchets at the rear.

Napoleon Victory was not messing about. The importance and success of General Grafton's mission was paramount. The general knew this, and would use his men and the fire power, that he possessed, to their full potential.

The Majestic Wood was not on the new map. The name had not been scribed upon it. Just like the old map, that had been ripped to pieces, the trees would be too, by Blackheart blades and missiles. Then, whatever remained, would be burnt to ashes, in a maelstrom of Wulfdaeden fire.

Chapter Sixteen

High, up on the ledges and crevices, above the vast entrance, of the Fantaellen mountains, dozens of eyes watched, as the riders entered the rocky pass. An unforgiving icy wind blew down the narrow rocky corridor, to chill the purple robed riders, to the bone.

The mountain trolls on lookout duty, passed hurried messages to each other, with a series of calls and shouts, as they continued to watch the riders with caution.

Robert Scotten looked up, just in time to see, all the trollian scouts, disappear in a sudden flash. Gently, he carried on stroking the mane of his steed, who had been spooked by the noise from above. With the sudden disappearance of the troll scouts, came a sense of unease. Robert could sense this, in his men, and so he moved to reassure them.

'Don't worry men. The silence means, that the message will get back to their Elder. Trogar and I, go way back. He and his troll's are our allies.'

A few flakes of snow had begun to fall. It was not a significant amount, and soon it slowed to nothing. Robert, was used to the weather of the mountains, having visited on numerous occasions. It could be so unpredictable, to the point of being very dangerous. So, he always had his wits about him, where the weather in those mountains, was concerned.

The rocky corridor had suddenly narrowed, to barely the width of a single rider. The high, vertical rock face, either side of them, gave some of the riders, a sudden sense of confinement and containment, as they firstly entered, and then continued their ride, onwards.

The icy wind had subsided, and the silence from the ledges and the crevices above remained. The only sound, echoing around the corridor, was that of the hooves of the steeds, as they negotiated, the rocky pathway.

Trogar, the elder of the Fantaellen mountain trolls, watched the riders with interest. Stroking his long, straggly white beard, his gaze remained upon them, until they completely disappeared, from view.

The troll, wondered why his friend, had ventured into his mountain range, when he clearly had problems towards the south, judging by the large plumes of smoke, spotted by his scouts, and the glowing orange hue on the horizon, the previous night.

Trogar, had been joined by his wife, Anje. She adored her husband, and he adored her. In his eye, (he only had one, due to a fight with a Wolfdog, a few years ago,) she was the most beautiful female troll, he had ever seen. He loved her kind nature, and her superior intelligence, compared to his own. She was indeed beautiful, by troll standards. Her big, wide green eyes were so full of life, and her long, dark lashes, frequently charmed him. Trogar, loved her long, black hair, that flowed behind her in the wind. He even loved the stubble on her chin, which was the envy of many of her subjects, male and female. She was also built to wrestle. Having challenged and fought, many male trolls and won. Trogar, was not one of her conquests. Choosing instead, not to try his luck.

Elder Trogar was himself, a beast of a troll. He made up for his lack of height, with his width. He was twice as wide, as any other troll, in his mountain. The width was also pure muscle. His, hardened hands, the size of small diggers, with numerous scars, across his knuckles.

He does indeed, only have one eye, and occasionally wears a patch, if the icy wind annoys the void, in his thick, hard skull. He sports, a white Mohican hair style on his head, which compliments, the long unkempt white beard, on his wide chin. He can be grumpy, unpredictable and downright nasty. However, to his close friends, he is loyal.

And one of those close friends, was presently riding through his mountain pass.

Trogar, briefly looked at his wife, who had carried a concerned look on her face, for the past few hours. He had known that something was not right, beyond the safety of his mountain's. Especially when, he had received the sketchy intelligence, about an invasion, and the unthinkable fall, of Guinlance and its castle. And, until he had seen the smoke from the south, he had not believed the validity of such information.

Seeing, Robert Scotten now riding at speed, towards him, Trogar appreciated that the situation was indeed grave. He knew that he had to be there, to greet his friend. With a quick signal to one of his troll's, and a kiss placed tenderly, upon his wife's bristly cheek, Anje was then taken back into their cave.

If the invasion of Fantaellen had happened, then he and his subject's, would be obliged to support the Fantaellen's. As, the subsequent invasion of their ally's soil, would also impact on them.

Am I and my trolls, ready for war?

That would be a question, not to be answered now, Trogar reasoned. Winter was on its way, and the invaders, would settle into their new surroundings, without instant retribution.

Nevertheless, come the spring, he and his trolls would be ready. Ready, to fight and die, for their freedom and the freedom of all their fellow Fantaellen's. But firstly, he must listen, to a first-hand account of the situation, from his close friend, Robert Scotten.

It was going to be, a long, hard, and bitter winter, he said to himself.

★★★

Jonti Quixall, took a goblet, and filled it with fresh, cool water, from a pitcher, on the elaborate wooden table. The Peace Room was quiet, and the fresher air that circulated, around the room, was most welcoming. He drank deeply, for several minutes, desperately trying to quench his thirst. Patiently, Jonti waited for Theo the troll, to arrive. The young knight had a plan in his head, that he wanted to share with the troll. However, it had been Theo, who had sent a message, to say that he wanted to see Jonti, regarding a matter, most urgent.

Jonti, suddenly became aware of something around his feet. Looking down, he could see a small furry mono opti, looking up at him, with its one eye. Jonti, gave it a gentle push away, with his foot. He knew that the creature was now harmless. Still, he had seen one of the same creature in its previous form, rip the flesh, from a man's arm. Hence his caution.

'Go away, Flesh Goblin!' He exclaimed, as he kicked out, with more force, upon the return of the creature.

Feeling the impact of Jonti's boot, forced a little squeal from the furry ball, who then shot off towards the doorway, as it rubbed its little hands, on its backside.

'I see, you still share the love of the cute furballs.'

Jonti looked around, to see that Theo had entered the room. The young knight smiled weakly at the troll, who in turn, had a beaming smile across his chubby, red face.

'You look weary, my friend,' remarked the troll.

Jonti did not reply, preferring to cut to the chase, and hear what Theo, had to say.

'It's good, that we can have a chance to talk,' the young knight stated. 'I presume, that is why, you wanted to see me?'

Theo could trace the weariness, and yet, a sense of urgency, in his friend's voice. So, the troll, approached Jonti, and cleared his mind, before he spoke.

'The Blackhearts are coming here,' Theo, suddenly declared.

'And, you know this how?' Jonti asked.

'A hunch. Plus, some intelligence, that I have received. Look, you are not stupid, my friend. The enemy have spies everywhere. And so, do I. A battalion of knights and engineers, with a couple of your trebuchets, have been seen, marching in this direction.

Victory will know that the prince and the princess, are here. He too, is not stupid.' Theo paused for a moment, before carrying on. 'We need to get the twins, away from here. As safe, as this place is, it is not impregnable. Come on, we all thought, that Guinlance Castle was. So, all the more reason, to act quickly. What do you think, Jonti?'

'I have thought about it too, my troll friend,' began the young knight. 'Majestic Wood, as vulnerable, as it looks, that vulnerability, is its best defence. I know, what Oakengarne, and his fellow oaks and beeches, are capable of. This place is still one of the safest havens, in the country. There, is another place. Now, that winter approaches.'

'The Fantaellen mountains.' They both suddenly said, in perfect unison.

The young knight, and the troll, instantly smiled at each other.

'It's definitely the safest place on the planet, in winter,' Theo stated. 'We will have to move quickly Jonti. The winter will be upon us in days. More pressing, the enemy, will be here within a few hours.'

'I do have a plan too, Theo. It does, involve the mountains. Hear me out.' Jonti took a drink from his goblet, before carrying on. 'The impending snow and ice, in the mountains, will indeed make it impossible for the Blackhearts, to enter the mountain pass. No disputing that. My plan is a damage limitation exercise. I have the upmost faith, in Oakengarne and his trees, of holding back the enemy. But we need to half the burden, for the Great Oak. If both children, were to fall into enemy hands, it would be game over. Agreed?'

'Agreed,' replied Theo, cautiously.

'The Blackhearts will attack The Majestic Wood. Oakengarne and his trees, will be ready. So, we split the twins up. You and I will sneak the prince away to the Fantaellen mountains and spend the winter there. By doing this, we hopefully keep both twins safe, at separate locations. If the worst happened, and one of the twins were to fall into enemy hands, then we still have the other one. By, taking Josh, the eldest with us, I feel, we can almost guarantee his safety, till spring. If, we leave, as soon as possible. We can pray, that Oakengarne, will hold out and keep Maddie safe, here. However, as you said, we will need to act now.'

'Yes, we will.' Agreed Theo, before quickly falling silent, as he processed, Jonti's plan through his head.

The young knight watched, as his troll friend, quietly spoke to himself, and occasionally muttered, 'Yes,' as he paced, up and down, the room.

'As dangerous, as our undertaking will be,' the troll slowly began, 'it could, just work.'

'Yes, it could Theo. Look, I have already spoken to Oakengarne, and he agrees with the plan, stated Jonti.

'Oh! I see,' mocked Theo. 'You, were going ahead with the plan, anyway.'

'Oh Yes!' Laughed Jonti. 'Of course. I knew you would agree.'

'Yes, I would,' agreed Theo.

'Listen. I need to brief Geremi. He will be remaining here. He will have my authority, to lead, in conjunction with The Great Oak. Before we go, I must speak, to the children. They need to understand, the situation. Understand their lineage.'

'Yes. No problem,' replied Theo.

'Remember, we need to look inconspicuous Theo. Be ready in one hour.'

'Can I still bring, my sword and axe?' asked the troll.

No reply was forthwith, so he took Jonti's silence, as a yes.

Truthfully, Theo was glad, to be going back home. He had been, but moments, from running back there anyway, if his own plan of taking the twins there, had fallen on deaf ears. The troll had a Blackheart bounty on his head, for the slaying of one of Napoleon Victory's closest advisors, some years previous. If word, had reached the enemy battalions, that Theo the troll, had sought the shelter, of Oakengarne, it would have given them, more reason to burn the wood to the ground, and to take him back to Victory, for punishment. For, the troll with a price on his head, was worth double, still alive, rather than dead.

At least now, Theo would keep himself alive, whilst doing his country, and the World of Portaellen, a huge favour, by taking the prince to safety.

The name, Theo the troll, would be present, in many songs in years to come, he told himself, as he made his way down the corridor, to his room. He began to hum a random tune to himself, before an unexpected, sense of panic overtook him, suddenly.

'Quick!' he shouted. 'Out of my way.' Theo the troll was going home, and he had less than an hour, to prepare himself. 'Out of my way! Please.'

★★★

Maddie began to cry, as she ran, towards her brother. Geremi, quickly took hold of her, and hugged her.

'It will only be, for a few months, Maddie,' Geremi reassured her. 'Just, till the winter has been and gone.'

Jonti, looked at Josh, who had his head bowed down, sobbing. Gently, the young knight, placed his hand, on the boy's head, before kneeling, in front of him.

'There is a reason, for doing this,' Jonti, began to explain, to the young boy. 'We don't do it, to hurt you both. I know that you have never been apart. So, this decision, was not taken lightly. It is, for your own safety. And the good of the kingdom.'

'The kingdom?' spluttered Maddie, suddenly.

'We don't have a lot of time,' stated Jonti. 'But, you both need to understand, one thing. You two, are precious to your people, your second country, your second world. And, the blood given right, that flows through your veins. Your lineage.'

'I don't understand,' Maddie cried out.

'What is lineage?' asked Josh.

'Lineage means, that you and your sister are special. You both, have royal blood flowing through your veins. Your father was a king. Your mother, a queen. You Josh, are a Prince, and the oldest, making you, the next in line for the thrones. You Maddie, are a Princess, and second in line, for the thrones. This is what lineage is. Your lineage.'

'You, said thrones? There is more than one?' Josh, who had stopped crying now, had suddenly become, more inquisitive.

'There, are two thrones. The Thoriron Throne of Fantaellen, and the Diamond Throne, of the Sovereign of Portaellen.'

Jonti, still knelt in front of Josh, and he could see a small flame suddenly ignite, in the boy's eyes. Josh had wiped away his tears and stared at the young knight. It was the same flame, that Jonti had seen, in the eyes of the boy's father, the flame of a king. Jonti, now smiled at Josh.

'By, the right of your lineage Josh, those thrones are yours.'

Jonti, let what he had just told the young boy, sink in. He saw the flame rise, in Josh's eyes, just momentarily, before he continued, 'But, we have a problem. Your uncle has invaded your kingdom and has thrown this world into a war. He, has stolen your throne's, and we believe, that he wants to capture, both you and your sister.'

Jonti paused once more. He had not wanted to be so forthright with his words, and his explanation, but he had seen that flame, in the boy's eyes, and he knew, at that moment, that Josh was ready for the truth. To his surprise Maddie had stopped crying, and listened intently, to what he had to say. Jonti, decided not to mention, that their uncle, would probably have killed them, in a heartbeat. He felt that the twins, did not need to know that.

'Is this why, you have decided to split us up?' asked Maddie.

'Yes, it is. By keeping you apart, it gives your uncle, two headaches, if you like. Listen Josh, you will be safe in the mountains with me and Theo. We will be kept safe, by Theo and his people, in a winter wonderland. Maddie, you will be really safe here, in the inner sanctum, of Oakengarne. I am just being extra cautious. Come spring, you will both be back together. I promise. And Maddie, there is somebody, I would like you to meet, he needs a friend.'

Jonti made his way over to the doorway, where he appeared to be speaking to someone, and beckoning them forward.

Henri, the royal physician appeared in the doorway, with his arm around a shy looking, young boy. Following obediently, was a black hound, his head the shape of a wolf. Maddie gasped, at the sudden appearance, of the fierce looking hound.

'Maddie. This is Arami.' Jonti announced. 'His hound is called Zevarn. They both, really need a friend.'

The room fell silent, as both children, stared at each other.

'Hello,' Maddie said, somewhat cautiously.

'Hello,' replied Arami, extremely shyly.

Zevarn, now slowly crept towards Maddie, who nervously backed away. She had never seen a hound before, and she wasn't sure what to do.

'It will be all right Maddie,' affirmed Jonti. 'He is being inquisitive. He wants to smell you. Get your scent. He knows that you are not a threat. He wants to get to know you. Be your friend.'

With Jonti's reassuring words, Maddie stopped backing away, from the approaching hound, and slowly walked towards it.

Within moments, she and the hound were entwined in an embrace of wet canine licks, and cautious rubs of a strong, short haired body, that stayed gentle, yet excited, as the young girl, gained her confidence, with her newfound friend.

Jonti watched, as Maddie became more assured with the hound, to the point, where she was in control. Within moments, Zevarn was sat at her feet panting, with the young girl's hand, placed upon his wolf shaped head.

'I think, you have a new friend, there Maddie,' Geremi remarked.

'What about, Aunt Grimshaw?' Maddie suddenly asked.

'Your aunt,' Jonti began, 'when she wakes up, will be different, to what you remember. In time, as she gets better, she will become the aunt, that your father entrusted, with your safety and your wellbeing.'

Maddie felt calmer. She looked at her brother, who smiled at her and nodded. She looked at the filthy, grubby looking boy, who just stared at her. She smiled at him warmly. Arami, had a distant look in his eyes, a lost look, but also a look of defiance. Maddie suddenly felt sorry for him.

'We must leave, as soon as possible.' Declared Jonti, suddenly.

Brother and sister now lovingly embraced. Josh, instantly promised to see his sister soon, and he asked her, not to worry about him, as he was going on an adventure.

It was, in those few moments, of truthful conversation, and confused, childlike emotion, that Jonti had seen the twins, gradually begin to change. He had seen a fledgling resilience, a newfound courage and a willingness to embrace their destiny, their lineage.

As he shook the hand, of his best friend, and his second in command, he pulled him to one side, and declared his optimism, for their future.

'We have had some dark days, recently my friend. Even now, we stare into a great, fiery abyss, of evil. Nonetheless, before us Geremi, in this room, is our future. You and I must guard these two children, with our lives. Seeing, the prince and princess together, warms my Dual Blood heart. Their destiny, will hopefully mirror, the destiny of this world, and one day, the natural balance, will be restored.'

'Amen, to that,' agreed Geremi.

The two knights embraced and shook hands once more.

They were shortly joined by Theo, who wore a black cloak. In his hand, he carried his sword and axe. He looked anxious, and a little on edge, as he began to speak.

'My brother has been seen, on the edge of the wood, skulking in the shadows of the saplings. He has a companion with him. A Wolfdog.' Theo began to pace, back and forth.

'Stay calm Theo. They will be the scouts. We have time. Not much. But we have time.'

The time had most definitely come. They did have to leave now, Jonti told himself.

Jonti, shook the hand of Geremi, one final time, before he grabbed a few belongings, that he had bought with him.

As the three, made their way down a long corridor, towards a secret back entrance, out of Oakengarne, the Great Oak, quietly bid them farewell, and good luck.

It took a little while, but eventually, the three cloaked figures, spied the daylight of a secret entrance, that only a few, knew of.

As they neared the daylight, Josh saw a lone purple flower. He noted how alone, but beautiful it looked. As, he bent down to pick it, Theo the troll, placed a firm hand on his shoulder.

'Don't, take that purple Tulip, from the ground,' he warned. 'It stands alone, as a sign of hope and rebirth. If, it is picked, it will die. And, along with it, hope and rebirth, dies.'

'Sorry.' Uttered Josh.

On the outside of the entrance, tethered to a tree, waited Braern and a smaller white steed. The rain had stopped, but the dark clouds remained.

It wasn't long, before the three, black cloaked figures, had raced away, from the safety of The Majestic Wood, and across the open fields.

Mounted, on the smaller steed, was Theo the troll. On the other, Jonti with Josh, who clung on for his life, as Braern was encouraged, to race away, as fast as his hooves could carry them, towards a gathering mist, in the distance. Jonti, briefly looked back over his shoulder, and prayed that they had not been seen.

From, the shadows of his hiding place, in the younger oaks, Normauss turned to look at the horizon, and spied a couple of riders.

Time to report back.

Those riders were Blackheart scouts. General Grafton and his battalions were here.

★★★

General Grafton was buoyed by the intelligence, from his two scouts. Normauss and Wulfrik, had raced against each other, to be the first, to give him, their report. The general loved, winding up, both the troll and the Wolfdog, who each had such an intense hatred of each other. He used that hatred, for his own purpose, and he loved to watch, as they tried to outdo each other. Today, had been no different. He had listened, as the two scouts had tried desperately, to talk, then shout over each other, as they had relayed their intelligence to him. As, the two creatures had spoken, shouted, shoved and pushed each other around, he had heard, the news that he needed to hear. Nobody had left The Majestic Wood.

The general then laughed, at the sight of Normauss and Wulfrik punching, biting and kicking, the living daylights, out of each other. For the moment, he would leave them to it, he told himself.

He would then send the troll and the Wolfdog, off in different directions, to do something of use, once more. He had received his intelligence, and now it was time to act upon it.

★★★

Out, of a low-lying mist, a Wulfdaeden war machine thundered into position, upon the edge of The Majestic Wood. A battalion of calvary, were placed to the north. Archers, to the eastern edge, and knights on foot, to the south. The engineers, with their trebuchets and huge fire boulders, were placed to the western edge. The wood was now completely surrounded.

Along, the western and eastern edges of the wood, small fire pits were hastily dug, and buckets of tar, brought forward.

General Grafton, then called his officer's over for one final briefing. He quickly became quite animated, as he went through every detail, once again. Before, he dismissed them, the general lit a torch and pointed towards the wood.

'Once, we have chopped, hacked and crushed those pompous, arrogant, oaks and beeches, and taken the twins, from their sanctity, then, we will finish the deciduous filth off, in the almighty fires, of a Wulfdaeden hell.'

General Grafton threw his lit torch, towards the wood. The evil pumped through his body, as his officer's ran to their posts.

Soon, the attack on The Majestic Wood would begin. The ground would shake, and the earth would be scorched. Oakengarne and his trees, along with a number of trained Fantaellen knights, and a few hundred refugees, were all that now stood, in defiance of the invaders, who had come to take the twins, and raise The Majestic Wood, to ashes.

★★★

A Blackheart Officer, watched the stormy black clouds, race across the angry sky, as the colossal, dark waves of the Stoirim Sea, slammed into Needle Point Rock. The wind whistled around and through the rocky alcove, where he stood, high above the thundering, crashing waves, that smashed into the Fantaellen coastline. The water was deep and extremely dark, in this particular alcove, and the rocks below the surface, would serve their purpose.

The elements, seemed to be throwing everything at his men, as they pulled on their ropes. A driving rain, and a vicious wind combined to slow their progress, as the engineers slid helplessly, on an energy sapping mud.

Fifty men had been required, to lift The Thoriron Throne from its deep foundations, at Guinlance Castle. Double that amount, now dragged it up, a steep, muddy, grassy bank, to the highest point, above the alcove.

Through, an unrepentant gale force wind, and a rain, that quickly turned to needles of ice, the ancient throne of the Fantaellen monarchy, was gradually dragged to the top of the alcove.

As, the throne was pushed to the rocky edge, a tremendous gust of wind, took two Wulfdaeden engineers, over the edge. Their screams were immediately lost, in the tremendous noise of the storm, and the crashing waves, below.

The officer directly barked out an order, for all his men, to take hold of the throne, and for them to dig their heels, into the soft earth.

On his order, that was barely audible above the storm, the Wulfdaeden engineers, began to push and shove, the Thoriron Throne, towards the edge. Despite, their numbers and their combined strength, it felt as if the elements, of wind and driving icy rain, that smashed into them, was creating a natural barrier.

Slowly, they pushed through the storm. Their combined force of strength and determination, driving them on, until there was no more ground, and the throne teetered, on the edge, of the rocky alcove.

For, a split second, time stopped.

The elements had ceased their roar. The engineers had stopped pushing, and they held their breath, as they watched in wonderment, at the throne balanced on two legs, held in suspension.

The officer in charge of the engineers, roared an order at his men, and pushed two of his closest engineers forward, towards the throne. Their momentum carried them forward and into the throne. This was enough, to take them and the Fantaellen throne over the edge.

The Thoriron Throne, quickly disappeared into the wall of thundering, crashing waves, before hitting the surface of the deep, dark, rocky waters.

Slowly and hauntingly, it fell into the cold, inky blackness of the depths below. To, be evidently lost, forever.

★★★

Robert Scotten, watched the two steeds, enter the narrow rocky corridor, into the Fantaellen mountains. From the safety, of the mouth of their cave, he and Trogar observed with caution, as the troll's scouts called out their messages to each other, from the ledges and crevices, in the distance.

When the riders, came to the part of the corridor, where it narrowed to the width of a single rider, Robert recognised Jonti, as one of the visitors, and Trogar saw his fellow troll Theo, upon the smaller steed.

'Who is the child?' enquired Trogar.

Robert remained silent for a moment, before answering. Upon realising, who the child was, and instantly, admiring the young knight's ingenuity and cunning, he, then laughed to himself.

'I think, my troll friend, that you will find, that the child, or should I say, the boy, is our future.'

Robert Scotten's heart, suddenly burst with joy. In his hand, he held a scroll. The newly, inked words, would be used to gain reinforcements, and Jonti would be his man, to deliver those words, once the coming winter, had thawed.

At the feet, of the Guardian of Fantaellen, was a purple Tulip. A flower of hope. Never to be picked. Even, in these dark and desperate times, the robust flower, was seen, as a sign of hope and rebirth.

The winter snows would soon cover the Fantaellen mountains and the land beyond. Nonetheless, come the spring, the hope that would keep them warm, through the ice and the snow, would be ready, to be put to use. The Fantaellen fight back, would begin, with the warmth from the two suns, that would eventually melt the snow and the ice.

***

The strong smell of death hung heavy in the air. The fields, as far as the eye could see, were bathed in blood.

The smell of burning flesh, choked the advancing lines of Blackheart knights, as they checked, for any breathing corpses.

The two battalions had carried out their master's order's, by making sure that their newly gained land, remained their master's, and had no foreign creatures, living and working on the land.

Up on a small hill, overlooking the massacre of the centroll and gigahominum allies, one lone gigahominum still lived, just. He, had numerous Blackheart arrows, embedded in his body. From several cuts and slashes, he bled. His breathing was laboured, and his pulse, very weak.

The creature was sprawled on his back, the fading sight of his eyes, looking up at the dark, storm clouds above. His name was Gorgas, and he was the son of the chief, of the gigahominums. He had been kept alive, for this one moment.

Gorgas's head and upper body were lifted from the ground with ropes, that had been tied around his neck. As he choked, a Blackheart stood over him, and raised his sword, above his head.

'This is our land!' He screamed.

Within an instant, the Blackheart bought the blade of his sword, down upon Gorga's neck, with such an immense force, that the gigahominum's enormous head was immediately severed from his gigantic shoulder's. Blood shot directly into the air like a fountain. The thick red mass, instantaneously covering a large area of the ground.

Gorga's head was placed on a spike in the ground, next to the countless other, centroll and gigahominum heads, as heavy rain, began to wash away the blood, and douse the flames engulfing the innumerable corpses.

In the distance, virtually due east, and just before the horizon, thick, black, rising smoke can be seen, in the direction of The Majestic Wood.

Across the land, once known as Fantaellen, winter would soon be upon it. The clouds and the wind would weaken its sun's and bring snow and ice to blanket the ground. There, would be no joy, no happiness.

And the Dark Epoch, would prevail.

The End

Author's Notes

For many years, I had tried to speak to the last known surviving veteran of that terrible war, known to all Dual Bloods, as The Third War of Portaellen. My targeted subject had repeatedly refused my offers, to meet and talk. The people, who knew him, said that he had become a virtual recluse, locking himself away, from the world. Thus, refusing to speak to anyone, especially, about his war experiences.

Frustrated, I finally gave in, and tactically retreated.

However, the hope of meeting the enigma, that was that man, remained throughout my thought processes and deliberations, as I toyed with the idea, of still continuing my project.

One winters afternoon, as I stared out of my living room window, at the wind and the rain, I suddenly decided, that I would write my story anyway. Of course, it would have been nice, to hear the first-hand experiences of someone, who had been there. Especially, such a great man, and a fierce warrior.

As it was, I had gathered as many historical facts as I could about the war, through books and archived sources, including old maps, hidden deep within the ancient vaults of the libraries, financed by Dual Blood patrons. You will hear more about how those libraries operate, in the next volume. Also, by speaking to other Dual Bloods, whose family members, had been involved in the war, I felt I had enough details and facts to proceed. I would use, all of this information, to write my story.

Then, one evening, my home phone rang. Which was unusual, as that phone never rang, because I gave nobody my number. Cautiously, I picked up the receiver, expecting somebody, to instantly start selling me something, and before I could say anything, a frail voice suddenly spoke.

'I got your number, from the card you pushed through my door.'

'Who is this?' I enquired, as I did not recognise, the voice.

'How, many war veterans, do you know?'

'Who is this?' I asked, once more.

No reply came. Then, it slowly dawned on me.

Could, it be?

'Jonti? Is that you?' I enquired.

'I, am ready to talk.'

And, with that, the line suddenly went dead.

I could not believe that he still had my card. It must have been, five years ago since I pushed it through his letter box. I was stunned, and yet, suddenly excited.

This was it.

Two days later, I knocked on the solid, purple wooden door, with the crooked, rusty numbers, six and nine. A tall, well-built man, in his fifties, eventually answered the door.

'My Grandfather is in the living room,' he stated. 'He has been waiting for you.'

As, I walked into the poorly lit living room, I saw a frail, old man, sat in a leather chair, propped up by his cushions. He did not look at me for a moment, as he slowly pulled himself up.

'Hello, Mr Quixall.' I said.

The old man in the chair, looked up at me and that is when, I saw the first set of tears, streaming down his face. He was in obvious distress.

'I am ready,' he suddenly sobbed, 'I am ready to talk.'

For Jonti Quixall, a proud Dual Blood, of English birth, and Fantaellen lineage, being able to talk about his experiences, in The Third War of Portaellen, would hopefully be his beginning.

I learned, very early on at our meetings, that he is very much, a closed book. For many visits, we sat in silence. Others, he would say just a few words, mainly about the weather that day, and how similar the weather patterns were, in England and Fantaellen. Then, he would remind me, about the awful winters in Portaellen, during the Third War. They had been brutal, he would remark. No subsequent winters would ever compare to them, he would state.

It took, a lot of gentle persuasion, and patience, to get to where, we are now. Even though, his account of what happened, is not all of my story, there are large parts, that are. After all, he was the guardian, and ultimately, in charge of the welfare, of the two most important children in Portaellen, at that time. So, their story, entwines with Jonti's.

Let me briefly, tell you about the remarkable, elderly gentleman, that is James Jonti Quixall. He is in the deep, winter of his years. I have not yet seen, his birth certificate, but he has quite solidly stated, that he lost count of his birthday's, after one hundred and ten. His thin, wrinkled face has numerous scars, across it, which he states, have come from death, blood and sweat. When, he looks in his mirror, he studies them, as each one reminds him of his days, in two world wars, that he says, were so different, yet so similar. He tells me, that the screams of the dying, and the voices of the dead, fill his nightmares. He is a shadow, of his youth. And, the darkness, is gradually taking his sight.

Every time, I shake, his giant, but frail hand, it is obvious that he is a man, who is still a fighter, a warrior. Not only, are his scars visible on his face, you can see them, in his eyes. Jonti, is still fighting a battle, and a war today. And, he will be, till his last breath. For, he is a warrior.

Despite, Jonti having to leave his home, for good, a few months back, to receive the proper care, that he needs, we continue, to meet regularly. One particular day, not long after he had moved into his new home, (which also has a purple door, and the numbers six and nine upon it), he placed a battered looking diary, into my hand.

'You will need that', he started 'when, you've finished, this story.'

When, I thought he wasn't looking, I turned over the cover, and I saw a scribbled title, written in pencil. I smiled to myself, and put it in my pocket, for safe keeping.

'That story, will have to keep,' he said.

'It'll be safe, with me,' I stated.

'I know, it will,' he replied.

It wasn't long, before the commanding, yet frail voice of Jonti, had me hastily jotting down more notes, and checking my voice recorder, to make sure, it could pick up, his voice, as he began. He had my total attention.

Despite, his elderly, frail appearance, I am still, in awe of this once great warrior. I could sit and listen, to his tales, forever.

It is those great tales, and all the historical facts, from the books, that I have read, that inspired me to write my account, of The Third War of Portaellen. This story is based upon, what I have gathered, and my poetic licence, to add a little of my own fiction. Men like Joseph, Mathew and Wilfred, whom I placed, on the huge walls of Guinlance and its castle, are a part of that fiction. Reading, accounts of the First Battle of Guinlance Hill, it appeared that there were countless men like those fictional characters, fighting desperately, to repel the enemy. There, is also written evidence, of the head of a Fantaellen knight, with a grey beard, being held aloft, on the ramparts of the outer wall of Guinlance Castle, as some sort of signal to General Grafton. Unfortunately for the fictional Joseph, it would be his head, that I would use.

Regarding, Captain George Corder. He is not fictional. His name is still told in heroic stories, to this day. Jonti, had met him once, he had told me. His name is listed as missing in action, on the roll call, of the battle at the South Western Fortress. The way, I have described that battle was based upon eyewitness accounts, and an account from the regimental diary. And yes, some of my poetic licence was also used. Just to say, that Captain George Corder's body, has still never been found. So, the words 'missing in action' still stand. It would fall, to his son, still a little boy in this volume, to eventually take the battle to his father's enemy.

I also found an account, of a sea battle that took place, a few days before the invasion. It did not last long, judging by the short amount of text afforded, to the clash of the two navy's, ever taking place. It seemed, that the Fantaellen ships, were not only outnumbered, but were also, far less capable vessels, than those of the Wulfdaeden's.

You will have seen my reference to the Wulfdaeden flag, on several occasions throughout, the story. The tri lance was designed by Napoleon Victory, upon his inception, as the king of Wulfdaeden. It had a red background. Within its centre, was a large black heart, that had the merest showing of a smaller silver heart, in its centre. Engulfing that heart, was another blackheart. Running behind, the larger blackheart, were three lances. Each lance ran from the emblems base. One centrally, protruding up and out of the centre. The other two, protruding up and out, either side of the central lance.

I made no reference, to a Fantaellen flag, as it was being redesigned, on the orders of the king and sovereign before his death. I hope that I can unveil, the new design, as it were, in a later volume.

With all the facts and stories, of this awful period, in Portaellen and Fantaellen history, finally being told, I just hope, that I do Jonti, and all the others, justice. That is my mission.

For, I am not a warrior. I am a writer.

The author

C.P. Bird was born in 1969 in Nottingham, UK.
He studied for 2'O' levels in English Language and
Literature. He spent 35 years in retail and 25 years
in Health and Beauty Retail. He became interested
in reading any kind of book from a young age.
Reading became his form of escape which fed
his vivid imagination and carried him through
his school years. It was only two years ago that
he decided to follow his dream and write his
manuscript. C.P. Bird hopes to encourage people
to follow their dreams, to trust in their abilities
and to take a leap of faith. He loves reading,
writing, watching films, football and history. He
is divorced, has two children and has been living
with his current partner for ten years.
This is his first manuscript.